"Powerful… [La Sala] is a model for what an authentic queer writer can be, and it comes through in his debut."

—Medium

"Stunning and terrifying to behold."

—Hypable

"A unique, clever fantasy with a strong protagonist."

—Booklist

"Joyously, riotously queer."

—Kirkus Reviews

"I don't know that I've ever encountered a book quite like *Reverie* before. Queer, dream-bending mystery fantasy may well be the next big thing, and I'm here for it!"

—NPR

"A spectacular, imaginative tale unlike anything you've read all year."

—Paste magazine

"*Reverie* makes a strong, late-season case as one of the best young adult fantasies of the year."

—Tor.com

"[A] gem of a novel that is as affirming as it is entertaining."

—Bulletin of the Center for Children's Books

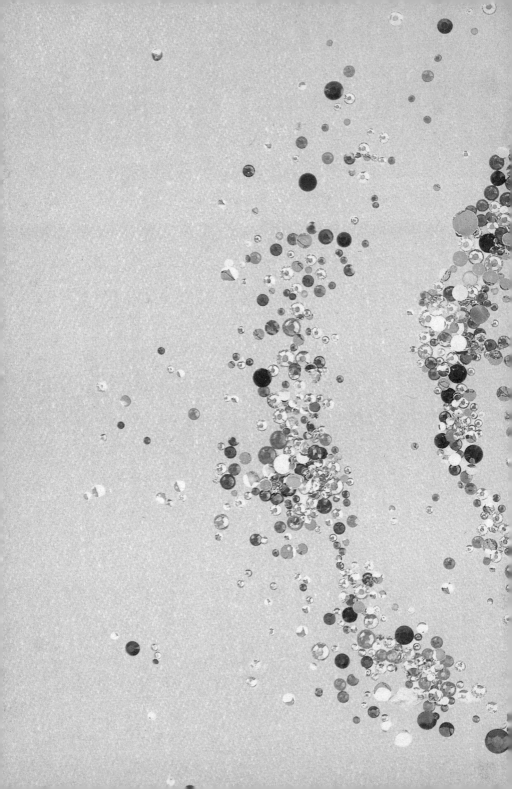

BE DAZZLED

Ryan La Sala

sourcebooks
fire

Published by Sourcebooks Fire, an imprint of Sourcebooks
P.O. Box 4410, Naperville, Illinois 60567-4410
(630) 961-3900
sourcebooks.com

Library of Congress Cataloging-in-Publication data is on file with the publisher.

Printed and bound in the United States of America.
LSC 10 9 8 7 6 5 4 3 2 1

For Sal, because duh <3

ONE

- - - - - - - - - - - - NOW - - - - - - - - - - - - -

The Boston Convention Center has good security, but it doesn't have missile launchers, which means it would have a pretty tough time defending itself against Evie Odom.

My mother.

If she knew I was outside this place, she'd probably descend from the low clouds on this foggy Boston morning like some sort of alien doomsday spacecraft and vaporize me.

And if she knew I was standing out here in a costume that can only be described as "fungus chic" for all of Boston Seaport to see? Well, what's worse than being vaporized? Whatever it is, *that* is what she'd do to me.

Some might think I'm being dramatic. Which, okay, fine. Maybe they'd be a little right. But mostly, they'd be wrong. This is Evie *fucking* Odom here. The self-made millionaire artist turned gallery director. The woman of onyx eyes and champagne lips (according to her *Times* profile, which was for sure penned by a gay man).

But in my opinion, Evie is just sort of evil. Like a fashionable Antichrist sent by the art world to look down upon all things pop culture, cartoon, and craft. So her son, Raphael Odom, the boy currently stumbling out of an Uber dressed *as* a cartoon made *out* of crafts, on his way *into* a pop culture convention? Evie would hate it. Actually, she *does* hate it, but we're a two-person family—we can't discuss the things we hate about one another without polarizing the entire house. So, to survive her wrath, I hide my crafting and my cosplaying. And I pretend I don't spend hours fashioning incredible costumes out of hot glue and household hardware. And I lie. And I sneak. Basically, I do *whatever* I can to avoid Evie's particularly flamboyant form of hate.

What Evie hates, she destroys. It's her thing. For a while in the early nineties, she was famous for hating and destroying replicas of her work. Usually she did this in front of an audience, often for a lot of money.

So as you can imagine, I'm not trying to get caught sneaking into conventions. I'm rushing, dragging my friend May behind me as we exit the car and dive into the crowd of con-goers loitering outside. May is slow in her clunky costume (100 percent my fault, I built it—sorry, May), but we don't let two tons of foam and hot glue stop us from hitting warp speed. People scream and scatter in our wake. Maybe someone loses an eye. I don't know, I don't care about injuries. There's only one—only *one*—force I trust to keep me safe from my mother, and that's the group of ladies that runs check-in at Controverse. I don't know if they volunteer or if they're paid handsomely; I only know that if you're not on their list, you're not getting into the con. Not if you're the president, not if you're Jesus H. Christ, not even if you're Satan.

And yet…

Evie is Evie, so just in case they can't stop her, I've taken every precaution to make sure she doesn't know I'm here in the first place. She thinks May and I are camping. *Camping!* Out in the Blue Hills of Massachusetts, like some plucky settlers of CATAN! It is the most outrageous lie I have ever told her, and I was downright offended when she accepted it without protest, only saying, "Do not bring any ticks into my house, Raphael."

"Out of my way," I snap at a group of girls trying to take photos of us. They lower their phones and drift apart, letting us pass to the front of the crowd.

"Raffy, will you just calm down for two freaking seconds?" May protests.

I certainly will not.

"Come on, they just want photos with us."

"You're not even on your stilts, and we still need to do final touches."

"Oh, you mean when you make me sit on the floor so you can glue mold to my face?"

"It's not mold, it's *moss*, and it's not just glue, it's *spirit gum*. It needs to look real, like little organic puffs."

3

"The little organic puff," May says in her *grand* voice, which is just her normal voice but with an affected Maggie-Smith-in-*Downton-Abbey* accent. "That's the title of your memoir. *The Little Organic Puff*, by Raphael Odom."

I continue listing all the things we—or really, I—need to do before we hit the con floor.

"And then I have test the power packs for the LEDs and check to make sure the vape cartridge is full, and you need to practice walking in those stilts, and I need to touch up some of my toadstools. There's a lot to do. I don't want anything hitting social until we're perfect."

Typically, you show up at a con ready, but with all this sneaking, we have to get ready on the go. Not ideal, but necessary. Lucky for us, the bigger cons now have changing rooms so people can suit up on location. This is why I have a rolling suitcase.

"But the moss—are you sure I need to wear it? It's itchy, and besides, my mask nearly covers my whole face."

"Yes, I'm sure. It's all about being fully in character. The judges will appreciate the detail if they ask you to remove the mask, which they will. You'll see."

May scrunches up her eyebrows.

"Fine, fine, you can mold me," she says. "Sometimes I think you get off on these things, Raff."

"May, gross. I'm gay. And so are you."

"So what? Gay people do all sorts of things. They wear, like, harnesses and leather straps. Just out and about."

"So do horses, but no one kink-shames them. Now drop it."

She murmurs, "Oh, you can bet I'll drop something. And I'm sure you'd love to watch me pick it up real slow."

May basks in my discomfort. She is doing me a huge favor this weekend by competing with me; putting up with her weird jokes is the least I can do. If I weren't so anxious, I'd be laughing and joking around, too. But I am anxious. I'm *always* anxious about something, but on competition days, I'm anxious about *everything*. And usually, I have ways of calming myself down, but this is the biggest show I've ever competed in. This is *Controverse*. It doesn't get any bigger than this, so nothing is going to calm me down. Not listening to music. Not meditation. Maybe tranquilizers, but probably not. Only winning.

Once I win, I'll relax. Once I take home the top prize, it won't matter that Evie will probably, eventually find out that I'm not camping (and have never camped a day in my seventeen years of life). Once I become the youngest person ever to take best in show at Controverse, I'll be a legit award-winning crafter, and Evie will finally have to admit that this whole "arts and crafts obsession" of mine is not a phase.

Or...

Or she'll promptly fake her own death out of embarrassment and then start over in Toronto or something, but that's okay. Because if I play my cards right—which I will, which I *am* by showing up in this sickening look—winning Controverse is going to come with something even better than my mother's approval.

5

Sponsorship! In the past few years, Craft Club has been giving major sponsorship deals to the crowd favorites at Controverse. And other businesses are starting to tap into the young, influencer-driven craft market, too. The cosplay scene at Controverse has become a hotbed of recruitment and sponsored content. And if I want to have a future after high school that isn't passing mini Bellinis at my mother's shows, I need to make it happen.

Put simply, I need money to pay for art school, because Evie is *not* about to waste her wealth on that shit. She doesn't believe in formal arts education at all. She says that any artist worth their paints is guided by talent and instinct. *She* didn't need college to be a success, after all. And it's a major point of pride for her. (She has many points of pride; she's a sea urchin of prideful points.)

I'm less prideful and far less pointy. I know I need to go to art school. And I will need money to pay for art school. And, to a lesser degree, I will need money for food and Crunchyroll dot com.

I'm not just here to win a competition or my mother's respect. At the end of the day, I'm after one thing: a future, on my terms.

"Name?"

We're at the tables where they give out the badges. I pull my ID from the pocket I smartly sewed to the inside of my robe.

"Raphael Odom," I say.

The lady looks at my ID, then at me. My ID says that I am seventeen, that I am five foot six, and that I have brown hair and brown eyes. In this moment, though, I am an ancient spirit of the forest, a druid, wearing six-inch platform heels. My face barely shows beneath a hooded robe clotted with fungus and ferns. One of my eyes is pure black due to the scleral contact lens I spent the entire Uber ride trying to put in.

But then the registration lady's scrutiny breaks into gleeful recognition.

"You're Evelyn Odom's kid, right? I grew up with your mom in Everett! We went to high school together! Oh, she must be so proud of you. She was always an eccentric one, too."

"And I'm May Wu," May says grandly, cutting off the conversation like a benevolent guillotine. I suffer through check-in, refusing to look at anyone else directly until the woman finally hands us our badges.

I pull May into Controverse, one determined step at a time. No matter what I make myself into, there is no escaping who I am. No amount of makeup will cover it. Not the thickest of latex. Not even platform heels make me big enough to escape my mother's shadow.

But this weekend, everything will change.

As we enter Controverse, I start to breathe a little easier. These are my people. Geeks and weebs, but also a handful of nerds and a dash of dorks. The kind of people who sit through family dinners silently contemplating the fact that Carol Danvers got a haircut between appearances in the Captain Marvel movie and the final Avengers movie, which means that somewhere in the MCU, there are scissors powerful enough to cut the hair of a woman who has broken *several* spaceships apart with just her body. Without suffering a single scratch! Thanos should have grabbed those scissors and added them to his bejeweled oven mitt.

This is *the* con in Boston; it materializes every October, gathering together a million-person family made up of every fandom. Lately there has been a lot of Marvel and DC because of the movies, of course, but if we're being honest, the anime contingent (to which I proudly belong) holds the con together. And then there's the noble Star Wars fandom, which has more rules than a ballet academy for assassins. The Trekkies used to be like that, too, I hear, but now they spend most of their time chasing after their little grandkids, because all of them managed to couple up and start nerd families. Weird. Oh, and of course there are the Doctor Who people. Every single one of them put on their TARDIS dresses this morning thinking, "No one will see this coming."

I kid. I like the Doctor Who people. But they get very, very angry if you don't have an opinion about which one of the seemingly infinite number of actors who have played the Doctor was best. Oops.

Fandoms, families, fans—they form a buzzy, diverse congregation that makes the annual pilgrimage to the Boston Convention Center at the city's seaport once a year to celebrate their mythologies and their lore and, of course, pay tribute to their gods.

And by gods, I mean cosplayers.

Trust me, cosplay is *the* cool thing to do at these events. Costumes don't just transform the people wearing them; they transform the world around them. At a con, one second there'll be just a crowd, and then Goku enters, and suddenly *everyone* is screaming. But not just *regular* screaming. I mean full-on, throaty, anime-power-up screaming. It's something else.

I love cosplay. I've always been good at creating things, but I only got big into creating cosplays in the last couple of years. It took convincing. And, admittedly, some spite. I kept watching other people's follower counts skyrocket after they put on ratty shake-and-go wigs and called themselves Sailor Mars, and it annoyed me. I always said to May, *Why doesn't anyone brush out their wigs? Do they like looking like microwaved showgirls? I could do so much better.* And she was finally like, *Okaaaaay, then why don't you?*

So now I do. And I was right. I'm great at this. I create almost compulsively, my stuff isn't bad, and I've even won a few titles at smaller regional cons. I'm not big or anything, but like a young god, I have gained a small but devoted following. About fourteen thousand people, give or take a thousand, tune in to watch me hot glue shit together on my Ion livestream twice a week.

But that count is going to double by the time I'm done with this year's Controverse. For the first time, I'm entering the Controverse Championship of Cosplay (Trip-C, pronounced "Tripsy" if you're cool). It's the biggest, baddest cosplay competition in Boston—a multiday contest famous for its weird rules and twists. Just about all the criteria change from year to year, except one: People must compete in pairs. Controverse famously considers cosplay a team sport.

Enter May and myself. We're doing a twist on the classic game *Deep Autumn*, in which the hero gets trapped in an enchanted forest and must battle through each season to escape. The character designs are nuts. Perfect for a team of cosplayers looking for a recognizable but difficult build.

I'm dressed as a druid, a keeper of the Spring Temple, and May is dressed as a Pinehorn, a low-level beast common on the temple grounds. Except we've been corrupted, which means we've been overtaken by fungus and mushrooms, turning us evil. As a result, I've taken the usually playful design of *Deep Autumn* and rendered it with gory realism.

I straighten May's helmet and step back to admire my work.

May is gone. In her place is a creature hunched atop four clawed-footed legs that bristle with pine cone scales. Glowing red eyes glower from beneath a spiked mask of deep aubergine, a lethal spike slicing up from the snout like a gargantuan Japanese horned beetle. A riot of leaves and rotting flowers grow from the creature's ridged back, where two ragged wings of transparent cerulean twitch. Its whole body sprouts clumps of neon moss and fungus that glisten in the fluorescent lights of the convention center. It looks powerful and decrepit and diseased at the same time. Shockingly monstrous.

"Perfect," I tell it.

I tell *May*.

"You look pretty good, too," she says from beneath the mask.

Whereas May's Pinehorn cosplay emphasizes illusion, mine is

a more subtle, though just as complex, build. My character—the Spring Keeper—is mostly human-shaped. But because I'm extra, I've fashioned prosthetics that give me a long, sharp nose, spiked cheekbones, and an overbearing brow. I've altered my exposed chest, too, creating tissue-thin, clammy skin over blue veins and spindly bones. The image of health.

Only the shine of my one black eye shows from beneath my hooded robe, which I've sewn and embroidered. It took ages to do, but the effect looks both whimsical and ghastly, as though I'm one blink away from being completely overtaken by nature itself.

We are unrecognizable. We are totally transformed.

We are for *sure* going to qualify.

"Remember the poses?" I ask her.

"Of course."

"And the cues?"

"Yup."

"And you can walk okay?"

"For a girl in a forty-pound costume, balancing atop four stilts? Sure. But Raff, next time can I be the one in the pretty mushroom dress?"

I barely acknowledge her sarcasm as I unfasten and refasten one of her straps for the eighth time. I'm afraid that the moment I decide we're ready, everything will fall apart.

"Relax, Raff. Listen, this is going to go well," she tells me. "We're going to *win*, and we're going to get you that sponsorship, okay? And then it's only a matter of time before those fancy-shmancy art schools will be begging to review your portfolio, okay?"

I force a smile (a small one—I don't want to risk dislodging my prosthetic cheekbones). I hope she's right. Everything—every dream of mine, every winking whim—rides on proving I can do this without Evie. In spite of her, in fact.

"And listen." May's voice turns solemn. "I know you miss him, and I know it was supposed to be him in this costume and not me, but—"

"Stop."

"Raff—"

"You know I don't want to hear about *him*."

"Yes, but Raff—"

I give her a warning glare, and she stops talking. There's one last reason why I'm here, but I won't let it be the main reason. I won't even let May say the reason's name. I only want to hear his name when the announcers award him silver right before awarding me gold.

"I'm just saying that you can do this without him," May says.

"*We* can do this." I give her a small nudge, and the Pinehorn armor shakes as we start our walk out onto the con floor.

"I'm doing this for you, but remember our deal? I get Sunday to set up at the Art Mart. There are some top online artists here, and I'm aiming to make some friends."

The Art Mart is where all the artist booths are set up, a huge room that bustles with shoppers looking for custom prints, gifts, shirts, phone cases, comics, and anything else you can imagine. It's a small nuclear power plant of creativity and bootlegged shit. It's May's Mount Olympus, and this year she's got a chance to drop in at one of the amateur booths on Sunday, where she'll be selling merch for her recently kinda-famous webcomic, *Cherry Cherry*. As a fellow art-trepreneur, I couldn't be prouder.

"Of course."

As soon as we hit the con floor, I know we've nailed our look. Within two seconds, people are calling out famous lines from *Deep Autumn*. Kids rush over, asking if they can take pictures with us. A circle forms around us, but at a distinct distance, like the moss on our skin is contagious, like its spores might float through the hot air of the con and lodge in skin, throats, and eyes, burrowing into bones and turning them soft with rot.

Perfect. May and I are ready. We get into our practiced stances, but before anyone can snap a picture, May turns on her stilts and lumbers off.

People are confused. *I'm* confused. I run after her.

"May, what's wrong?"

"We need to go."

"What? We just got here."

"Yeah, well, it's urgent."

I grab May's arm through the joint of the costume. We need to build up excitement now if we're going to have a reputation by the time we're onstage in front of the actual judges. I want people in the audience to know us, to *cheer* for us. I want to be recognized.

"Shit, I wanted to warn you," she says, stopping short as a

commotion begins in the crowd behind us. Whatever she wanted to warn me about, it's too late. I track the shouts. Is it Evie, here to take me home? How did she get here so quickly?

But it's so much worse.

A new couple has entered the room. The screams that go up are hysterical with excitement, people practically crawling over one another to see the latest looks. I hear a bellowing laugh over the racket; I see sunlight on the curve of a muscled back and the shock of white teeth in a broad smile.

No.

I see a girl slinking across the floor, stalking her prey. Not a girl—a deer. Arrows protrude from her back and throat, and blood streams down her lithe body in glistening ribbons that look fresh enough to paint with. It's an expert job.

She is dressed as Bambi's mother, shot dead and now risen with undead vengeance. I know this without even seeing her partner, because it's my idea. Down to the bloody ribbons, it's all my work. My drawings come to life, splayed out before me on the Controverse floor.

How could this happen? Who took this from me?

But I know who. I follow the eyes of the crowd to where her partner lies on the ground. His body has been completely airbrushed to resemble that of a deer, every muscle painted in soft browns and beiges. A bite mark on his upper thigh seeps blood, and the flesh around it is already zombified, the infection curdling his young flesh and turning his veins black.

He drags himself up and pretends to limp on the bad leg, desperate to flee the zombie his mother has become. But he's laughing. His smile is what slaps me. A smile that wins everything and everyone over. A smile that won me over for a long time, too, until it vanished from my life.

He's here.

Luca Vitale is here.

My biggest competition. My worst nightmare.

My ex-boyfriend.

Given how much TV I watch, I know tropes. Broken love is, of course, the perfect origin story for mortal enemies, so I guess that's ours, but I'm still not sure who the hero is. We hurt each other. The hard kind of hurt that doesn't heal up quickly.

I've clung to that hurt for a long time. It's what has kept me going; it's what got me here. But when I see him, the hurt abandons me, leaving behind an overwhelming, disorienting nostalgia. When I see him, I see us. How we came together, what we created together, what we ruined together. I see our every moment, and at the same time, I see us unraveling all at once. It's gutting. And the only way to understand how we fell apart is to understand what made us *us* in the first place.

TWO

- - - - - - - - - - - - - THEN - - - - - - - - - - - -
THIRTEEN MONTHS EARLIER

My filming setup is in the studio.

The studio is a converted garage behind our house that Evie sometimes traps artists inside when they're on deadline for a show. It's not in use right now, which means I'm living here. Yes, I have an actual room in the house, but the studio has everything I need: a loft space with a mattress on the bare wooden floor, a collapsing sofa, a kitchenette, and a bathroom. And of course, a fully equipped, climate-controlled, spectacularly lit artist space with more leftover supplies than a kindergarten class could use in a year.

Evie doesn't care that I live out here for months at a time. I don't think she really notices. She probably likes the quiet for the few nights a month that she's actually home. I think she knows, vaguely, that I'm making cosplays out here, but so long as I keep my dirty little hobby a secret from her, she keeps her temper in check. So I'm careful to clean up and to never mention this stuff around her or her art friends.

But, because I guess I love danger and irony, I *also* set up a camera and record myself crafting for the entire internet to see, twice a week. What can I say? Some kids do drugs. Some kids start fires. I embroider in the dead of night, for the attention of strangers.

I use Ion for streaming. Everyone uses Ion for streaming. It's sort of like this massive digital forum full of people talking into their cameras as they do their weird hobbies. But are they still weird if thousands of people watch and comment and subscribe? Not so much.

Some people eat and review takeout. Some people give personal updates while they polish silverware. Some people stream their latest virtual conquests in whatever games they're playing. Some people watch scary movies with their jumpiest aunts.

On my channel, I create stuff.

Or rather, I create cosplays and narrate what I'm doing. And then I open up the stream to Q&As at the end. I'm not a huge deal, but I've got a few thousand subscribers and tons of return views from other cosplayers looking for tutorials. Mostly people lurk on my channel, keeping their comments to themselves. It's hard to tell if people care, since users come and go and screen names change. Still, it's comforting to spend time with these random strangers. It makes the long hours of crafting feel not so lonely. And on the plus side, if my mother ever discovers what I'm up to, my most loyal watchers will have a live viewing of me being incinerated by her laser eyes. What could be more special than sharing that?

I adjust my camera, then turn it on. I give myself a moment before starting the stream.

"Hello! And welcome back to my channel, *Crafty Rafty*, the home of all things arts, crafts, and creation. I'm Raffy, and as per usual, I'll be talking through my latest costume creation, answering questions, and reviewing supplies."

I spin through my usual intro. I have rehearsed it many times in front of the tiles in my shower, which give limited feedback. Porcelain, as a material, is very hard to impress.

"Today, we're picking up where we left off with my latest build: Plasma Siren. I'm planning on wearing her to Controverse this year, and if all goes well, I might even be competing next year. So, what do you think? Is *all* going *well*?"

I hold up the garment so far. One day, it will be an incredible cosplay of my favorite, *favorite* mini boss from last year's indie breakout game, *Wake*, which is about haunted islands in the Bermuda Triangle. Right now, it's just a mottled mess of fabric, but today I'm applying scales and rhinestone fin detailing. This is actually something I should do after I've sewn the rest of the bodysuit together, but I'm too excited to wait.

"So, a huge shout-out to one of you. I have no idea who, but *one* of you must have really been listening during my last stream, because today I arrived home to a package from an unknown sender. And what did I find in it? The exact rhinestones I needed to bedazzle Plasma Siren's fins."

I pause, more to keep myself from laughing than anything else. Someone—a total stranger—bought *me* craft supplies off my wish list. It's a looooong list I keep updated on Amazon with the supplies I'm working with, and *theoretically* people can buy me stuff from it and ship the packages to my house without them having to know where I live. It's like a wedding registry, but for a single person, and that single person is single because of their ridiculously demanding preoccupation with arts and crafts. And I say *theoretically* because until now, no one has ever thrown money down for my cause. But, with these rhinestones as my witnesses, someone believes in me! Which means it's finally happening. My star! It's rising! I'm practically already the executive producer of my own Netflix show.

"So whoever sent these, thank you."

There is much more I want to say, but I need to act cooler than I feel.

"Anyway, there are many ways to stone things. Plasma Siren's fins aren't your typical surface. They're plastic, and even though they are opaque, you can see that the surface is super smooth. That's not great for glue. So before we get to gluing, we're going to need to give the glue something to grip."

As I talk, I pick a patch of sandpaper.

"I'm sanding the plastic in small circles, carving out tiny

scratches that the glue is going to fill. This gives it some tooth. That said, make sure you wash off the plastic after doing this to get rid of the dust. I also suggest swabbing the plastic with alcohol to clean off any residuals."

I pick up the fins I've already sanded. I hold them up to the camera, letting the light show the newly textured surface.

"Now that our plastic is treated, we can get to gluing. For gluing to hard surfaces, I recommend an industrial-strength adhesive, like this E6000. But because I need to mask the seam between the stiff material of the fin and the fabric it protrudes from, I'm also going to use some foam clay to smooth out the gap, and then this liquid cement, which comes in a fabric formula." I hold up both. "Whatever you use, always make sure that it's going to dry clear. You don't want a bunch of dry white stuff all over your beautiful jewels."

I hear myself and cringe.

"Sorry, Mom," I say to the camera, playing it off. Evie is, of course, not watching. She is backpacking in São Paulo with one of her artists, a man who only produces one painting per year, applying the paint directly over his last painting. She's got him booked at a gallery in SoHo in a few months, where he'll complete his next layer.

"I'll be handling the gems with a picker tool so I don't get glue all over my hands. I can tell that the glue is going to get every-where if I don't use something very fine to administer it. So what am I using, you might ask?"

I fan a fistful of syringes at my audience.

"These are glue syringes. They're perfect for getting glue into very small spaces without making a mess."

I adjust the camera to look down at my hands, and I begin. As I work, I sometimes forget to talk. I'm most chatty when I'm nervous, but I calm down when I work and just go dead quiet with focus. It's like I've only got enough electricity to run my hands or my mouth. Never both. But I have to make the effort to narrate or else it'll be quite a boring show.

"Not all rhinestones are created equal. Did you know that? There are tons to pick from, and for almost all your cosplay needs, you're going to want ones that are flat-back, which means the backs of them are flat, which is perhaps obvious… I don't know, maybe it's not obvious, but whatever. They have flat—Oh, shit."

I've pricked myself with this stupid glue syringe, and a stray stone has drifted out of its spot. I shut up and correct it. Then I show the camera my work so far, hiding my bloodied finger.

"See how pretty that row is?"

I do another row in silence.

"This is a gorgeous color," I say. "What would you guys call this color?"

I check the chat. Someone has responded with: blue lol?

"Well, yes. They're…blue. But can anyone guess the specific color?"

I make myself do another row before checking again. When I look up, I see that someone by the name of Striker9 has said: Sea Foam Dream #6.

"Well, someone's been on the Craft Club site!" I grin. "Yeah, the exact color of these is called Sea Foam Dream, and number six is the size. It's super hard to find enough of them, since they're a specific size *and* color."

Truth is, I've gone to Craft Club twice in the last week to buy every bag they had.

"And you'd think one pack would be enough, but trust me, once you get going, you can burn through five or six of them in just one build. I've only done half of this fin, and I can already tell I'll need to pick up a few more packs. But thanks to my generous benefactor, I've got enough to get a ton done tonight."

As I bedazzle, I manage to keep talking. I try to keep it funny. Upbeat. A facade, because behind my act, there's my typical uncertainty.

I wonder if what I'm creating will be enough to make me into what I want to be. I wonder if my mother is right, if I'd be better off putting my skills to use in the back rooms of fashion houses, handing off garments to assistants who smell like cappuccino and have massive iPhones. Working in fashion is glamorous if you have Evie's high-society sensibilities, but for me it would be failure.

That fate feels far away from here and now, though, as I bedazzle a costume using gems donated by the internet. I've earned this, I tell myself. I am worth my best effort and a bag full of plastic gems at *least*.

"I'm out of gems! But I got both the arm fins done and half of the dorsal."

I get ready to sign off. Usually I'd take a few questions, but it's late, and my eyes are tired from staring into the glinting depths of five hundred little sea foam dreams.

"Thanks to everyone for tuning in! If you're curious about previous steps in Plasma Siren, check out my other videos below! If you enjoyed this and want to see more, subscribe! And lastly, if you'd like to support me, a link to my wish list is posted below. You can either buy me some supplies or just throw down cash. Whatever works for you. Every patron's money goes toward helping me make new cool stuff and record videos for you guys."

A bubble pops up in the chat.

Striker9 is typing.

"And for those of you who tuned in at the end, my name is Raffy, and I'm getting this cosplay of Plasma Siren ready for—"

The bubble vanishes. Striker9 has stopped typing.

"Ready for—"

It shows up again.

Striker9 is typing.

It vanishes again, then shows up again. What are they trying to say that's so hard? I've zoned out wondering about this, so I zone back in.

"I'm getting this costume ready for this year's Controverse, held right here in Boston at the Boston Convention Center in the Seaport. For those wondering, no, I won't be competing, but I will be on the con floor both Saturday and Sunday, so come say hi! And—"

Striker9 is typing.

"—and don't be afraid to reach out with questions! Till next time, happy crafting!"

I power down the stream, leaving Striker9 to hammer out whatever novel they've been working on in the chat. It's only then that I realize they're the same person who knew the exact name of the stones I've been using for the last hour.

"Striker9, then?" I murmur, looking at myself in the dark mirror of the windows. "My bejeweled benefactor. Thank you."

THREE

- - - - - - - - - - - - - NOW - - - - - - - - - - - - -

Luca is here.

We've been broken up for like five months, since Blitz Con in Providence in May. Long enough that the devastation isn't constant. Now it just comes at me sideways sometimes, knocking me down into my thoughts. I knew he'd be here, and I told myself I wouldn't freak out, but when I'm down, I'm down. I can't stop thinking about him. Even in this moment, when I should be at my best, I feel my smallest. I am obsessing over how he took my idea that I wanted to do *with* him and executed it with Inaya instead. My former friend.

My replacement.

The betrayal is made worse by the fact that they did a good job. A really, really good job.

Fuck.

"Raffy, there are kids here."

Sometimes I don't realize that I am swearing out loud.

"My nose," I say.

"Fuck your nose?"

"No. Stop. My nose is coming unglued. There's spirit gum in the bag. Can you reapply?"

May hastily unscrews the small amber bottle and brushes the adhesive onto the portion of my facial prosthetic that's peeling off. It's entirely due to the grimace I let contort my mouth just now. She holds it in place for a few minutes, and we're forced into silence, which helps me clear my head.

"Did you know what they were wearing?" I finally say.

"No, they kept it a secret. But Inaya posted right before they arrived. I wanted to tell you, but you were so focused."

"Let's just hang out here," I say. "Then we can get to prejudging early."

May nods. She knows I'm not okay, which is why she does me the courtesy of not asking.

Most cosplay shows have two parts. The actual show, and before that, prejudging. Prejudging is a chance for the judges to see the cosplays up close before you walk across the stage and get your actual score. The stage part is more for the audience—a performance—whereas prejudging is all about craft and deliberation. Usually the prejudges ask questions, flip seams, look at the undergarments. The goal is to see the work up close, like it deserves.

This year, they've asked every team to show up at once for prejudging. It's taking place in a closed-off hall, and we need to show our official competitor badges to even get in. Cosplays from every universe mill through the room, friends catching up as they recognize each other beneath layers of plastic, makeup, feathers, and armor. I see none of it. I'm scanning for Luca, but he's not here yet.

"Are they going to do prejudging in front of everyone?" May asks.

"Fucking better not," I say. Usually it's more private. Just you and the judges. But this is more like a mixer than a competition. Everyone knows Controverse likes to change it up, but are the twists already starting?

"Just relax, Raffy," May is saying. "If you cry, you're gonna lose your contact or something. And if you start sweating now, you're gonna be totally ripe by the time the judges get up close and personal."

"Gross, May," I say, but she's right. I do need to get it together. I've already wasted precious moments letting Luca distract me. I can't give him another second of my time.

I used to tell myself that over and over: *Don't let him waste your time.* But he did it so easily, and he did it so well. And for a time, I loved letting him.

I suck in a deep breath and hold it, something I've watched my mother do when she's about to lose her cool. I don't know what she imagines, but I imagine that the breath is cooling within me, condensing into a spinning fog, then a crystal of ice. I embed the crystal between my lungs, pushed against my spine, cooling me from the inside out. This isn't a place for emotions. This is competitive arts and crafts. It's serious.

"I'm cool," I tell May.

"Good, because I think I just saw Irma."

"*Irma? As in Irma Worthy?*"

"Yes. Irma as in Irma Worthy."

Irma Worthy is the head of Worthy's Craft Club. A crafting legend who took over the few Craft Clubs in Massachusetts and turned them into a national chain sprinkled from coast to coast, like sequins strewn across a map. She's the mastermind behind Trip-C, using the competition as a vehicle to advertise for her stores, and she is my idol. My everything. The woman I am determined to grow up to become, then overthrow.

When Irma enters the room, half the people start to scream, and the other half go silent in reverence. She's in her sixties, with a face that looks like it was made to break into laughter. Dormant wrinkles give soft outlines to big cheeks, a big chin, big eyes.

And her hair is humongous. It's rumored to be a wig—a sort of meta-advertisement for the wigs sold at Craft Club—but no one has ever had the nerve to verify that. If it is a wig, it is masterfully styled and expertly imperfect, better than anything a casual cosplayer could manage. In a way, it affirms her authority. We cannot actually tell if she's in cosplay, costume, drag, or just her Sunday best.

Like fish, we slide into a school that follows her down the length of the room until we're gathered in a tight circle. Irma talks with a few of the con staff, then turns her starry eyes to the room full of cosplayers.

"Well, well, well, look at *you*. I do *love* getting everyone together." She beams. "I figured I'd say good luck before everything got cutthroat, but looks like we're already feeling a bit monstrous, am I right?" She claps for us, and the crowd cheers back.

Irma can barely get her next sentence out as the cheers threaten to overflow the room. She's not shouting, but her voice carries with the clarity of a lady who knows how to put on a show.

"This year marks the sixth annual Controverse Cosplay Championships, or Trip-C, as you all call it. As it does every year, Controverse has chosen to partner with Craft Club to bring the competition to life, and we couldn't be more excited about all of you, our fantastic cosplayers. We've also got an incredible panel of judges to reveal."

Reveal? She carries on while we murmur.

"And, of course, we have our fabulous coordinating staff: clubbers from local Craft Clubs in the Greater Boston area. I'll hand things off to the professionals in a bit," she jokes, jerking her huge hair at the cluster of nervous-looking adults with tablets and earpieces, "but I just couldn't help popping in to get a look at all your work. Now remember: measure twice, cut once, and give up never."

Irma exits to riotous cheers, and I'm breathless. I've been coming to Controverse for years, and I've been sneaking into her store for many more years, but I've never seen her. I wasn't even sure she was *real*. Seeing her in all her dolled-up, constructed glory actually makes her seem less real, yet so much more important.

The clubbers take over from there. A representative from Craft Club is always in charge. This year, it's a tall brunette lady with a pixie cut and massive circular glasses. She peers down at us with bird-like apprehension.

"Hello, everyone. My name is Madeline, and I'm the head of marketing for the northeast division of Craft Club. I'll be handling operations and logistics with the clubbers these next few days. You all should have received the official rules and guidelines upon acceptance of your applications," she says, doing away with all of Irma's warmth. "If you haven't had a chance to read the rules, I encourage you to spend your waiting time making sure you have what you need for today and tomorrow. Anyone who isn't ready to compete won't compete."

"Yikes," says May as several competitors turn to their partners.

Madeline covers the ground rules with the efficiency of a NutriBullet. I zone out. I know these, anyway. Controverse is known for twists, but the basic structure of the competition is always the same. There are two days of competition—Friday and Saturday. On Friday, today, there's the qualifying round. On Saturday, there's the primary round for the finalists. Quals, then Primes. Simple. Each round involves private prejudging so the judges can see the details and then a stage show so the general con population can cheer for their favorites.

You get most of your points in prejudging, but the shows matter. Sometimes, a show can win you the title, if you do something awesome and the crowd loves you enough. That's why people love Controverse and Trip-C—anything can happen, no matter who you are.

And of course, people love the twists. Usually the twists are something like an absurd budget restriction or a strange material everyone has to incorporate. This year's twist? Quals has a theme, Double Creature Feature, which explains the paired-up monsters all around us. There's no twist for Primes yet, but we're all expecting something to shift. It's just the way Irma runs her shows.

No matter the twists, Trip-C requires its teams to produce four separate cosplays. It's a *lot*, even for two people. And May, while awesome, isn't much for crafting, so it's been mostly on me. I don't mind the work, though. In the months after Luca broke up with me, work was all I had, all I wanted to do. In a way, it was the work that pulled me up, put me back together, and got me here.

Still, now that I'm here, I can't help feeling like something is missing. May is great, but my monster was supposed to be Luca.

Madeline finishes her explanations. The clubbers pass around tablets with even more paperwork. After we sign, we're told to wait until our names are called. I still don't understand why they've kept us all together until May says, "Look, Raff. Cameras."

Sure enough, there are camera crews sweeping into the room, setting up. For a moment, staring into the dilated black cyclops eyes of the camera lenses, I'm reminded of my setup back at home. I feel the excitement of looking into that lens, that digital oblivion, knowing that someone is watching me back. Someone is noticing me.

I don't know who's on the other side of this lens, and I don't really care; tons of people are going to be photographing us. Still, the quality of this crew piques my curiosity.

"Are they allowed to film us like this?"

"Raff, there's a photo release in the application. Our parents had to sign it."

"Oh, I forged that."

"And we just signed another thing on those tablets. Did you even read it?"

I'm too scattered to read just now. I just punched through the pages and signed, passing the tablet off to May.

Then the judges enter. I don't recognize them like I expect to. They have a small meeting with the clubbers before calling out the first couple's team name. I barely pay attention, because I've just now pinpointed where Luca is. He's at the back of the room, and he's watching me.

Luca used to play this game with me. We'd be watching a movie or working, and he'd just look at me. And he wouldn't look away until I finally looked back. I used to be so enamored by this; I loved looking up and seeing him smiling at me.

But he'd do it all the time. At shows. While I was driving. While I was talking to someone else. And I realized after we broke up that it wasn't about me. It was about *him*. He wasn't admiring me; he was giving me a chance to admire him admiring me.

I feel his stare now. As the judges call May and me, I let my robes billow, and I make Luca look upon what he's lost.

"Which one of you is Raffy?" one of the clubbers asks. I raise my hand.

"I follow you on Ion. I've been looking forward to seeing this in person. And it's—"

Another clubber hushes the first. The judges whisper to one another at their table, then indicate that we should begin. I start talking right away.

"For the Double Creature Feature, it was important that we pick a pair that was symbolically similar but not redundant in technique. We wanted to create a companion build that showcased needlework, and so we came up with the Spring Keeper and the Pinehorn from—"

"From *Deep Autumn*? Holy shit," one of the judges says, recognition hitting the panel. They sit back, awed as they mentally compare our grotesque appearance with its cutesy origin.

I begin my rehearsed breakdown of the materials I used, the techniques I incorporated, and the time I spent. You have to be quick—most prejudging only lasts about five minutes so the judges can get through everyone and still have time to eat bad con food. To help them, competitors also bring build books, printed-out guides to their work with reference photos, progress pictures, and detailed notes.

The judges get to ask questions, too.

Where do you get your supplies?

Did you drape the robe, pattern it, or a mix?

How did you build the Pinehorn's stilts?

Did you design the embroidery pattern on the robe?

Who did what?

I'm prepared for all of this, especially that last bit.

"We worked together. May is a talented illustrator. I'm good with sewing. It was a team effort."

"Well," says one of the judges, "for a team, you certainly do a lot of the talking."

This shakes me, but I just give her a bow. "I'm the Spring Keeper. The forces of the deep forest are mine to command and care for, corrupted or not."

The judges are visibly impressed, both with the costumes and my in-character retort. They thank us, and we thank them. A hush falls over the other competitors as we walk back into the crowd of costumes. Everyone is staring now, and I let them, reveling in the weight of their attention.

I finally glance at Luca. He is the only one looking elsewhere.

FOUR

I, Raphael Odom, a.k.a. Raffy, a.k.a. Crafty Rafty, have died and ascended to heaven.

And by heaven, I mean Craft Club on a Sunday morning, when the rest of Somerville is still asleep and I have the whole place to myself. I practically hear the harp music sweeping over me as the doors rush open, pulling me into the bright, funky-colored universe—my favorite place, forever and ever.

The store in Somerville is Craft Club's unofficial headquarters. It wasn't the first store, but it is the largest, at least for now. Craft Clubs are popping up all over Massachusetts, bringing an astounding variety of crafting supplies to a craft desert near you. They have it all: paints, papers, pens, fabrics, flowers, frames, scissors, sheers, cardboard, glue guns, heat guns, staple guns, and increasingly, cosplay supplies like thermoplastics and wig wefts.

I'm here to grab more rhinestones, and since I came all this way, I might as well pick up a few other supplies, too, right? I could get a lot of my supplies online, but there's something so inspiring about being surrounded by such abundance. So much material! So many projects in so many parts, just waiting for the right hands to assemble them.

I like being here. And besides, I hate ordering stuff to the house. Evie has a camera on the stoop, and she's nosy. It's better if I just get what I need here and smuggle it in. For the same reason, I use cash. Untraceable, dirty cash. When it comes to Evie, the fewer questions, the better.

Evie is…a lot of things. Just a lot in general. But most of all, she is a Very Serious Art Person. She despises anything crafty, and she especially hates Craft Club. In fact, it's a hobby of hers to sit at Jurassic Perk, the coffee shop next to Craft Club, and bemoan the state of art as shoppers walk by, loaded down with bags. It's because she hates accessible art. And the people who partake in casual creation? They disgust her. *Hobbyists*, she calls them, pronouncing it like it's a four-letter word. Like if she sees one more DIY tutorial on Facebook, she'll fall into a self-imposed coma. To a woman who is defined by her taste and curation, the very idea that people dabble in art without lofty intent is, by default, sacrilege.

So that makes Craft Club the equivalent of a satanic temple. And here I am, her son, breathlessly rushing inside first thing on a

Sunday, ready to go absolutely bananas in aisles *full* of horrifically accessible art supplies.

I float through the store, turning into the seasonal decorations aisle instead of walking down the central one, where clubbers (the employees, dressed in branded, bright-magenta polos) hand out promo cards. (I have my coupons on my phone, like a professional.) I walk through shrines of glittering gourds and life-size robot witches cackling over cauldrons. One of the witches has been knocked over, and her top half has dissociated from her legs. As her head turns this way and that, it looks like she's writhing on the white tiles. She is, quite literally, cackling her ass off.

"Same, girl," I say as I step over the twitching witch and into the kids' section. Surrounded by watercolor kits, I pause to review my list.

I need:

◊ GEMS—SEA FOAM DREAM #6
◊ ADHESIVES—E6000 X 2
◊ ADHESIVES—GLUE GUN STICKS
◊ FABRICS—NETTING FOR TRAWL SHAWL, 3 YARDS
◊ FABRICS—CROCHET COTTON LACE (EYELASH EDGES), 1.5 YARDS
◊ FOAM—CLAY
◊ FOAM—BEVELS

I push my sunglasses farther up my nose. I'm sneaking—in disguise. I pop the collar of my coat like a cartoon spy, and I get to finding.

Most of the list is easy. I fly through the fabrics first, knowing that'll take the longest. When a clubber asks if I need help, I say, "No, just browsing," as kindly as I can, and they drift off.

I pick up some new scissors, since my fabric ones are pretty worn. I also get a few fresh box cutter blades. Then I start looking at respirators, since the ones they have here are much nicer than what you can get online.

"Basket, Raffy?"

I jump; the clubber talking to me is much closer than I realized. She registers the surprise on my face, and the skin of her nose crinkles, amused. She's got a basket for me, and I smile thankfully before I dump the many items I've collected into it. The clubber gives me a wink before she goes.

I heave my basket to the gem aisle, knowing I've already stayed too long. Am I really here so often that they know me on sight? I'm thinking about this when I accidentally clip another shopper with the corner of my basket.

"Sorry," I mumble, keeping my eyes down. I pass the individual packets, then find the bulk gems. I'm annoyed that the store is slowly filling up, and I'm annoyed that my palms are itching as I begin to overheat from carrying around this basket, which I've filled with too much stuff. Stuff I don't need. Nonessentials. Indulgences. And now I'm rushing to find the one thing I actually really need—these idiotic stones. I pull the label from my pocket, checking the name, and begin searching for the exact color.

"Sea Foam Dream, right?"

It's a clubber helping another shopper. The person I just bumped into.

"Ah, here they are. We've got a few sizes. Anything else you need?"

The clubber looks at the shopper, who is looking at me, but I am looking at the stones. The exact stones I myself am here to buy.

"This *is* what you were looking for, right?" asks the clubber.

"No. I mean, yeah. Thank you, I'm all set," says the shopper. He's as young as me, by the sound of his voice. But he sounds unsure, even embarrassed, and I don't know why. The clubber goes away, and then it's just me and this guy looking at the same jar of Sea Foam Dream rhinestones. As with almost all product labels at Craft Club, the face of Elizabeth Worthy, founder of Craft Club, mother of current CEO Irma Worthy and iconic wearer of ringlet curls, stares back at us with a warm smile. We return her inviting smile in silence, until:

"Raffy, right?"

I nearly drop my basket. What is happening? Why does everyone know my name? Instead of sprinting away, I face him. The first thing I register is that this guy is soaking wet. And then I register his smile, and the strangeness of his appearance is immediately eclipsed by the realization that I have never, ever, *ever* seen a more beautiful face.

He's got dark hair and dark eyes. He's in some sort of sports uniform, his shorts revealing tan thighs brushed with grass stains, and slumping white socks pool around his narrow ankles. His tank top is tie-dyed with sweat. The tank clings to his muscular body, and he plucks at it bashfully.

"It's Luca. From bio?"

At first, the image of this boy doesn't fit, and then it does. Luca Vitale.

"Oh, I didn't recognize you. You're so…wet."

"I play soccer. I had practice this morning. It's why I'm gross." He shrugs, and I force myself to blink rather than stare for another second at the sheen on his exposed shoulders. "I'm not usually this gross. Or wearing cleats. Or, I guess I do wear cleats a lot, and I guess I play soccer a lot, but, like…" He rocks on his feet, rambling, and I hear the *click-click* of his shoes on the tile floor.

"Usually I shower right after practice," Luca says definitively.

"But today you went shopping?" I ask.

"Yeah."

"At Craft Club?"

"Yeah."

"For aquamarine flat-back rhinestones."

He shrugs. I look at the wall of glittering plastic gems and pearls. I look at Luca, who appears to be uncomfortable in front of me but unaware of how out of place he is here in general.

"So, I'm Luca," he says again, smiling.

I roll my eyes. "I know."

"And you're Raffy." A playfulness threads his brow, like he's guessing. Is he flirting? He's not flirting. People don't flirt with me.

"Sorry if I stink," he says, but he's not sorry. I know because he gathers his big arms across his chest, flexing so that the small muscles near his elbows jump. His skin glows. I'm blushing.

"Yeah, I'm Raffy. And you're fine," I say.

I'm used to guys like this categorically avoiding me, as though interacting with me is going to leave them exposed to whatever gay contagion I suffer from. This guy is doing it all wrong. He's doing his best to connect with me. And he seems…interested. I've never received attention like this, but I've seen it in movies. By the way Luca leans in, I think he's seen the same movies.

I scramble for a question to ask him. I come up with: "What are you making?" I know I need to go, but I'm not sure when else in my life I'm going to have such a distinct upper hand. Here in Craft Club, I'm on my own home turf.

"What?"

"What are you using the rhinestones for? I'm looking for this color, too."

"I'm not making anything," he says quickly. "I'm picking them up for someone else."

I'm a little let down. I liked the idea of Luca bedazzling something, like…a shin guard. I grin at this idea as I scoop up a bag for myself and then a bag for him.

"You can buy a smaller package, but in my experience, they don't go far. You're better off having a little extra than not enough. Otherwise you'll have to come back here all over again."

"I like it here," Luca says. "It's…fun. What about you? What are you making?"

I am not about to tell this boy that I'm working on a lifelike version of a zombified mermaid who haunts a nuclear submarine. Instead I say, "Just a small project."

"For school?"

"No, for something else."

"What kind of *else*?"

"A super geeky *else*."

"What sort of super geeky *else*?"

"A video-game-related *else*."

"What game?"

I sigh. "It's called *Wake*. You've probably never heard of it. It's not, like, *Call of Duty* or something."

"Maybe I have heard of it," he says. "Maybe I've even *played* it."

"Have you played the secret bosses on Death Mode? 'Cause if not, you're not gonna know what I'm talking about."

His eyes narrow. He smiles smugly, like he's got me right where he wants me.

"Plasma Siren."

I give him the gratification of my shock. I haven't even made it that far in Death Mode. I've just watched other people do the boss battle on Ion. Who is this person?

"Wait, you've played against her?" I ask.

"Nah, I'm just familiar."

He's smiling like he's got a joke I'm not in on. I find myself adjusting my basket, heavier every second, like I'm about to make a break for it.

"I'm gonna go explore a little bit. Want to come?" Luca asks me.

"No," I say right away. "I mean, no thanks. I've got to go."

"Oh, that's okay. See you tomorrow?"

"What?"

"At school. Remember?"

"Right." I return his fist bump. It is the most bizarre thing I have ever done with my hand, which, for a seventeen-year-old overly into arts and crafts, is truly saying something.

As I pay, I keep my face down. I do this because I don't want to be recognized again. I also do this because I cannot seem to stop smiling. I'm Elizabeth Worthy's face on those labels, my cheeks drawn back into an eternal, glowing grin. Then, right before I rush out of the store, I turn. The doors sweep open, the warm air breathing into the cooled store, bringing with it the smells of dust and grass and water evaporating off pavement. I look back at the milling shoppers and the bright pink clubbers, realizing too late that I'm looking for one last glimpse of Luca. As soon as I understand this, I stop. I turn. I leave.

"Hey."

I'm an inch from the door, and he's there again.

"Striker," he says. "It's my position in soccer."

He grins again, taking in my shock with satisfaction. Striker9 was the name of the person who bought me those stones.

"You think you're gonna need more of these?" he asks, holding up his bag. "Or are you good?"

"I think I'm good," I manage.

"Cool," he says. He smiles. I smile. The door tries to close, impatient, and then jolts open again.

"I'm going," I say.

"So go," he says.

And, still smiling, I do.

FIVE

Con food can be rough. Usually at Controverse, May and I leave the con grounds to hit up a pizza place in Southie, a few blocks down from the convention center, and take photos in our cosplays as Southie residents look on in horror and text their group chats. But this year we're competitors, and they tell us everyone's got to stay put in the back hall, so we don't even get bad con food. People protest, but clubbers ignore questions as they separate us into smaller groups and take turns leading us out a back door, *away* from the main con floor.

Luca and Inaya are in the first group. May and I are in the second group. The third group is kept in the prejudging room.

We're told to wait in a darker hallway and not talk as clubbers trade notes with the film crews. Whatever the other group is doing, it takes about an hour. May is allowed to remove her helmet, and people sit down. Then the clubbers are back, getting us up and walking us through the dark; the only light is the bloody glow of the exit signs. We pass by the first group of cosplayers going the other way, and all of a sudden, Luca jumps out at me. He whispers, "Be ready, Raffy."

Then Inaya drags him back and he's gone, and my head is spinning with more shadows than the ones in the hall around us.

Finally, we reach a door that says QUIET, SHOW IN PROGRESS on a whiteboard, and we go silent.

"You two—you're first," whispers a clubber, pulling May and me forward through the door.

May and I exchange a concerned look as we're ushered into a dark passage beyond.

We are about to be murdered, aren't we? I ask her with my eyebrows and a downturned smirk.

If so, let death take me swiftly—it has been a good life, she responds with a shrug and a dignified nod of her head. She puts on her mask.

"Now," the clubber whispers, pushing May and me through a curtain. "Good luck!"

Then, like cannonballs hitting placid water, spotlights crash over us. We are on a stage in front of a crowd that responds to our baffled expressions with ecstatic cheering.

"Can we do that once more, but this time, can we get the monster to enter second?"

The voice is huge, blasted at us from speakers above the stage.

The crowd murmurs, agitated. How many people are here? It must be more than a hundred, bigger than any Quals audience I've ever seen. Then, when nothing happens, I realize they're talking to us. To May, the monster.

A hand pulls us back behind the curtain. Someone counts down.

"Three...two..."

I think quickly, adding the clues together like materials. The film crew. The fact that Irma showed up personally. The huge crowd, the cheering, and the staged production. Controverse has a twist this year, all right, and the twist is that Quals has gone from being a con sideshow to the main freaking event.

"So *this* is what that release form was for," May whispers as I think, *So this is what Luca meant.* She elbows me, and I remember that no matter what surprises we're thrown, we're here to win.

"One."

I'm ready.

We enter, confident this time, moving across a wide stage. Cameras are trained on our every move. On instinct, I find myself posing. May follows my lead.

The crowd screams until a voice booms over the racket: "Good. Now approach the judges."

The judges—*new* judges—are seated on a raised platform at the end of the stage, watching us with blank faces. And I realize that the performance portion of Quals has started. It's happening right now. And if they're doing all this for Quals, what are they planning for tomorrow's Primes? I shut down my apprehension, determined to make it through Quals so I can find out.

"You ready?" I say.

"Fucking Controverse," May says back, but with a tone of resolve that I know means she's ready to rock this.

Just like we rehearsed, we drop into a low hunch, then stagger upright suddenly so we look contorted by the corruption eating our skin. While May hisses and jabs at the crowd, I reach inside my robe for our secret weapon, a totally awesome prop I've been saving for the Quals show. It's a hanging incense burner like a priest might use in a real temple, except I've fashioned this one to look like a hanging orchid plant on chains wound with ivy. As I swing it, the small vaporizer I've installed starts up, and we're surrounded by undulating vapor and floating petals. In the lights, it's nothing short of pure magic.

Our illusion grips the crowd by the throat. They're cheering "*DEEP AUTUMN!*" as we hit the raised platform, and the judges are grinning with appreciation. I've never felt cooler.

We bow, letting them know that we're done with our antics. Things quiet down. For a moment, I think we're in trouble, and then that voice returns.

"Good. Thanks. Person in the monster outfit, take two steps to your right, and then cheat left so we can see the wings. No, your other left."

Somewhere among the cameras, someone is directing us. They make a few more minor adjustments to where we're standing, and the room goes quiet as we wait. Someone is giving notes to the crowd, instructing people to turn and face the front, rearranging so that certain faces are in the shot as the cameras zoom in on our outfits.

Finally, *finally*, the judges come to life. It happens all at once at an invisible cue, like animatronics at a theme park. They beam and cackle at one another like old friends, and I'm able to see them clearly for the first time as the lights find them. They aren't the people from prejudging. These are new, camera-ready judges, and I realize I recognize several of them from the cosplay big leagues.

"This? We haven't seen this yet today. *This* is fun," says a man with bright blue hair and bright blue nails. They click as he flutters a hand up and down. "This is everything we come to this competition to see, am I right?"

He's Waldorf Waldorf, a famous designer. I recognize his inch-long nails, and the iconic contrast of his electric-blue hair, crowning the cool brown of his face. I just watched him get those nails applied on Instagram a day ago. He was in LA then. Why is he here? How is this real?

"But is it fun *enough*?" asks a lady in thick-rimmed glasses. When she talks, she cocks her head to the right so that she's looking at us down the angle of her pale, wide cheekbone. Her frizzy bangs bounce as she shakes her head critically. "Can you be an expert in fun? We're looking for experts here. The best. And while I appreciate camp—Waldorf, you know I love camp—can this be considered fun next to some of the cosplays we just saw?

I'm still thinking about that Bambi look. How can I care about this when I've seen that? *That* was fun."

"I'm not sure how you can care about anything other than finding scissors to cut off those bangs, but okay," Waldorf Waldorf shoots back. The crowd whoops as the lady leans over, swatting at him. I expect her to karate chop his throat, but she's laughing. They're friends.

"Raphael, which one are you, under all that makeup?"

This is from the second-to-last judge, an older woman with warm, tan skin, who is in an outfit seemingly made entirely of loops and loops of crochet. Her hands gleam with rings as she points at me, her eyes on her tablet. I think her name is Yvonne. She's got a super popular crafting channel on Ion.

"I'm Raffy," I say. I suppress the urge to curtsy.

"And you're the mastermind behind this look?"

I glance at May, inscrutable behind her helmet.

"We both designed it."

"You both did?" She looks at her tablet again, frowning. "Designing isn't executing. Who built it for you, then?"

"Raffy built most of it," May jumps in, but her voice is barely audible.

"I love it," says the last judge, a man with the least amount of neck I have ever seen on a person. His head is mostly embedded in the mass of muscle that makes up his hulking back. Next to the lady with the rings and crocheted outfit, he looks like an interloper from an entirely different universe.

And I know exactly who he is: Marcus the Master. He's a famous cosplayer specializing in metalwork and armor builds. He's known for winning Controverse years ago with a Viking-inspired reimagining of Optimus Prime, and he makes a living running armor workshops at cons.

"Still there, Raffy? What about the moss? You've done a good job of distressing it, but it looks a little muddy from far away. Some of that lovely, rich green is getting lost," says the lady with the glasses. "There are higher-quality materials you could have used, I think."

I point at the moss on May's shoulder armor. "*Hypnum cupressiforme*, a sheet moss." Like we rehearsed, May drops into a perfect hunch and holds it as I go through the blooms rustling on her back.

"Asiatic lily. Celosia. Alstroemeria. A few varieties of roses. Yarrow. Gypsophila. They're all fall-blooming flowers. We planted them in the spring. The moss was easier—you can blend it up and paint it onto the fabric, and then it grows under the right conditions. We thought about airbrushing it for a better green, but we liked the idea of keeping it real."

"You *grew* those flowers?"

"Not all of them. Some are made of satin that we airbrushed."

May strides to the edge of their platform to give them a good look, saying, "We grew the fungus, too. The itch is *very* authentic. Want to touch?" The tension of the room breaks into laughter, which breaks into applause. In a flash, Waldorf Waldorf has descended from the judging table, spinning me around to inspect the blossoms on my shoulder.

"Fascinating," he says. "Exquisite! I can't tell what's real and what's artificial."

"That's the point," I tell Waldorf.

"So how are they staying on? Does the moss grip them?"

I smile. "No, sometimes we in the cosplay world just need to use a little hot glue."

Waldorf Waldorf claps for the small joke, and I take what feels like my first breath since walking onto the stage. I don't relax yet, though.

Someone offstage calls the judges, who nod in acknowledgment but never actually turn toward the cameras. The lady in the glasses is smiling deviously as Waldorf returns to his seat. May and I begin to leave the platform, but she stops us.

"Now, you said you both spent the summer on this build, am I right?"

"That's right," I say.

"Interesting, because I heard from another competitor that Raffy started these builds by himself, and you only teamed up a short while ago. Is that right?"

I feel that familiar choke in my throat. Did Luca tell the judges about us? Or Inaya? I'm about to try lying again when the judge says, "Raffy, we've heard a lot from you. Why don't you give May a chance to explain some of her work?"

May goes still under her huge costume. She's a confident

person, but all the confidence in the world wouldn't prepare a person for this scenario. The silence stretches on, and the crowd, seeing us pause, begins to titter.

"It was my greenhouse," she finally says. "We used my greenhouse for all the plants."

"How about the construction? Did you guys split the work?" asks Marcus the Master.

"Yeah, we helped each other get dressed."

"No, not getting dressed. I mean building the suit. The props. Can you point out a portion of this build that you're responsible for?"

I help May remove her mask, expecting her to be dumbfounded. But she's got on her own natural mask. And I'm glad she let me glue that moss on her cheeks and jaw. She looks threatening.

She says, "We split the work. I'm a visual artist—I helped produce the concepts for this—but Raffy is the one who put it all together."

Even this is stretching the truth, but it's the right answer, and I can tell the judges are trying to create some sort of narrative for the cameras. I'm glad May lied, but as we walk back up the stage, all the goofiness is gone from our performance. May is nervous and knotted up.

"I'm sorry," she whispers to me.

"Don't be," I say.

At the back of the stage, the people in headsets indicate that we should step up onto the top tier of some risers, then indicate we'll be there for a while. And they're not wrong. For the next hour, we stand and watch as the other couples enter from backstage, walk the runway to the judges, and get torn apart. Then they're led back to the risers to wait with us and agonize over their performance. Some are crying by that time.

Waldorf Waldorf appears to be the expert on concepts and design. He's the nicest. The lady in glasses is a master sewer. She is extremely harsh, but I am amazed by how much she can tell about a look just from inspecting the seams. I decide she is psychic. Yvonne is basically who I aspire to be with my own Ion channel. And then, of course, there's Marcus the Master. I am thinking about him shirtless when May catches my attention.

"Finally," she says, relieved. The coordinators are back, collecting all the couples who have been judged and arranging us in a single-file line as we exit the stage. The crowd is silent as they watch. Tired. A man is standing onstage with a clipboard, talking to the judges, who have been given sandwiches.

"Not a word to the other competitors," says the coordinator as we're led into the dark corridor. The final crop of cosplayers huddles backstage, silent, drinking in our defeated parade as we're pushed past. They have no idea what's coming. I remember Luca trying to warn me despite Inaya's hushing.

Anyone would feel grateful for that warning. Faced with a person like Luca, anyone would feel grateful in general. But I don't. This is my world. My competition. For him to think I need his help—it fills me with a cold blue fire, pulsing beneath the silicon gripping my skin.

I am not doing this for Luca. I am not doing this to spite Luca. I am doing this for me. This is my only opportunity to secure my future. This is my big chance to propel myself into my destiny.

And if I succeed, it will be because I am good enough alone.

SIX

It takes me nearly an entire week to decide that my conversation with Luca in Craft Club must've been a hallucination. A very vivid hallucination, likely induced by the glue fumes I'm inhaling while I bedazzle Plasma Siren's fins. And even while awake, the hallucination continues. Luca and I have two classes together, which I've always known. But now that I've spoken to him, it's like his presence is *all* I know. I feel so dumb, so easily absorbed into this infatuation with a guy I barely would have acknowledged a week ago. And he makes it hard. So hard. When he stands at the front of the room presenting, or when he answers a question, his eyes always find mine, and his lips always pull together in a triumphant smile. It's like he's been waiting for me to watch him, because every time I do, he's already watching me. But we don't talk, which is good. We only talk online, when Striker9 asks me kinda flirty questions during my stream and I pretend not to know who my new admirer is.

> How do you keep your hands from getting sticky?
> When you create a sewing pattern, do you leave a
> seam allowance in case you get a raging boner?

It is, admittedly, very strange to flirt with an apparently-not-as-straight-as-I-thought jock through the time/space chasm that is the internet, then to pine for him every day in real life like *I'm* the one doing the chasing. It's like in person, we reverse roles, and maybe that's why it feels like a hallucination. Outside of Craft Club and the internet, I don't feel all that remarkable, yet Luca watches me anyway. It's how I know I'm dreaming, and it's why I'll never make the next move. I don't want to snap out of whatever this is. In fact, if glue fumes caused this hallucination in the first place, I might as well inhale all the fumes. Every fume. Not a fume in this town is safe from me, in fact.

Ironically, I am in the school's art studio, spray painting beneath the spray booth, the next time I encounter Luca.

It's late after school, the art wing totally free of students and teachers. Before me on a slab of cardboard, I've laid out a series of rough bangles. Or they will be bangles as soon as I finish painting them. Right now they're just foam rings, carved and pocked to look like rough metal. All that's left to do is Midas the whole affair with gilded spray paint, then apply some rust.

Suddenly, the spray booth jolts. Never a good sign; usually it means something's about to explode. I scream and flail backward, colliding with something right behind me—a person who catches me just before I fall over. Together we hit a table, and then it's their turn to flail backward.

"Are you kidding me?"

I look at Luca, who has a fresh gold stripe sprayed up the armpit of his shirt, over his chin, and onto the corner of his mouth. He must have knocked on the spray booth to get my attention, and my hand tensed on the nozzle right before I fell. I throw the spray can down, my own hands coated from where it caught me, too.

I don't know what you're supposed to say when you accidentally spray paint a hot person gold, so I say, "I was working. You shouldn't surprise someone when they're working."

Luca starts to speak, but paint drips into his mouth. His eyes go wide, and I spring into action, dragging him to the sink where we wash brushes. I expect him to wash out his mouth, or maybe just run the water over his lips. But like a puppy, he shoves his whole face into the stream, and he shouts, "BLEEEGHHHHH."

I am about to react when he squints open an eye to make sure I am watching, then resumes his fake vomiting noises.

"Look, can you be quiet? I'm not even supposed to be working in here by myself."

"BLEEEGHHH!"

"I know you're not vomiting. I can *see* you."

"BLAAAAGHHHH!"

"Luca, come *on*."

He stands up abruptly, his head soaking. Water cascades off his nose as he smiles down at me.

"You remember my name?"

I thrust paper towels into his damp chest. "I *knew* you were faking."

Luca takes the clump and dries his face. There is still a lot of gold smeared on his neck and chin. He gives me a very sad, very tortured look, and it's a beat before I realize he wants me to help him wash off the rest.

"C'mon. I know you want to." He grins, as though he is doing me an incredible favor by allowing me to bathe him.

"Why is it that all straight boys think they are undeniably attractive to gays? Do they think we're all just waiting around, desperate for their attention? Do straight guys think they're the only people with access to porn?"

Luca's grin widens. I am, admittedly, baiting him with this line.

And then he says, "Correct me if I'm wrong, but you're the one who shot into *my* mouth just a second ago."

I nearly black out.

Luca's laugh fills the studio again, and I shut him up with a hand. His eyes continue to laugh at me, his breath hot on my palm. I snatch the towels and drag them roughly over his chin, the underlit hollow of his neck.

"So you're Striker9?" I ask.

The curiosity I saw earlier vanishes, replaced by a well-practiced nonchalance. "Yeah."

"You've been watching?"

"On and off."

"Why?"

Luca rubs at his neck like he's not sure I got all the paint off (I didn't—this *is* spray paint—but I did my best).

"*Wake* is like one of my favorite games. Plasma Siren is a bad bitch."

"Do you cosplay, too?"

Luca scoffs. "Nah."

"You think it's dumb, but you watch my streams?"

"I don't think it's dumb. I could just never do it. My parents already think I'm into freaky shit with the games I play. They'd kiiiiiiiiiillll meeeeeee if I came home with a wig."

This doesn't surprise me at all.

"Why do you do it?" he asks me. "Just because you love making stuff?"

I drift toward the spray booth, turning it off. I scoop up the can of spray paint and turn it over in my palm, the nozzle leaking pure gold onto my skin. His breath was so warm. I held his smile.

"I do it for attention," I say. Luca scoffs again, then sees I'm being serious.

"I've always been good at making stuff, yeah, but if I just wanted to make stuff, I wouldn't set up streams. I wouldn't enter cosplay competitions. I want people to see my work and recognize it as work. I want…"

"Respect?"

"Yes! Yes. Exactly."

We both go still, like my naked ambition deserves a moment of silence.

"Okay, you know Craft Club, right?"

Luca nods.

"So, they run competitions in the area, and if you do really well, sometimes they'll offer to sponsor you. And recently, with cosplayers becoming such a big community, those sponsorships have really started to mean something. Art schools have started sending recruiters to the competitions, too. Last year, RISD gave a girl a full ride based on some textiles she did."

"Tiles? Like in a bathroom?"

I grimace.

"Yeah, the Rhode Island School of Design has a world-renowned program in bathroom remodeling."

Luca nods, accepting this. "Cool, cool."

"I'm kidding."

"Oh."

Luca is looking at me with that slow curiosity again, like he's on the verge of understanding the alphabet that makes me up. "Isn't your mom, like, a famous artist, though?"

"Artist turned gallery director, yeah. She discovers other artists."

"Why doesn't she discover you?"

I look at the bangles in the spray booth. They are half painted, and they still look terrible. I look at the cheap spray paint on my palms and the school studio's cheerful clutter. I don't know how to answer Luca's question.

"I'm sorry about your shirt," I say.

Luca plucks at the shirt, dripping wet like when I first met him in Craft Club. The water has blurred the paint into swollen stains. The shirt is ruined.

"Shit," he mutters.

"Is your family going to kiiiiiillll youuuuu if you come home covered in spray paint?"

A smile breaks through Luca's contemplative expression, but his lips never part. It's a performance of restraint. Boyish coyness. He knows what he's doing.

"They might," he says.

"Do you need another shirt? I feel bad."

"I might," he says, and now he is smiling with those teeth. "Why, do you know how to make shirts, too?"

"With a sewing machine, yeah."

"You have a sewing machine?"

"Not here."

"Where? Your studio?"

I nod.

Luca scratches at the gold on his neck. He makes me watch him as he considers what I've offered. What *am* I offering? I don't even know. But I am hoping with every stitch that makes me up that he'll say yes.

"You could show me," he finally says, rubbing at the paint on his hands. "I could learn. How to make stuff, I mean."

I nod.

"Should we go now?" he asks.

And, smiling, we do.

SEVEN

The stage vanishes behind the doors, and then we are through the concrete hallways and back on the con floor.

The brightness and noise of the con makes it feel like we've waltzed through a portal and into another world. I should feel relieved, but I'm not. I should feel accomplished, but I don't. Between Luca and the promise of even more surprises, my rigorous preparation now feels subpar, and my glorious daydreams of winning Trip-C are coming undone. Reality right now feels a little ruined.

We head to coat check first so that May can extract herself from the Pinehorn costume. As I pack it into the suitcase, I remember how the judges looked at other people's costumes: with derision, doubt, and dismissal. I find that focusing on that brings me a dark joy and settles my nerves. I'm not proud that I'm resorting to the dark magic of gloating to make myself feel better, but part of me knows I'm also being logical. Not everyone got the applause we got. Not everyone should have. We worked hard.

I worked hard. I always work hard.

So how come I never feel like I'm working hard enough?

"You're brooding. Why?" May asks as she stretches, newly freed from her stilts and helmet. Moss still covers her face, but it's not the weirdest look on the con floor, and she for sure doesn't care.

"I'm just confused. I don't know what that was."

"That," May says as she hands some cash to a vendor selling popcorn, "was high production value. Did you see the cameras they were using? They looked like rocket launchers."

"I guess Craft Club's going big this year," I say.

"Here," she says, handing me the popcorn. "I'm gonna go pee, but then can we swing through the Art Mart?"

"Sure."

"Are we free for the rest of the day?"

I shrug. "I think so? Those coordinators told us they'd be emailing the finalists tonight."

May scratches at the fake moss on her face with reckless indulgence, and I wince as my work is ruined.

"Fucking finally. Oh my god." She hisses with relief. "Are you keeping Pinehorn intact, or will it also be cosplay composted?"

May knows I have to be very careful about holding on to cosplay, because each piece has to be kept hidden from Evie. I have a few bins of costumes I store at May's place, but I deconstruct most of the larger builds and keep the reusable parts, then trash the rest. I try to think of a scenario in which I'll need Pinehorn or Spring Keeper again. I've already done my making-of videos. We did our couple photo shoot during our makeup test last weekend. I did detail shots this morning before we left May's house. I should be good to deconstruct both, yet I feel like I'm missing something big. Then it hits me.

In my mind, there is a memory I have yet to color in. A plan I have yet to realize. It's a picture I've looked at a million times in my head, a picture of two boys dressed in moss and flowers, sitting beneath the brushing fingers of the willows in the Boston Public Garden. Luca and me, in full cosplay, together.

A picture like that would absolutely rock on Insta. But it's not even worth thinking about anymore. It's never going to happen.

"We're all done with these builds," I tell May. "You can take off the rest of your makeup if you want. I'll meet you at the Art Mart. But let me take the coat check ticket so I can grab everything later."

May whoops in relief, slapping her ticket into my hand before skipping toward the bathrooms.

I stand still, pure sadness crashing over me. My green-stained fingers clutch the ticket. May left her popcorn with me, too. Gross. It's one of those immense plastic tubs that people only eat a few handfuls from before their bones begin to disintegrate from the salt. May will absolutely be able to finish it, and she will absolutely vomit some of this up tonight at my place.

I am suddenly very annoyed to be holding May's future upchuck. I shove it under my arm and start pacing through the crowd. It's midday, and the crowds are clogging up the aisles, looking at books stacked in teetering towers and figurines in lit-up glass cases and taking photos in front of the large, bright displays. Instead of going directly to the Art Mart, I swing through Controverse's core, where all the food vendors have set up shop, and then out into the open area where photographers buzz around cosplayers. Here, the crowds crush and swirl, backing up to clear space around the cosplayers so people can take turns snapping pictures. It's hard to focus on where you're going when there are so many wonderful costumes.

Many people recognize Spring Keeper, and as I wave back at the ones shouting for my attention, I begin to forget my anger and anxiety. Eventually, I have to put down the popcorn because a few people want pictures, and soon I've gathered my own crowd. I'm not huge on performance usually, but right now I play along. I pose for the photos; I give the cry. I throw myself into it, and I'm rewarded by a few photographers asking me if they can take some portfolio shots.

They mean for their own portfolios—a lot of photographers come here to build their socials. They offer me cards in return for my poses, and I throw them in my bag. I will try to remember to follow up online, introduce myself and so on.

There are a million reasons for a cosplayer to want to be on the floor, but none of them are why I'm here, and I know it. I'm hoping to see Luca. I want him to know his presence hasn't fazed me, not one bit. And soon I am rewarded.

"Raffy!"

I hold my pose and glower into the lens of a camera. It lowers, the photographer shows me the shot, and I nod in approval.

"Raffy!" Luca shouts again.

I was an idiot to come here, I realize. I just wanted Luca to see me, not talk to me. But there's no going back now. He appears all at once. In the glow from the skylights, I can see every detail of his work.

(Well, Inaya's work.)

He is wearing nearly nothing, just hide shorts with a flared tuft of a tail that quivers as he slips through the crowd. Someone asks him for a photo, and he pivots like he's never not ready, and I get a full view of his back. Soccer, I reason, should be considered a performance-enhancing drug in the world of competitive cosplay, because it has absolutely weaponized Luca's body in a way that cloth and foam cannot match.

"You look great," he says. His eyes shine like onyx beads against the soft white makeup masking his brows and head.

"Fuck you."

Shock curdles Luca's posture, and a few photographers lower their cameras. I'm just as surprised as they are. The sound drains from our small pocket of Controverse, and I race to pour something into the emptiness I've created. In my rush, I pour in a lot of nastiness. It's what I have ready.

"You could have called," I say. "Or texted. Or even paid me back for any of what we made. But you just went dark, and then you show up here with Inaya, and you're dressed as *my* concept? Does she even know that? Or did you tell her it was your idea?"

Instead of backing up, Luca steps forward. He's bigger than me, but he can't intimidate me. Not when I'm dressed like this.

"Abandoning me for Inaya wasn't enough? You had to give her my idea, too? And after everything, you think the best way you can re-enter my life is with a compliment? I don't want a compliment, Luca. I want an *explanation*."

I meant to say exactly none of this. I meant to say, "Hey."

But I mean every word.

Luca gets real close. The next words he says are only for me to hear.

"Don't do this here. Don't ruin this for both of us."

"Ruin?"

I stare back at him. Then there's a flash, and, surprisingly, it's not the anger punching through my brain. It's a camera, then another camera. People are mistaking us for a pair, seeing his fawn costume paired with my floral robe.

In my mind, I page through the visions of me and Luca from the future, a destiny we will never inhabit. I had so many plans for us. So many ideas to create. And here, in the midst of our fight, the vision of being photographed together in cosplay is happening. But this isn't right; none of this feels good.

Luca and I still pose, masking our fight. And other cosplayers join in. Suddenly our argument is taking place through the other people modeling with us.

"I told Inaya it was your idea," Luca whispers to me. "She told me she checked with you. I would have checked myself, but you have me blocked on everything. Still."

"We go to the same school."

"You know I can't say shit in person. You know that."

I'm tapping my foot. "Inaya didn't check."

"Well, that's not my fault."

"It's not that simple," I snap back. The other cosplayers between us shift away, hearing the edge in my tone. They give us a confused look before the next people take their place.

"It *is* that simple," Luca spits back. "Sometimes, shit is simple, Raffy. Not everyone is one of your complicated little projects."

I don't get a chance to respond before Inaya, in all her zombie-deer glory, lithely slips through the crowd to join us. People see the two deer costumes side by side and start to cheer and laugh, finally getting it, and I am suddenly on the outside again.

"Raffy, you look amazing," Inaya says, air-kissing me. I don't move a muscle. She says, "Wasn't that wild? I can't believe Craft Club sprang for that stage! And all those lights! I've never been in a competition like that before. How'd you do?"

I turn to go. Luca is one thing, but Inaya wants to pretend like we're friends now, too? I know myself, and I know my anger. I better go before I say something I can't take back.

"Raff, *wait!*"

A hand digs into the flowers on my shoulder, crushing a few blossoms. The grip is firm. Desperate.

"Please," Luca pleads.

"You stole my idea." I say this right to Inaya's face.

Inaya laughs. "Are you really trying to take credit for this? You don't even touch gore makeup. You were never gonna pull this off." She smiles. "Not like this."

"Inaya, come on," Luca cuts in.

I really, *really* want to be anywhere else right now.

"No, *you* come on," she snaps back. "If Raffy wants to talk about it, we can talk about it. You don't have to protect him."

"No, Inaya, *look*." Luca pulls her around, and I turn, too. We're facing into the bright lights of two cameras balanced on the shoulders of two people wearing clubber outfits. A third person has a mic and is talking to the cameras excitedly, our little fight the backdrop for whatever they're recording. And then they turn to Luca.

"And here we have three of the youngest competitors. Luca, tell us about how you pulled off this amazing look," the interviewer says.

"He didn't," I cut in. The interviewer turns toward me, eyes shimmering.

"These two aren't much for complicated projects, or complications in general," I say to her in a bright tone. I try to slam on the brakes, but my mouth keeps working. "It's why Inaya chose him over me, because he's a lot hotter, right? And Luca lets people use him for his looks as long as they make him look good."

The interviewer is confused. Luca is confused.

"It's an inside joke," Inaya says. "We go way back."

"So you know each other from outside the competition? Drama! What can you tell us about being friends with your competitors?"

None of us says a thing. It's super awkward. All I want to do is run, but Luca's got his hand on my shoulder still.

"Raffy," he whispers. "Please."

"What is the deal with you three, anyway?" the interviewer asks, nervous now.

How can we answer this without admitting what we used to be to one another? I look right at Luca, who isn't out yet. After everything that's happened between us, there is still a trust that I would never break. Bruise, maybe, but never break. I would never out him like this. I would never out him at all. But as noble as I think I am, Luca's face is full of fear that I know I've put there. It makes me hate myself even more, knowing that when he sees me, he sees me with my dagger raised and ready. He fears my temper. I fear my tongue. It's why I keep him blocked. Luca ruined us once, but I've been so busy being hurt that I knew if we talked before I was ready, I'd ruin us forever.

I need to *go*. I shrug out of my robe easily, the heavy garment pooling at Luca's feet as I snatch up May's dumb bag of popcorn. I lurch away, but my foot catches in the cloth, and suddenly I hit the floor. Luca reaches for me at the same time and we knock heads. Then we're both on the ground, clumsily tangled in a storm of fabric and flowers. And popcorn. Oh, there is popcorn *everywhere*.

"Get *off* him," comes a familiar voice. May, barreling out of the crowd, shoving Luca off me so that he slides away in a cascade of popcorn and petals. I shakily stand, aware that the space around us has doubled. Two security guards push through the crowd, and when she sees them, May thrusts a finger at Luca and shouts, "He started it!"

"We weren't fighting," I say, but the guards are already herding us away from the crowd. Luca, for once, is agreeing with me, but they want us out of here.

I throw a last look at May. She's still got some moss clinging to her ear. *Text me*, she motions solemnly. Inaya stands next to her, somehow looking completely innocent while covered in zombie gore. Then she turns back to the cameras, the interview becoming all hers.

Shit.

Luca and I are led through a set of back doors. The guards ignore us as we beg them to listen, eventually pushing us into a small conference room full of boxes of lanyards. One stays with us while the other talks on his radio in the hall. After a long time, the door opens, and in walks Madeline. The person running Trip-C. She regards us with restrained annoyance and…is that fear?

"She wants to see you both."

EIGHT

As soon as we get to the studio, Luca ducks into the bathroom to strip off his shirt and try to scrub away the paint. A little baffled by the whole situation, I do what I always do when I'm nervous: I get to work.

I consider pulling from my brand-new Plasma Siren fabric, but something tells me Luca won't want a shimmering gossamer tank top with scalloped, eyelash-edged lace. What else do I have? A few months ago, I did a simple Chihiro cosplay. She's the main character from *Spirited Away*, a Miyazaki classic. At the beginning, she wears a simple shirt with a fat, horizontal stripe in frog green. I made it roomy so it'd give me the look of a kid, but that means it'll still be a little tight on Luca. I find it crumpled up at the bottom of one of my many bags, hidden in the studio's cedar closet. It's wrinkled, but it's nothing my steamer can't handle. Easy.

But I don't want easy. Somehow, this boy, flecked in gold, has followed me all the way home. Maybe he's straight, but maybe he isn't. Either way, just handing him a shirt feels terribly anti-climactic. I've got a live audience for once, and I want to show off.

The water shuts off in the bathroom, and Luca emerges shirtless and damp (yet again). I suddenly wonder why I'm racing to put a shirt on him at all.

"I have an idea," I tell him.

And that's how Luca and I end up collaborating on a tank top. It's just a simple garment, but he takes it very seriously when I tell him the fabric choice is up to him. We spread scraps from previous projects all over the table, and Luca considers each one with the care of a vintage wine enthusiast. When he finally does pick one, it breaks my heart to tell him that he's chosen wrong.

"But I like the color."

I take the fabric from him. It's a bright orange canvas, waxy and inflexible. Maybe he is straight after all?

"We need a knit fabric. It's got to be able to stretch."

"Knit? Like a sweater?"

I pull out a swatch of jersey knit in viridian, leftover from a hipster Midoriya cosplay I did last year. "See?" I say as I stretch it out. "This is knit together, and it has good recovery. It stretches, but it takes back its shape when released. Perfect for tight clothing."

"But I like the orange."

I scan the heap before us. There's no other orange. But then I get another idea. I race away and return carrying a toolbox full of sewing supplies, popping it open with such a flourish that Luca lets out a whistle.

"That's a lot of needles."

"They're pins."

"What do you do with them?"

"Pin things."

I find what I'm looking for: a length of neon orange bias tape.

"What if you pick a workable knit and then we finish it with an accent trim in this bias tape?"

This sentence, while perfectly reasonable to me, earns me a few slow blinks from Luca. I'm ready for what's coming—a scoff, or maybe a taunting laugh as he strolls out of here—but instead he says, "Say that again, but with different words."

"Want me to just show you?"

He crosses his arms and smirks. I do my best to keep my eyes on his. His smirk opens into a smile, which he wipes away with a cupped hand. "You know what you're doing, don't you?"

Not really, I think.

We end up going with a cotton blend rib knit in a rich forest green. I consider using his ruined shirt to make a quick pattern, but again, my efficiency fails in favor of flare. Instead, I made Luca stand still as I take his measurements.

This takes me one hundred years to get right. I hold one hundred breaths. I'm halfway under his arm when I realize I have not written down a single number, and I start over again, hoping he doesn't notice. The whole time, he watches me with amusement.

"You're shaped weird," I tell him.

"What's my shape?"

"Somewhere between anime man and upside-down Dorito. Very triangular torso."

"Are you calling me top-heavy?" he gasps, clutching his chest.

I'm a little self-conscious, aware that at any moment, the conversation could turn to my own body. I'm not like Luca. I am soft and round almost everywhere. I don't want him thinking he has some sort of upper hand because of his athletic figure.

"Just busty," I say, tapping the tape.

Luca just grins, watching me.

While I cut the fabric, I pretend I'm streaming on Ion. At first, it's much weirder to have a person to actually talk to, but then it's the easiest thing in the world to narrate as Luca peppers me with questions. I let him do some cutting, and I like how careful he is with the scissors. I let him do some pinning, and I am enamored with how delicate his fingers can be. When we get to sewing, I sit him down in the chair, introduce him to the pedal, and coax him into stitching a seam that starts out wavy but is pin-straight by the end.

"Good, see? You're a natural."

I handle sewing on the bias tape, since it's tricky. As I feed the garment through my sewing machine, Luca sits on the other side and gathers it into his palms, whistling with amazement. And then we're done, and I recognize the glow of accomplishment that hovers around Luca as he pulls on his new tank top.

"It fits!" he exclaims.

"Of course it fits. That's why we measured."

"You didn't write any of that down, though."

I shrug. *Stay cool, Raffy.* I'll admit I'm a little disappointed he's dressed again, but then he asks something that totally disorients me.

"Can we bedazzle it?"

I slow blink, astonished. Maybe not as straight as I thought, then?

"Nothing crazy," he adds. "Just, like, a few jewels. Someplace my parents won't see, though. Like when an artist signs their work."

Dazed, I drift over to the gems, pluck out a few Sea Foam Dreams and some E6000. I return to Luca, and he's standing so rigid that I pause.

"Just do it," he says through clenched teeth, like I'm about to tattoo him.

I look him over in his new tank top. It's perfectly fitted, and the dark green works with the garish trim to make a sort of military combination. Gems will look weird wherever I put them, so I elect to put them on the inside of the collar, where only Luca will see them. He consents to this, and we're quiet as I carefully dot on glue and press the stones on with my fingertips.

"Sooooo," he says while we wait for the glue to dry. "Your mom just lets you do whatever in here?"

"It's a multipurpose space. If we have an artist living with us, they use it as a workshop, but we haven't had anyone here since May. So I use it."

The studio is a converted garage, insulated so that it stays cool in the summer and warm in the winter. We order in brand-new supplies for whoever is here, and the space is set up for a bunch of different media. The last person here was a wood-carver, so right now the sunny brightness of the studio is laced with the smell of sawdust and scorched aspen.

I watch Luca's eyes land on each object as I describe the loft, the couch, the TV, and the bed. I watch his eyebrows carefully, but they betray no intent. I tell him about how May and Inaya and I have game nights in here, and the occasional party. Evie either doesn't care about those, or doesn't notice.

"I recognize this," Luca says, picking up a mannequin head. It's a wig form, but right now it's bald. "I thought this place would be smaller. I guess you just use that corner, though."

I remember belatedly that Luca has seen my videos. I still find it hard to understand.

"Do you watch a lot of cosplayer streams?"

"Just yours," he says. He glances back at me, and I find myself drifting after him. Before I make it too far, I force myself to stop, one hand gripping the table. Then, because I'm sure I'll forget myself again, I sit on the table and crush my hands under my thighs.

"You're so fast," Luca says. "I'm always amazed at how quickly you make stuff."

"I've been doing it for a long time."

"I wish I could do what you do. I have all these ideas I would make if I knew how to do it."

Luca's voice contains an entire reality that only he can see. One full of characters and costumes that live in his head, not at his fingertips, like in the reality I've shown him.

"You're good at other stuff," I say, rocking on my hands. Luca crosses behind me, but I keep my eyes ahead on the glass of the cabinets, watching his reflection.

"Like what?" he asks.

"Soccer, I assume."

He stops moving, turning to smile at my back. Then, catching my eye in the reflection, he leans against the table.

"You like soccer?" he asks.

"No."

"But you like soccer players."

The question catches us both off guard. I decide I have no reason to lie, having just taken in, washed, and clothed this boy after he interrupted me painting. Finally, I turn to face him.

He's closer than I thought. And blushing. He gives me a sort of slick expression, like he knows he's charming, like he knows he's guilty of maneuvering the conversation into territory where neither of us has control.

"Fine, yeah," I say. "Maybe I do."

He leans toward me. I watch him splay his hands out and see the shadows carve into dimples on his shoulders as he leans over the table.

"I make you laugh," he says.

"I make you clothes," I say.

We will kiss.

I know, because like everything else, a kiss is a sum of parts. It began a long time ago, at Craft Club, with Luca's shouldering his gear as I handed him a bag of jewels. Then at school, the particles of gold soaking into Luca's clothes, drawing from him the dramatic performance he gave me as the faucet poured water over his lips. And here, the kiss waited patiently between us as I sewed an entire shirt out of nothing, out of the hope that it would keep this boy captivated by me a little while longer, his eyes memorizing the shapes of my fingers as I fed fabric beneath the hopscotch of a needle and into his waiting palms.

And now, as he crawls up onto the table with me, turning me around to wrap my waist in his arm and my mouth in his breath, the lead-up to the kiss ends. It ends with our lips fitting together, my laughter pushed back down my throat to wait inside as I let myself enjoy what I've created. The kiss ends like all my projects: amazing and whole, the fragments of many moments joined together to create something entirely alive and real. Something incredible, out of nothing.

Minutes later, we need to breathe. The pause is long enough that we both consider what's happening, what we've created.

"Have you ever—" I begin to ask.

"Not with a guy," Luca says. "You?"

"Yeah. Only guys. But only, like, twice. Do you want—" I breathe deep, not sure when my next chance will be. "I mean, we can do that again if—"

"Okay, but…" Luca trails off.

"But what?"

"But I want to keep the shirt on."

"Of course." I smile, lean in. We're kissing again when Luca stops us.

"Not because I'm, like, not into you," he assures me. "I just like the shirt. I'm very much into you. And into this."

"Okay, Luca."

He evades my lips one more time.

"Not just physically. I think you're cool. I think what you can do is amazing. And I'm sorry if buying you those gemstones was weird. My plan was to get more and give them to you in school, but then we met in Craft Club. That was dumb luck, I swear. This wasn't, like, a plot to get into your pants, I promise."

I stifle a laugh. He looks down, mumbling now.

"I just really like watching you work."

"Luca."

"What?"

"It's cool. You're good. You can watch me work later, okay?"

His arms tighten around my waist. His nerves settle. Mine don't, but I try to play it cool.

"Is that an invitation?" he whispers, lifting my chin toward him.

The afternoon sun fills the narrowing space between us with golden light. We close over it until it's just a glowing seam between two things, finally joined.

NINE

We're led from the conference room to an elevator, then up to a hallway with windows overlooking the con floor. From above, there's no trace of the calamity we caused. In the open areas, people are back to taking photos with cosplayers. On the other side of the hall, we can see down into the aisles of displays and booths. The density and color of the slowly churning crowd gives the dizzying impression of some sort of multicolored seascape. A coral reef carpeted in anemone, an invisible tide keeping it all moving.

"Wait here," Madeline says, leaving us in the hall. The guards go with her, and Luca and I are left before a pair of double doors. We stand there in silence for a long time. Surely whoever we're waiting on has better things to do than attend to two delinquent boys. The moments become minutes, the awkward silence in the hallway emphasizes everything left unsaid between Luca and me.

"I'm sorry," he says finally.

I turn away from him, pretending to look out over the con floor. The glass is tinted; probably no one can see us. I watch Luca's reflection, but he keeps his eyes down as he talks.

"I should have made sure you were okay with us using your idea. It was shitty of us to develop something you came up with. I really thought she checked. I'm sorry."

I watch him in the reflection, and finally he looks up at me. I look away, back out over the crowd.

"And if it's any consolation, the judges thought it was good, but simple. They called it 'sensational,' but, like, not in a good way. I'm not even sure what they meant."

"In this case, it means provocative. Like, you took an idea and made it edgy. Shock value, basically."

"I knew I could get you to talk by giving you a chance to make a jab at me. Feel better?"

We make eye contact in the reflection of the window now. It reminds me of one of my earliest memories of us: We're sitting in my studio, watching each other in the glass cabinets and waiting to see who will make the first move. Who will start the story of our *together*.

We're so far from that now.

"Not really," I say.

"Do you want to talk about it?"

I can't help it. I turn and look Luca dead in the eye.

"What I said to you was shitty. It was even shittier to say it in front of all those people. I was mad, and I was trying to leave, and my mouth…just got the better of me. But now it doesn't matter who's the better builder, because we're both done for."

"Yeah." He shrugs. He actually shrugs, as though this is one of the many cons he was planning on getting kicked out of today. And his cavalier attitude slaps me like a frigid wave. I'm breathless with perspective, suddenly. For most people, this is a fun activity. It used to be just fun for me, too, but recently it's felt like so much more. Like everything. Without the Craft Club sponsorship, was any of this even worth it? The only silver lining is the boon of followers I'll probably get from being the infamous moss creature who made a mess.

I know that now is the time to hold myself together, but I start to cry. I'm here with Luca, the boy I loved and the boy who broke my heart, and we're alone together for the first time in months. All those feelings—I forced them into my work, my craft, my dream, into shaping my future. But now, with that future going up in flames, the prison I built around those feelings is gone. They're free to surge forth, and they do so with the full intensity of the day they were hatched from my breaking heart.

Luca hugs me, and I let him. I don't worry about the mess I'm making of my makeup or the streaks of green and black that smear over his biceps and chest as he embraces me.

"I'm sorry, Raff," he says. "But you're going to figure out a way to fix this. You create stuff, remember? You can make anything. And that means you'll find a way to make this right."

I pull away, dabbing at the tears stinging my eyes. I badly want to rip off this prosthetic nose, but I need a special releaser chemical to do so. Still, it's started to peel, probably from all the frowning. And as I force down sobs, petals and leaves drift from my crown and fall to the floor. My careful costume is coming undone.

"I'm sorry, too," I say. "I'm sorry I'm so angry. I can't help how I feel."

"Me neither," Luca says.

"What do you mean?"

"I mean that I still feel a lot for you, and I don't know what to do with it all. Inaya and I are close now, but we're just friends. We just cosplay together. But you and I were more, and I think about it a lot. I think about you a lot. And…"

"And what?"

"And I know it's terrible timing, but I still really want to kiss you. But only if you say it's okay."

Through the window past Luca, the crowds are cheering as someone takes up a microphone. We can't make out the words through the thick glass, but we can sense the excitement vibrating in the silence. I pretend the cheers are for us.

It's okay.

I imagine saying it. But I don't say it, because just then, the double doors open.

"Boys," says Irma Worthy.

Luca and I push apart. I laugh—actually laugh in shock at the sight of Irma Worthy appearing out of nowhere.

She's smiling at us like I'm not a sobbing mess covered in literal moss and leaves.

"Well, sounds like you created *quite* the scene down there," Irma says.

"We're sorry. It won't happen again. If you allow us to keep our passes—"

"Keep your passes?" Irma throws back her head and fills the hallway with a crackling cackle like snapping electricity. Her curls bounce as she shakes off the amusement. "You think I came here to confiscate your badges? Honey, I have a *job*. And it's not *that*."

Her laugh surrounds us. She puts out her hands for us to take, which we both do without hesitating, as though she's our mother. She leads us over to the windows so we're all watching Controverse from above together.

"Listen. I understand the hard work that goes into these projects, probably better than most," she says. "I know the time and money a person's got to spend if they want to make something, or make something of themselves. More than anything else, I respect that effort. Maybe too much. I look at all this"—she gestures at Controverse—"and sometimes I have trouble seeing it as an experience. As a convention. I tend to focus on the parts instead of the whole. The time, the effort, the creativity. The people. I see all of them, and all of their *work*, and sometimes it's easy to lose sight of the big picture we're all creating together."

She looks between us. I find that I'm nodding. I get this.

"Controverse wants you two gone, and I understand why."

Irma sighs. "I heard about what happened just as we were tabulating the final scores of today's judging. It would be the easiest thing in the world to knock you both out and let the competition race on without you."

She looks at Luca with adoration, a maternal glow that he can't help but smile under. When Irma looks at me, the glow cools into a smoldering fixation that I cannot make sense of. I don't have time to dwell on it.

"But I want you both in this competition. And the other judges agree. You scored very high. So high, I couldn't let the convention staff kick you out. I'm going out on a limb here, boys, for the big picture we're all making together. Do you get what I mean? I'm making promises to people, but you've got to keep them for me. *With* me. Are we clear?"

We're both stunned. I can tell Luca's nonchalance is slipping. He's just gonna go along with whatever, so it's up to me to ask the question on both our minds.

"You're letting us stay in the competition, but in exchange for what?"

Irma looks up at me with the same stern contemplation. I can't help but compare her to Evie. The difference is that while Evie loves me, Irma respects me.

"All we ask is that you give us the best show possible tomorrow. You're both moving on to the final round. Take tonight to prepare. Don't make a scene on your way out. And not a word to the other teams about our little chat, okay?"

She winks. Luca winks. I don't know how to wink, so I nod. Then Madeline emerges from the double doors, her trusty tablet lighting her neck and jaw with a ghostly glow.

"Madeline, they've agreed to compete. Isn't that nice?" says Irma.

Madeline, as per usual, is the image of poise. But there, just at the edge of her mask, I see a wisp of apprehension seep out. Her nostrils flare as she sets her jaw.

"Very nice, but are *you* sure this is a good idea?"

"I am, dear. No more questions. I'll answer to the board if they need some convincing."

Madeline's lips tighten. She gestures for us to leave with her. We're led through a maze of back passages down to the convention center's employees-only parking lot. A car is waiting.

"Luca, security has your bag. I'll escort you. Raphael, this car is for you. Your items from coat check are in the trunk. The driver's instructions are to take you straight to your house."

I climb in, and Madeline closes the door without a goodbye. The car isn't an Uber or a Lyft. It's a private car, like a president might ride in. Is it Irma's? I don't know. Inside, the driver gives me a quick glance and checks a mounted phone with my address preprogrammed into it. He says nothing, and we turn away from Controverse on silent wheels.

As the convention center vanishes from view, Irma's words buzz in me like a large fly, swatting against my lungs. She saved us, but I can't help but feel the cost is going to be a big one, and it's going to come tomorrow. But no matter what happens next, I've been given a second chance. Now, more than ever, I'm determined to prove that I'm worth it.

TEN

The day after we kiss for the first time, I can't bring myself to look at Luca in class. After he left my house, I replayed the strange sequence that led me into his arms and decide it was definitely an anomaly. An aberration. An irregularity, never to be repeated. But then, as I'm walking in the hallway, a shoulder nudges mine, and I look up to find Luca strolling beside me.

"*Psst*," he whispers. "Can I come over later?"

"I've got work to do," I hear myself say.

"Okay, and? Take out your phone."

I do. Luca swings to the other side of the hall, across from me. People fill the space between us. My phone buzzes, asking if I'd like to accept an AirDropped photo from an unknown number. I do, and a picture downloads of Luca, shirtless, a phone number printed on his biceps.

I roll my eyes at him. He's got his tongue between his teeth, his eyebrows arched. Playful, but restrained for him. Then he flashes open his zip-up. I see the green; I see the orange. He's wearing the tank top we made together.

With a finger to his lips, Luca backs down the hall, our eyes locked in a playful battle until my blush forces me to look away.

I wait six whole minutes to text him.

⬦ - - - - ⬦

Luca shows up, and he keeps showing up. Every time, I pretend to be surprised, but the truth is that it only takes me a week to get used to our weird routine. He comes after soccer, sweaty and smelling of grass, and there's always a small chase around my worktable until he captures me in a gross hug. Then I make him shower, using the precious minutes to get as much done as I can before he's out and demanding I teach him something.

Our lessons are small. They're usually about things I've streamed recently for Plasma Siren, because those are the supplies I have accessible, and it seems important to Luca to frame this as him helping me. I play along with that. Why not? I think it's cute, but the truth is that I usually redo his work later and just don't tell him. I don't mind. Like, at all. Which is *very* strange for me. Wasting time is the one thing that makes my anxiety go through the roof, but somehow with Luca, time never feels wasted.

I have no idea what we're building together, between us. But as with all projects, I am determined to find out, and I put in the work to make it the best it can be. Luca does, too. He starts bringing homework over. He starts staying later. The pizza place near my house memorizes our order. We start working less and kissing more. Sometimes, we don't work at all. Sometimes, like today, we collapse into each other and just watch anime, and I marvel at this strange new person I'm letting Luca make me into. A person who isn't obsessed with working on something every minute of every day. A person whose hands are content to be still, so long as Luca's the one holding them.

Late on a Thursday night, I wake up because once again I'm overheating in the vise-like embrace Luca winds me into every time we end up together on my couch.

I didn't mean to fall asleep, but as soon as I'm conscious, I regret being awake. By the way my arm is numb, I know we've been asleep for a while, which means it's probably past the time when I need to send Luca home so his parents don't freak out. Which means I need to wake him up. Always an ordeal.

We fell asleep on the loft couch, and the only reason I woke up was because the opening song of the anime we've been marathoning for the last week is *full* of electric guitars. It's a horror anime, Luca's favorite, and as I rub at my eyes, I watch a montage of characters race through the opening credits in a parade of slashing blades and spraying blood.

"Luca, come on, we fell asleep," I say, poking him. He doesn't budge, but I know he's awake. Luca is forever falling asleep while I'm doing work, and he always sleeps with his mouth open. But right now? His face is perfectly serene except for his lips, which are puckered for a kiss. He's faking it.

"Luca," I say.

Nothing. I can see the muscles of his mouth twitching, trying not to smile. I groan and finally give in, kissing him. But because this is Luca and everything has to be dramatic, he's not waiting for *just* a kiss.

Smiling, I exhale onto his lips gently, and all at once, he comes alive.

"THE BREATH OF LIFE!" He surges upward, throwing the blanket over his shoulder like a cape. Then he kneels before me. "My master, you have breathed life into me, and now I serve you as your loyal totem."

It's a line from another anime—I never can remember the name—that we finished last week during another "work" session. And now, anytime we fall asleep watching something, Luca insists on me waking him up this way. Sometimes he'll wake me up with a poke and then fake sleep until I give him the breath of life.

"For the hundredth time, it's golem," I say. "Sirastros creates golems from clay before giving them the breath of life. Not totems."

"The subtitles said totem."

"The subtitles are wrong. Golems are from Jewish lore. Read the manga, Luca."

"You know I'm not allowed to have that in my house."

I give him my best pitiful *boo-hoo* face, and he returns it with a sleepy grin, asking, "What time is it?"

Using the light of the TV, I spot my phone at the edge of the couch.

"Midnight thirty."

Luca pulls the blanket over his head and lets out a scream. I muffle him as best I can, not wanting my mom to hear. She's seen Luca coming and going but hasn't really asked questions. However, if she knew we were still in here, she might check on us, and all my supplies are still out from the work I was doing before Luca busted in and demanded we order pad thai and watch cartoons.

Luca's yells turn into laughter as his arms encircle me.

"Can I stay?" he asked.

"You've got soccer in the morning, and you know your mom would flip out if you didn't come home."

"She thinks I'm at Calvin's with the boys."

Luca and I are both hiding what we're up to. I'm hiding my projects from my mom, and he's hiding me, a whole-ass person.

"The boys," I say, mocking the name he has for his group of guy friends. "Why don't you hang out with them anymore?"

"I do. At practice. And at school. But that's not what you're asking, is it?"

It's my turn to grin, but I don't yell or anything. Luca is good at guessing what's going on in my head.

"You're really asking, why does Luca come here all the time and watch anime with me?"

"It's 'cause they'd make fun of you for watching anime," I deflect.

"I could watch anime at home on my phone."

"So then why?"

Luca does this thing where every time I finally corner him into almost revealing something unspoken, he pulls me into a kiss. I'm not sure when I'll stop being stunned or when the edge of excitement will wear off, but for now it's a welcome distraction, and it works on me every time.

More screams from the TV pull us back down to earth.

"We have to start this one over," he says, feeling around for the remote.

"No, no," I say, pulling myself off the couch. Luca blinks up at me from beneath the blanket. He looks like a dejected nun.

"You need to go home and not act totally suspicious. And every time you're late to soccer, you find a way to blame it on me."

Anyone observing would see my point, but Luca knows I'm leaving something out. He raises an eyebrow.

"And," I grumble, "I want to finish what I was working on before you showed up."

"Work!" Luca flaps his hands at the ceiling. "Always with the work! Why can't you ever just relax? Go with the flow?"

I feel my heart tighten a little bit.

"I've *been* going with the flow since you showed up. *You* are the flow. And now the flow is *going* home."

While Luca finds his shoes, I descend from the loft and sit back down at my table. I've got the whole weekend ahead of me, but I'm not sure it's enough time. Plasma Siren is looking pretty messy, which is how a cosplay always looks right before you put it all together, but I'm still anxious as heck. The fins are done, as is the bulk of the sewing. But the armor needs a ton of work. What makes her hard is the clustered barnacles and spiral seashells that appear to grow right out of her shoulders and hips. I could have used actual seashells, but that would have weighed a ton, and so I elected to sculpt them all out of foam. And it's taking me five hundred years. Six hundred, now that Luca has derailed me for a few hours.

Still draped in the blanket, Luca drops down next to me. I expect him to hug me from behind, which he's taken to doing when I'm set up at my station, but he waits until I've put down the foam clay I was kneading. He hooks his chin over my shoulder, slinks his arms beneath mine, and picks up the foam seashell I was working on.

"You haven't done a stream recently," he says.

"I know. I'm so bad."

"You're not bad. Tell me what you're doing."

I snort. I know he's lingering here, and while it's a little annoying, I also love it. "Like I'm streaming?"

He nods on my shoulder.

Jokingly, I begin with my intro.

"Hey, guys, it's me, Raffy, and you're watching *Crafty Rafty*. I'm back, working on Plasma Siren, and as you can see, today I'm joined by a special guest. Would you like to introduce yourself?"

After a beat, Luca says simply, "I am the flow."

"And where do you hail from, Mr. Flow?"

Another beat, and Luca supplies, "I am from the beyond, the space between space, the world beneath the world. I am from the abyss."

I throw a cheery smile at my—our—invisible audience.

"Great! So glad to have you on the stream, Mr. Flow. It's not often that I'm joined by an interdimensional horror, but wow, am I glad you're a hot one! Does every eternal creature from your dimension have dimples?"

"Just me. I'm the cutest."

I twist, because I suddenly need to see his dimples, and I can feel him smiling. I kiss him.

"Keep going," he whispers. He tightens his arms around my chest like a living parachute pack, leaving me to lift up my project to the big, empty windows.

"Well, right now, I'm using foam clay and EVA foam to create seashells. Once the foam clay is dry, I'll be using a Dremel tool—"

"A Dremel?"

"It's like a little rotary tool thingy with sandpaper on it, and I'm going to use it to give the shells definition and texture before soldering finer lines into them."

"Show them," Luca encourages.

My Dremel tool is within reach. I pick it up and grab one of the dry shells, a smooth cup that will soon be etched with wavy lines.

I demonstrate a few strokes. I don't want to do much, because I should really be wearing my respirator for this.

I end with, "And that's how you make a fake seashell out of foam! Any questions?"

We both wait expectantly, longer than we need to, aware that this is absurd, resisting the urge to break into laughter. I crack first, but Luca's been waiting on my cue, and he bundles me up in his blanket. Under it, I can barely see him, but he's warm and close.

"You work really hard. I like seeing you chill out."

I lean into him. It's easy to need something like this, and it's hard to tell myself I need to stop. This is fun, but I've got hours to go before I can rest. I need to work. I can't fully turn into this person he wants me to be.

"I'd be a lot more chill if I didn't have so much to do," I say.

"I can help," Luca insists. "I don't want to stress you out."

He rocks me back and forth, back and forth. I note the difference between his words and his continued distraction. I know he's slowly making his way toward some sort of point. Why else would he be stalling?

"I was thinking we could do this together," he finally says. "Not just making stuff. I mean, like…"

"You want to cosplay? I thought you said this was the nerdiest thing in the world."

"Yeah, I mean, it's fucking nerdy, don't get me wrong," Luca says. I can hear the smile on his face as he rocks me. "But you love it, and I…"

"What?"

"…want to go with your flow."

"I think you love it, too," I say. "You're, like, much nerdier than me, you know that? You've seen every anime. You've played all the games. It's incredible that you've kept so much of this a secret from people for so long."

Luca's grip loosens. He unlatches from me, stands, stretches, then sits down besides me at the table.

"My mom hates this stuff," he says, gesturing at the cosplay materials. "She thinks it's for kids."

"Because it's arts and crafts?"

He shrugs. "It's just not what guys do in my family. She worries about me."

"She worries about you wearing costumes?"

Luca's cheeks puff up, and he blows out a breath. He's wrestling with something inside him, and I give him time to say it his own way.

"My parents don't know a lot about me," he says. "I tried to talk to my mom about maybe being bi a few years ago, and she freaked out. Not 'cause she's homophobic or anything. But I think she knew my dad would have an issue with it, and she said we shouldn't tell him. I kinda feel like he knows something is up, though, you know? Anyway, after that, she got all sensitive about what I was watching and reading and doing, especially when it came to anime and video games. She's old-school. She thinks doing this stuff influenced my sexuality or brainwashed me or something. Whatever it is, it was easier for her to focus on than the actual issue, so I hid all that stuff away. And I got really into soccer instead. And working out. Which she was much happier with. I like that stuff, but it's also part of proving to my folks that I'm still the person they knew."

"So does your mom still think you're bi?"

"I think so. I don't know," Luca says, picking up some felt and running it between his fingers. "But I don't care, either. I'm not going to live there forever. And I can watch all the anime I want here with you, right?"

"Right."

We sit together in the golden light of the lamp. I hook an arm around Luca's back and push my temple against his shoulder. He's always so warm.

"You don't have to do anything you don't want, and you don't have to be anyone you don't like."

"I want..." He stops. He puts down the felt and picks it up again. "I want to make something amazing, too. I want people to see me the way I see me."

"You'd really cosplay?"

After a moment, he slips back into the boyish, elusive persona.

"Sorry, no can do." He puts on this smug masculinity that he knows annoys me. It's an act, but being dismissed this way still makes me itch. "I've got soccer, remember? Can't spend the night drumming up seashells."

"*Dremel*," I counter, but the switch hurts. Luca is Luca until you push him to a point just past his comfort zone, and then this version shows up. Bored, boyish, brooding. And as much as I hate being shut down, I know I need to work. This is a flow I go with whether I want to or not.

"Right, soccer. Ball play. Very masc," I say, picking up my next shell like I'm about to get back to work.

"You know it." He puts a hand on the back of my neck, pretending to headbutt me like he and the boys do. I think they think it looks tough, but it's a strangely gentle motion that always reminds me of young rams learning how to charge. It's extremely homoerotic.

I haven't told him this, because he'd stop doing it.

"You sure I can't stay?" he checks one more time.

"Luca, you already told yourself no in the past. You made me promise to tell you no in the future. The future is now. It's happening. Your *no* is here to send you home."

He pulls back and makes a big show of grabbing his bag, then his jacket. He fishes out his keys and jangles them at me, all angry. I turn back to my work. But then I feel him watching me from the door. I know from experience that he'll watch until I finally relent and look up. Then he'll grin like he's won a bet with himself. As far as contests go, it's a pretty cute one. After a beat, I look up from my crafting.

"Maybe," he says.

"Maybe what?"

"Maybe I'll dress up. Just for you, though."

I roll my eyes. There's no way he's serious about cosplaying.

"We'll see," I tell him.

"*You'll* see, but only you," he tells me back before slipping into the night.

ELEVEN

I basically kick my front door closed as soon as I get into my house. The driver walked me and my big, dumb suitcase all the way to my stoop, like I might make a run for it. I'm annoyed. I'm tired, I'm hungry, I'm confused, I'm a mess.

But I'm still in the competition! I'm *still in*!

Take that, universe! Take that, Evie!

My thoughts are overly loud in my mind as the waves of anxiety drift away, returning me to my usual high-octane focus. Or maybe it's the adrenaline of being in my foyer in full cosplay, which is basically asking for Evie to arrive home suddenly and smite me. But the house is still around me, and her car isn't in the driveway, so I think I'm good.

I finally relax. And I finally think.

There is something so unrealistic about this that it feels like a conspiracy is maneuvering me around. Great mechanics working with me or through me, like I'm the needle operating at the very tip of a sewing machine, totally oblivious to the power that controls my motions.

Which, okay, fine. That's how life feels for a lot of teenagers, and I get that. But I feel like I've just glimpsed something I shouldn't have, talking with Irma. I've seen the outline of someone else's project with just enough perspective to realize I'm one of many materials being used to create something wondrous.

I shrug this off as I bundle up my robe. I don't really care about conspiracy theories. I care about arts and crafts. I guess I also care about winning. I care about proving Evie wrong. She won't be home until tomorrow afternoon, and by then I'll be back at Controverse, competing in Primes. I'll be in a new costume. I'll be a new person. A new Raffy.

Right now, though, I'm still a priest covered in mushrooms, and I'm falling apart. My whole body has begun to itch as the silicon cracks and breathes. I'm desperate to shower and change clothes—even to just undress. I consider going straight to the studio to change, but with Evie home tomorrow, it's probably safer to leave the studio in the pristine, blameless condition I left it in. My room is safer.

This means marching through my house and up to my room in full cosplay. A perilous task. If I leave a mess, Evie will find it. If I leave a single petal in the foyer, Evie will know, because her house is a world of industrial artsiness. It's a utopia of sleek gray planes, tastefully kitschy clutter placed *just so*, frosted glass walls, lumpy pillows the color of lips upon transparent chairs and low mustard couches, and so on. We basically live in one of Evie's galleries. And like every gallery my mother controls, it's all her. Everything has been perfectly determined by her taste. Dressed as I am, I'm the part that doesn't belong.

I heave my suitcase up the stairs. At the top, I check behind me for detritus, see a single fallen mushroom, and scoop it up. I'll have to incinerate this entire costume at some point, but for now I'll just hide it in one of my gargantuan plastic bins until Evie's next trip. In my room, I pull a bin free from its hiding spot under my bed and tip the robe off my shoulders. It pains me not to hang it up, but I try not to think about it as I begin undoing my underclothes. Eventually, I'm just in my underwear and exoskeleton, silicon prosthetics forming unnatural peaks along my collarbones and ribs. I spin for myself in the mirror, and because I look like a very fashionable larva, I pull my limbs into my best high-fashion pose. I am on my third pose when I notice something in the mirror.

The studio lights are on, and inside the studio, there are people. Many people. They press against the tall windows, watching me.

My legs collapse under me, and then I'm on my rug, digging through my bag for my phone. It's almost dead, but of course there are a million texts from May. I punch at her name and call her.

"It's us, it's us!" She laughs. "Jesus, did you just do a death drop?"

"A what?"

"Never mind. Listen, I know Evie isn't here, so I came here to wait for you 'cause you weren't picking up your phone. And then a few people wanted to meet up, so I told them to come over. But I knew you'd freak if I let people into your house, so I broke into the studio."

"The studio is, like, still my house, May."

"Not according to your mom."

"How many people are there?"

May doesn't immediately answer, so when she says, "Like a dozen," I know it's a lie.

"Is Luca there? Or Inaya?"

"What? Why? Should Luca be here? I thought he was with you. And what happened? You didn't answer any of my texts, and the next thing I know, you're flailing around in the window like a rehearsing TikToker."

"I'll explain later. Just…don't make a mess. Evie is coming back tomorrow. I'm gonna shower, and then I'll be right down."

I hang up. My heartbeat is stifled beneath my prosthetic ribs, but I can feel my pulse in the small of my back and the back of my knees. I put a hand on my chest, the fake skin warm, and I can't feel anything at first, but then I feel the smallest vibration hidden below my false flesh. Me, underneath it all.

I let my breathing even out. I think of my mom. I think of her seeing me as I am now, and I think of her disappointment. She wouldn't see that I scored high or earned a save by Irma Worthy. Technically, today was great. But I can't see it either, lying here envisioning her critical stare. In my mind, I hear her intone for the nine hundred and ninety-ninth time that above all else, art is about being authentic, that imitation like this is a form of cowardice, and that in this house, we do not abide cowards.

It's just in my mind, but it's enough to make me claw my fingers below my rubbery flesh and rip myself apart.

⬦ - - - ⬦

I can hear music from the studio as soon as I step into the backyard. The second I open the door, a loud *WHOOP!* goes out, and the studio vibrates with cheering, as though I'm a hero who has not only returned from war but who has clawed back up the dunes of death to survive another day.

Someone hands me a beer. I open it and pretend to drink from it even though beer tastes like rotten water.

I'm facing down a crowd of clowns. Of angels and monsters and mighty warriors and at least six Spider-Men. Most of the people here are from Controverse, many still in pieces of their costumes. I recognize at least six people right away from the strange prejudging, and then I recognize a few others from reviewing socials in the days leading up to the con. I don't know what May did to get all these people to show up, but it looks like I'm hosting the unofficial Controverse after-party.

May pushes through the crowd and hands me a second beer.

"Shit, Raffy, don't be mad, okay?"

A pair of nymphs are right behind May, and they nearly knock her over trying to speak to me.

"*Where is the coat?*"

"In my room."

"*The most amazing coat! Where is it?*"

"It was falling apart," I explain quickly, unsure how to handle these new people yelling at me. And then I realize they aren't yelling at me—they're praising me.

"*Amazing!*" one of them shouts, clutching my hand and looking at me with hazy vision. "*Teach me your ways!*"

"Thank you, thank you," I say, and then May is dragging me up the loft ladder.

"Listen," she says, still standing on the ladder as I scoot onto the loft's edge, "we are a *little* famous. Everyone thinks you're either getting kicked out of Controverse, which is legendary, *or* that we're going to make it to the finals."

"Wait, what? They don't know?"

"Don't know what?"

I shake my head, thinking through what Irma said about the results being posted this evening. They must not have gone out yet.

"We placed in Primes," I tell May. "We're competing again tomorrow in the big leagues."

May doesn't scream for joy like I would. She claps a hand over my mouth and says, "Don't say that! You'll jinx yourself. Or…wait, do you already know the results? Did they tell you after I left? Oh my god. So you're not getting booted?"

I mumble into May's hand, which smells like pizza. She removes it, wiping my breath on her jeans as she sits next to me.

"Irma Worthy intervened. *Personally* intervened, like some sort of fairy godmother mixed with a crime boss mixed with Martha Stewart, so, a crime boss. She said we're going to Primes."

May ponders this. Does she look a little disappointed? I guess I can see why. Maybe she thought me getting banned was her way out of more cosplay. She throws on a smile regardless and says, "Definitely don't tell anyone you know you're in. All anyone can talk about is how surprising the judging was today. Evidently, Craft Club streamed everything and posted it on Ion, so anyone in the world can watch Trip-C this year. It's like a surprise reality TV show. I heard a rumor that they're trying to get a real TV show next year. Everyone's a nervous wreck. People who would normally do great totally bombed in front of the crowd, and other people are sure they're up for Primes. Can you feel that energy? It's the energy of anticipation. If you let people know you know the results, they're gonna tear this place apart."

"I don't know the results," I say. "Just that Luca and I get to compete. And if anyone tears anything apart, my mother will kill me, and then resurrect my ghost, and then kill my ghost, and then force my dead ghost to lead her to you, and then she'll kill you, and kill your ghost, and—"

"Wait, Luca is in Primes, too? But he didn't do shit."

I shrug. She takes one of my beers from me.

"But I guess he is Western-hot," May reasons.

I don't like that she acknowledges this. I'll never have Luca's natural looks or his easy charm. He's a magnet for compliments just by being himself. I have to work so much harder. I know this, have always known this, and have always resented it. But even the resentment aims itself inward. Luca can't help what he looks like. So he gets off easy again, and I'm stuck holding my own hatred. Again.

The crowd of cosplayers below feels overly loud, like at any moment the thin walls of the studio are going to push apart and bring the skylights crashing down.

"I need some air," I tell May, handing her my remaining beer and climbing down the ladder. I take the long way through the crowd, forcing myself to say hello to people as a means of distracting myself against the freezing stiffness that webs through me every time I think of that moment with Luca in the hall. When I reach the door, I exit just as someone is trying to enter.

Inaya.

She's out of her makeup, in a fluorescent pink hoodie and leggings. Her black hair stands atop her head in three glossy buns.

We stare at each other, stunned, but only one of us deserves to be surprised. It's me, but I still find myself apologizing to her.

"Don't," she says. She points at the door behind me. "I heard you were having a party, and I figured I should show up to make nice before tomorrow. But I'm not gonna come in if you don't want me to."

I never know what to do with Inaya. She's always so…frank about things, like she stores all her artfulness in her fingertips. I will never get how such a ruthless person can create such soft, whimsical things.

"No, it's cool," I say, biting down on the inside of my cheek. As per usual, I feel a mix of awe and jealousy toward Inaya. She is smart, talented, and ambitious. I'm those things, too, but unlike me, she is rock solid. Unflappable. Perfect. It's as easy to admire her as it is to resent her, and that makes it even harder to compare myself to her, which I do constantly.

It doesn't help that she's gone from being a friend to a rival in just a few months. I liked her more when I wasn't straining to keep up with her.

"Cool," Inaya says. "And by the way, congrats. I talked to Luca. Guess we'll be in Primes together after all."

So she knows.

"We shouldn't say anything though, sounds like," she adds. I nod.

"For sure. We'll act surprised when the list gets posted."

Inaya smiles as I let her in. She smells like flowers and nail polish when she walks past. I barely register this before I see the second person waiting outside.

Luca. He doesn't ask for my permission like Inaya did. He pulls me away from the party, and suddenly we're on the back lawn together, cool grass licking my ankles.

"We need to talk," he says.

"About what, Luca? We had our moment. We said our sorrys."

"Not about that. Raffy, your mom just pulled into the driveway."

◇ - - - ◇

By the grace of some minor god, a call keeps Evie in her car just long enough for me to shush an entire party, force everyone under the studio tables, and make it back into the house with a few minutes to spare. By the time my mom walks in the front door, it's like there was never a party at all. I hope.

I am sitting at the kitchen table, a hastily slapped-together peanut butter and jelly sandwich on top of a paper towel in front of me. I have my laptop open, and I've just loaded a webcomic when she hits the kitchen and sees me.

The very first thing Evie does is scream. Like, *scream* scream.

I scream, too. I don't know why we're screaming until Evie cuts us off, presses the back of her hand to her closed eyes, and goes, "Raphael, that's enough of that. You scared me. I thought you were…in the woods or something."

Oh, right. Camping. Like a settler of CATAN.

"Mosquitoes," I explain. "They suck."

"Well, you would too, if that were your job." Evie wears driving gloves almost every time she's in a car, and she has them with her now, wagging in her bare hand as she gestures at me and my sandwich.

"What is this?"

"Dinner?"

She doesn't look convinced, which makes sense. We rarely use this kitchen. I eat most of my meals in the studio or in my room.

I turn the conversation away from the sandwich. "How was your trip?"

"Amputated."

My mother is always in these flowing scarves that billow from her like sails as she rushes around. Right now she's bundled in a vibrant chartreuse one with winking iridescent threads that create a strange grid pattern. It's so ugly it's awesome. I hate it.

Evie crosses the kitchen and plucks a chunky mug from the exposed cabinets, fills it with water, and then drinks it in gluttonous gulps. She does this twice more. My mother, who travels almost compulsively, refuses to touch airport bathrooms. So she rarely eats or drinks on travel days. This leads to a fascinating regimen of dehydration and malnourishment. From what I can remember, she was just in Arizona, which means she has likely been traveling for eight hours. She's bound to be irritable. I am absolutely petrified.

This must show on my face. She places the mug in the sink and asks, "What? What's that look?"

I'm looking out the back door at the studio without even realizing it. I see a light turn on, then off. I look back at her and offer a wan smile.

"Nothing. I'm good. Did you meet with the muralist?"

"Of course I met with the muralist," she says. "But she won't do walls outside of the Southwest. She says that she doesn't paint on walls. She paints on time. She paints on the temporal texture of a place, and she doesn't feel the same need to…what did she say? Oh—*dress up places that are too young for makeup.* Fascinating. I love her mind. I could eat it for every meal."

Anyone else would be annoyed by this, but Evie lives for the eccentric bullshit of artists. The more restrictive their rules, the better for her sales. The more bizarre, the better for her galleries. Right now, she seems to be entirely swept up in the assessment of surfaces as time canvases, and she's sweeping around our spacious modern kitchen with an air of disgust. Like she's about to tear off the backsplash with her bare hands.

"So what happened?" I prompt.

Evie is now at the freezer. She stands with the door between us. I cannot see her face as she says, "I found a buyer for her walls and a truck big enough to drive them to Miami. We'll tear off the front wall of the gallery to get them in and maybe leave it like that for the show. Just concrete and rebar ribs."

Evie plucks a microwave dinner from the freezer, tears it open, and then makes me read the instructions on the box to her. I can barely focus. She puts the dinner in the microwave, then goes to throw out the box. She stops, peering into the garbage.

"Raphael," she says, and I know she knows something is up. She gazes from the garbage to me, and there is no indication she's looking between literal trash and her darling child.

"Raphael, are you hiding something?" she asks, her eyes turning to slits. Quickly, she assesses my casual act, likely seeing it for the curated art it is. It's what she does professionally, after all. The hum of the microwave is the only sound in the kitchen, which suddenly feels like the whole world. And then there's a noise from outside. Someone laughing.

"Someone is here!" Evie exclaims.

I don't have time to answer before she pulls a knife from the knife block and charges past me, out into the backyard and toward the studio. I've barely caught up with her by the time she's at the door, and I get a hand around her elbow.

"Wait, stop," I say, pulling her around.

The knife slices through the air between us, but that's not the thing that gets us both to freeze. It's my hand on her elbow. We don't touch in this family.

I release her, but Evie's judgmental horror keeps me firmly in place as she turns and pushes open the studio door.

The studio is empty. I try not to make a show of my shock as we walk in and Evie glances under the tables. She checks one of the closets and finding nothing, gives me an annoyed look. Behind her in the loft, I see a whole crowd of shadows vibrating, but I keep my face calm as I say, "I forgot to lock it. I'm sorry. I'll be more careful."

"Yes," she says, drooping as though suddenly tired. "You will. Your access to this space is a privilege, not a right. This is not your home, it's—"

"Your investment, I know."

"Right. Here." She hands me the knife like it's much too heavy for her, and I carry it out of the studio. She locks the door pointedly, and we head back into the house. Inside, Evie gathers up the bags and packages she brought in from the car, then grabs her microwaved dinner and a plastic fork. Her heels click on the tile floor as she walks the length of the house to the stairs. I follow, the knife at my side, and I am conscious of every single thing that is out of place. I see a single petal from my costume on the floor, and I crush it with my heel.

"Raphael, I have something to tell you," Evie says, stopping on the stairs. "While I was in Arizona, I was visited by a vision. It came to me through one of the murals."

This isn't surprising coming from Evie. She loves Ambien. She doesn't love sleeping on it, though. She has all sorts of visions. Most of them involve traveling to ironically no-name places and staying at cheap motels, where she often has her best business breakthroughs. I fear what this latest one might entail, especially if she feels the need to tell me the details instead of just vanishing like she usually does.

"What was the vision?" I ask.

"It told me that I could help you. Now, I know what you'll say—that this defies everything I've taught you about self-reliance—but I think it's time to capitalize on all the opportunities for younger artists. It's time to modernize. To seek out new avenues of creation. Don't you agree?"

Evie can't see, but down the hall and out the back window, I see the lights in the studio come on again. Shadows pass quickly, fleeing. I play it off like I'm thinking hard about what she's saying.

"Of course I agree," I say.

"My vision told me you'd say that. It told me that not everyone is destined for greatness right away and that I need to give you time to find your…upward momentum. I think that's a nice way of putting it."

I bite down on my lip to keep from flinching. "Super nice, thanks."

Evie doesn't catch the sarcasm. With an air of benevolence, she says, "I know how much you like to make those…costumes. I think perhaps I've been taking the wrong approach, deterring you from it."

Is Evie about to get behind my cosplaying? Is she still high?

"So I've arranged to introduce you to an old friend of mine. Tobias Graham. He designs for everyone. Donatella, Dior, those sorts. He owes me several favors and several thousand dollars. I called him right away, and he offered to meet you for consideration as an apprentice. Isn't that kind of him?"

Evie says this with profound disappointment, as though the idea of her son going into editorial fashion design is a major step down from…I don't know. Whatever she does. From taking Ambien and talking to murals in Arizona.

"Awesome, thank you," I say. "That sounds great."

"I knew you'd see it that way," Evie says, relieved. I'm sure the last conversation she wants to have is one about cosplay.

"I'm tired," she announces. "I'm at the South End gallery tomorrow, but we can talk more on the plane on Sunday."

"What?"

"Sunday. The day after tomorrow. We'll meet Tobias for dinner, and if all goes well, you can spend a few days with him at his studio in New York. He has a friend with a room. I already checked."

A great silence pushes through the house, separating me from Evie, sweeping me off into the far reaches of my own mind. Evie has threatened to push me into various artsy scenarios before, but dragging me off to New York? Making a decision about my whole future based on a single drug-induced speculation?

Evie turns, ascending to the landing.

"What about school?" I say, fumbling for some reason not to go.

"What *about* school? If you do well with Tobias, you can skip all that and really make a name for yourself, Raphael. Isn't that what you want?"

"I don't mean college. I mean school. On Monday."

Evie shakes her head like I've said the most perverted thing possible.

"Priorities, Raphael," she clucks. Then she turns and enters her room, shutting the door behind her.

I'm outside in a flash, slipping back into the darkened studio.

"Hello? May? You still here?"

I shine my phone flashlight up at the loft, and an entire mass of costumed people blinks back at me. Belatedly, I realize I'm still clutching the knife, and I hide it behind my back.

"Party's over. Sorry, guys."

As quietly as I can, I lead them out the studio's back door, finding a few more cosplayers hidden near our garbage cans and in our bushes. I collect them all and release them into my neighbor's yard like colorful balloons drifting silently into the dark.

Back in the studio, it's just May and me sitting in the loft.

"Sorry," she whispers.

I shrug. I'm exhausted.

"We tried to clean everything up in the dark before she came out here. Did you get caught?"

"Nope," I say, and it sounds sad instead of relieved. And I am sad. Every interaction with Evie shows me just how little of me she sees, and this last one certainly takes the cake. A whole party—a whole *costume* party—was right in front of her, and all she's got on her mind is murals and Tobias Graham. I should be happy I didn't get caught, but even that would be better than my continued covert life among my mother's galleries.

"Good! That's good." May pulls several bloated bags of cups and beers out of the loft. I help stuff them into the trash outside, thinking it's risky to leave this much evidence in one place. But I'm the only one who takes the trash out, so unless I tell on me, I'm safe.

My phone buzzes in my pocket. May gets a notification, too. It's an official email from Trip-C with the list of teams who've made it to Primes. Even though Irma Worthy herself told me I was moving on, I still open up the list and scan until I find my name next to May's. Inaya and Luca are there, too.

"Congrats," May whispers, a smirk on her lips. "See you in the morning."

"See you," I say, and then I let her float off, too.

TWELVE

When Evie is home, everything goes artsy.

It's the music playing over the house's ancient intercom. It's the smells of incense and pot and perfume. It's the sound of rapid pacing from behind her office door. Mostly, though, it's the lighting.

She's very particular about lighting, and our house has billions of switches and knobs that control the billions of lights recessed into the ceiling or hidden in sconces or, in some cases, just floating in the open air of a hallway or staircase. They control brilliance, warmth, color, flicker—stuff that'd make a Broadway lighting designer drool.

Maybe that sounds cool, but it's honestly a pain. Evie's atmosphere is like living in a selfie filter. A constant performance, basically. And because she always accuses me of changing the settings even though I *never* do, I've taken to not touching the lights at all. I just navigate my home by daylight and, at night, with my phone flashlight. Like a Victorian countess dropped into a twenty-first-century art exhibit.

Evie is home right now, which means the house is currently in light-show mode. Almost everything pulses with mint-green light, like we live in the core of a radioactive spaceship. Except Evie has also taken to listening to flute music, so it's a radioactive spaceship powered by the Boston Symphony.

I'm in the bathroom, doing my makeup. I keep messing up my eyebrows. I'm nervous. Luca and I had our first real disagreement, and it was about tonight.

Luca is meeting up with May and me tonight at one of Inaya's shows. They're two of my closest friends, and they know Luca from school. They think it's funny that I'm hanging out with him, but they were impressed he wanted to go to an art show at all. Luca Vitale at a show? Points for Luca Vitale.

I'm worried about how Luca will do at an art show, sure, but what started the fight was, of course, Evie.

Luca offered to pick me up and even pop in to meet Evie, since she happens to be home this weekend. And I said no. It was an automatic reaction, and I felt bad right away when I said it, but I also felt secure in my choice. Evie doesn't care that I like guys, but one glance at Luca's classic looks and normal-boy clothes and she'd instantly make a permanent judgement. Luca, for all that makes him amazing, is careful to hide behind an illusion of normalcy that would drive Evie into a frenzy. And not a private frenzy, like most moms. A public one—an outright live critique session to Luca's face.

And if she found out he was a soccer player? World War III.

Maybe I'm wrong. Maybe it's wrong not to trust your own mom to be nice to your maybe-boyfriend. But that's the other thing. What are Luca and I? Boyfriends? Neither of us is eager to talk about it, and we would have to if Evie asked. And she would ask, especially if she sensed we were uncomfortable with the answer.

So I told Luca the truth.

> I've made up my mind, I'm sorry.
> I don't think you meeting my mom is a great
> idea right now. Let's just meet there, okay?

That's what I finally texted him. And he knew why right away.

> Yeah. OK.

And then, an hour later:

> I wish I could bring you to meet my mom.
> I wish I even had that choice.

That text shook me. I was embroidering when I got it, and my fingers just stopped working. They haven't regained their dexterity since. Which is why right now, I can't even do my eyebrows. Every time, I come out looking like a cartoon villain. Eventually, that's the look I end up settling on, because maybe that's what I am right now. Villainous.

But I do not feel bad about my choice. I like Luca, and I don't want him to run from me, and Evie would scare him. This choice hurts him, but it saves *us*.

May calls, letting me know she's driving. I text Luca a timing update, promising we'll talk about this later if he wants. Then I dress in the outfit I have out on my bed: a sleeveless turtleneck beneath a sheer black button-down. My skirt is thick black canvas with brass buttons. My rings are brass. My shoes have brass buckles. I hang a tote in the crook of my elbow (yes, it's black with brass) and assure myself that tonight is going to go well. It'll be good, even, once we're all there together.

My phone vibrates. It's May.

Outside.

I venture into the nuclear green of the house. I can hear different music coming from my mom's office. A comfort—it means she's working. I let myself relax as I skip down the stairs—they are lit from below, and the ribs of the railing flicker when you step near them. I don't use the front door, since Evie's bedroom and office overlook the front yard. Instead, I swing through the halls to the kitchen.

I should notice, but I don't…until it's too late. The kitchen lights are on, too. They have a motion detector, so they're only on when someone's making a cup of tea or microwaving takeout.

"Oh, Raffy, you're here," Evie says, stopping me mid-stride. "Good. Sit down."

She doesn't notice my outfit or that I'm clearly on my way out the door. Her command is light and dreamy as she motions to an empty stool. She doesn't even turn away from whatever she's got laid out on the granite island.

I sit, and I see what she's looking at, and suddenly all the artsy lighting in the world doesn't matter. My mind goes pitch black with fear. Before Evie lies Plasma Siren's gown. It's pinned like a butterfly beneath her critical gaze. With only a few weeks until Controverse, it's nearly done.

"Found this while tidying the studio just now. I presume it's yours?"

I could swear I put it away, but I was distracted by that text from Luca. I must have left it out. I'm done, dead, finished. Nothing can save me. Not Jesus. Not Goku. Not even One-Punch Man.

"Yes," I finally answer. "It's mine."

When Evie is considering something deeply, she steeples her fingers. Thumb, pointer finger, middle finger, and ring finger pressed gently into a scaffold, barnacled in rings. She always keeps her pinkies apart. She does this now, looking at the garment.

"It's poetry," she says. "The structure of the chest is a lovely shape, and the flow into the skirt is nice. Even flat, I can see how challenging it must have been to architect something with so much shape that's so lightweight. Did you use boning for these curves?"

She pinches the ridges of the skirt.

"Zip ties," I say. "They're cheaper and easier to install."

She looks at me now, a rare trace of appreciation knitting her brow. I glow with pride, but I'm still very scared of her. In another second, she'll figure out she's complimenting a cosplay.

"It's good work," she says. "Although…"

She lets the steeple of her fingers break as she uses her nails to peel up the seams and hems.

"These are messy. They'll bunch in the wash. You shouldn't use such a simple stitch, ever. It's neither durable nor impressive."

I see what she means, and through my fear, I find myself taking notes.

"And while I appreciate the execution, I'll admit the silhouette is somewhat"—she glances at me again—"cartoonish."

My mental notes incinerate as the blistering white fear returns.

"Who's this for?" she asks.

"May," I lie. "School project."

Evie, like some sort of immortal being who does not remember her schooling days eons ago, is easily tricked by this explanation. Or she just doesn't care, now that she's slipped in the dig of *cartoonish*. She said it with such pity.

"I see," she says, turning back to it. "I doubt your teachers will see what I see, but you simply must fix those seams and hems. And while the embroidery is nice, I suggest planning it out next time, like a print. As it is now, it looks rather too organic, like there's mold growing in the folds."

Which is what I want, I remind myself. I don't say this.

"Thank you," I say. It's the only reaction I or anyone Evie works with is allowed to have in response to her feedback.

"Here, I found some scissors in the studio, too. Maybe we can see about that skirt?"

Evie is holding my scissors. She fully intends to watch me make edits right here in front of her. In fact, I'm sure she was about to do them herself before I ran through the kitchen. I'm stunned, and seeing this, she considers me again. I see her notice my outfit, my bag, and my phone lighting up in my hand.

"Going somewhere?"

"Inaya has a show."

She assesses me from head to toe, because suddenly we are entering the world of her expertise: galleries.

"Where?"

"The Armory."

She shrugs, not impressed. The Armory is a community space, not technically a gallery. Evie pretends never to have heard of it.

"Send my love." She dismisses me, flexing her ringed fingers through the scissors. "You don't mind, do you?"

I look at the dress. Weeks of work about to be sliced apart. But what can I do? If I push too hard, Evie might take a deeper interest in what I'm trying to accomplish, and that might mean the end of all my cosplaying.

"Not at all," I say. "It's just a school project."

Turning away from it feels like leaving behind a child beneath the appraising gaze of a spiteful bully, but I have no choice. May is calling me now, over and over. I've got to move forward, and that means making hard choices. Choices that sting but also protect me, like not letting Luca and Evie meet. This is the same thing, but now I'm the only one getting hurt.

I tell May everything on the way to the show. About Evie finding my work, about Luca being mad at me for hiding him. It's a short drive, but by the time we park, I'm convinced I have done everything wrong. Not just tonight, but forever. Before Luca, I was careful. I had to be, between Evie and my work and pursuing my dreams. And before me, Luca was careful. He had to be, with his parents and his hobbies and his sexuality. We are two balancing acts, intricately and perilously put together, slowly collapsing into one another. The fallout will be impossible to hide from Evie or from Luca's parents.

"But do you like him?" May asks before we exit her car.

"Absolutely."

"And are you happy when you're with him?"

"Yeah, for sure." I'm not sure how to talk to May about how Luca brings me joy but also stresses me out a little bit. We've found a way of coexisting, but always in my studio, my space. Does every relationship feel like an invasion at some level? Tonight is the first time we—the pair, the couple, the combination of two boys—will be outside of our own small, carefully hidden universe. At first I was so excited. Now I'm dreading it.

I look at myself in the dark reflection of the windshield while May checks her makeup. "I'm just afraid the more he sees of my actual life—like, my life outside of the studio—the more he'll realize our worlds don't go together."

"Raffy, you're just panicking," May says. "You love control, and Luca brings you chaos. But maybe you need to learn to work with both."

"Maybe," I murmur.

We head inside, quiet as we slide through the crowds of fashionable attendees. The Armory is a huge open space with market lights crisscrossing a vaulted ceiling and a large stage, the curtain currently drawn. The floor's layout is mazelike, creating small enclaves for each artist to set up a mini gallery. Inaya's work is near the middle of the show, where the maze opens onto a reception area. Ambient music full of electronic pulses and chirps hovers above the crowd's din. Everyone here is stylish and self-conscious, like living art themselves.

"Have you ever thought," May says as we stand in front of a tessellated painting of a peach, "that maybe Luca knows what he's getting into?"

I think about his sad text.

"I don't see how he could know. If he knew, I don't think he'd be into me in the first place."

"You seem to have a lot in common," May offers.

"Like anime and games? Sure, yeah. But what about everything else? What about Evie and his parents? And what about cosplay and conventions? I feel like it's just too much."

"Too much what?"

"Too much…" I pause. "Too public. Too out. Too hard to hide."

I'm sure that tonight is going to be a disaster. If there's a place for Luca to realize he's making a mistake with me, it's for sure an art show.

May checks her phone.

"I wouldn't be so sure, Raff." She winks. Then she grabs my hand and pulls me toward the front of the show, like we're about to leave.

"May, wait, where are we—"

I run right into May as she stops short. She's got her eyes on the door, and she's grinning. I turn just as the crowd parts, everyone noticing the new face entering the art show. It's an unfamiliar face. A brand new one to this scene.

It's a boy, my age, but taller and decidedly broader. He's swathed in a fibrous black fur coat, so fuzzy that it nearly vibrates as he struts in. He lets it slide from his shoulders, revealing a torso clad in a skin-tight white cotton shirt, artfully torn to reveal patches of glowing tan skin. He wears a collar of thick, shining chain, and his pants are black with patent leather racing stripes down the seams. Combat boots would have been the obvious choice, but instead he wears high-heeled Chelsea boots, elevating the look to one that might be the most striking here.

He scans the crowd, his face expressionless beneath expertly painted brushed brows. Then, seeing me, he smiles, and I realize it's Luca.

WHAT?

Luca saunters toward us, cutting through the captivated crowd with gleeful pomp. He air-kisses May first, and I catch on to the conspiratorial smugness between them as they take in my shock.

"You did this?" I ask May.

"We collaborated," Luca says. He doesn't kiss me. Instead, we hug, and his hand leaves a five-pointed constellation prickling on my lower back when it lingers.

"But how?"

"You're not the only secret crafter, Raff," May says. "Just took a few trips to the Garment District and Goodwill and Sephora."

"But Luca—"

"Shh," he cuts me off. "I'm in disguise. *Art* disguise. Call me Vincent. Or Claude. Or something."

I step back. "Are you cosplaying *me* right now?"

May and Luca crumble into silent laughter, and I have to wait a whole humiliating minute before they're composed enough to face me again.

"But why?" I ask. "What if someone recognizes you?"

Luca is pure confidence right now. Before me is a totally different person. He's unrecognizable. He's incredible.

"I wanted to surprise you," he says. "Show you I can dress up, too, you know?"

At first, I cannot reconcile this new stylish person with the boy I found by the bedazzling supplies at Craft Club, sweaty and confused, but then the memories of every moment since bridge it all together. Luca *did* say he'd dress up, just for me.

"You didn't have to do this for me," I say.

"I know," he says. "But I guess I did it for me, too. I like it. I feel hot."

"You are hot," May confirms, and Luca winks at her.

Luca *does* look hot. He knows it, too. And then something occurs to me.

"Is this why you wanted to pick me up? So you could meet Evie like this?"

Luca stiffens, and without his confidence, the outfit suddenly looks like a costume.

"You told May about that?" he says.

"It's cool," May cuts in. "Evie is tough. I've met her a dozen times, and she still thinks my name is Mona. Raff was just telling me how he wished she were better with new people. Don't take it personally, Luca. You look great."

Luca smiles, but there's sadness tinting it. I feel that, too, imagining him putting together this look in order to gain not just my admiration but Evie's approval. And I stopped that from happening. He could have said something, but instead he chose to execute this perfect surprise, just to show me he could. Meanwhile, I've spent the last few hours doubting him.

He's more than I deserve.

"I'll be right back," I say, slipping away from them. I know I'm about to cry. I snake through the makeshift galleries, push through a door, and find myself in a dark expanse, somewhere behind the drawn curtain of the stage.

A second later, Luca joins me. I sniff and hold back my tears, but it's clear I'm upset.

"What's wrong, Raff? You don't like it?"

"No, no, that's not it. You look awesome," I say, emotion cracking my voice. "But you always look awesome. You could have worn whatever you wanted."

"I wanted to wear this," he says. "I like being with you, because I like being me."

That nearly makes me bawl.

"But…"

"What?"

"I didn't know how to put on…what do you call this?" He taps my cheekbone, where I've applied highlighter.

"Want to share?" I offer.

He smiles and lowers himself so we're face-to-face. I lean in, brushing my cheeks against his one at a time, sharing my glimmer with him. Luca holds perfectly still, eyes closed, lips parted, like I'm anointing him.

"There. Now you sparkle, too."

Luca grins. "You like it?"

"I like you."

"I like me, too, especially when I'm with you," he says. "Can you tell me why you're crying now?"

"It's dumb. Evie found some of my work, and I was anxious about our texts earlier. I'm sorry."

"Don't be. You can't help it. I can't help my parents, either."

I nod.

"We'll figure it out."

I nod.

"Can I kiss you?" he asks.

Before I can nod, May breaks into our small moment. She must have followed us.

"Enough," she groans. "This is a gallery, not couples therapy. Can we go silently judge some art, now?"

Luca and I clasp hands, and I notice he's even painted his nails black.

"Come on, let's go be artsy," he says. And we do, but we let each other go right before we re-enter the crowd. Instead, all night, I feel his eyes on me until I finally give in and glance back, drawing out his triumphant smile.

Inaya's exhibit is a world of colors and textures. She's got a collection of paintings that mix embroidery and acrylic, giving the paintings a distinct sense of movement and depth that's uncanny and beautiful. That sort of describes her, too, I think. I try to focus on the work, but seeing it reminds me of how far I have to go with my own work. The second I think of Plasma Siren, I shut my mind down. *Not now*, I think. Right now, I'm here to support Inaya, which I do by hanging out in her mini exhibit and talking up her work to potential buyers. As per usual, Inaya is swamped with interest. We don't really get to talk to her until a few hours later, after she's sold her last piece.

"That was quick," May muses as we walk out to the parking lot.

"I price them low," Inaya says, shrugging. "I'd rather they go on walls than in the trash. I've got other stuff to make. Plus, I've got to get going on some builds. Cons are coming up, right, Raffy?"

My stomach twists. I stay quiet.

"Luca, what did *you* think?" Inaya asks.

"You do really amazing stuff," Luca says. "I wish I could paint like that."

"Thank you, but I meant about the show in general."

Luca thinks about this. "It was cool. I'd go to another. I'm glad we're leaving, though. I'm starving. Can we get food?"

Inaya giggles. "Did Raffy tell you about our post-show tradition?"

I did not. I realize now that I never thought past the show. I figured by now Luca would be running. But he's still here, his hand brushing mine as we walk out together. Guiltily, I look up at him and ask, "How do you feel about karaoke?"

The karaoke place isn't your typical Boston bar. It's an Eastern-style joint where you book a room with just your friends and the staff leaves you alone unless you ring for food or drinks. We're not of age, but Inaya got tight with the staff last summer when she worked here, and we sneak in our own alcohol. The place has a confused theme that's a mix of old film studio and camouflage. The staff wears fatigue pants. Very camp. Even better is the name: Miss Sing, in Action!

Our usual room at Miss Sing's is the first one, which is the smallest. It has two doors in case a cop comes to check IDs and we need to make a break for it. The staff, recognizing me, waves us through the crowd of people camped by the elevator doors. Inaya drove with May, which means they got here way faster. Luca and I might have stopped for drive-through fries at Burger King.

May and Inaya are already at it when we enter, and they don't break their duet for us. They incorporate us, pushing us onto the couches so we can witness the chaotic end of "Let It Go" from *Frozen*. When they finish, they sweep into bows, and we clap boisterously. A staff member enters, throwing down some snacks, and after they leave, May busts out a few beers she's smuggled in from home. We drink and eat, and Inaya talks about behind-the-scenes stuff from the show. We shower her with more praise, which she accepts, and then it's time to sing.

I wonder: What now? Usually, I grab for the microphone right away, ready to scream my ass off to "MOON PRIDE" by Momoiro Clover Z, but with Luca here, I find myself suddenly shy. If I'm singing, he's alone with the girls. I resolve to sit and watch them instead to make sure he's good, but to everyone's surprise, Luca takes the mic next.

He's looking right at me when he says, "This one is for..." but then he throws a wink sideways and says, "...May. We don't know each other that well, but something tells me you'll like this."

And like magic, the opening notes to "Sora Ni Utaeba" play. May screams. This is her absolute favorite song from one of her absolute favorite animes: *My Hero Academia*. It's actually one of her favorite songs to sing herself, but the fact that Luca knows it and has prepared ahead of time to give it a go? I get chills. Inaya gives me a wide-eyed stare as if to say, *Where did you find this boy?*

Luca hits every word in his best Japanese without even looking at the words, and he even mimics some of the iconic character poses as the animation plays on the screen behind him. May watches, chin cupped in her hands, until Luca drags her up. They finish the end together, hand in hand. It sounds atrocious, but it also sounds wonderful, and I'm on my feet clapping. Clapping and cheering with abandon, because I don't just like what I've seen. I don't just adore it. I love it.

I realize that I was scared of this moment—of bringing Luca out of our own private world and into the world of my friends— but it's going so well. I'm excited, and I'm relieved. It's my turn to go next, and I'm not nervous now.

Inside, I'm already singing.

THIRTEEN

It is the night before Primes, and I don't dream.

But I don't *not* dream.

The entire night, I'm on the verge of sleep, of dreams, but I just hang there, too anxious to give myself over to my exhaustion but too stubborn to get up and get ready. The result is a long stretch of nothing until the sun starts rising and there's no denying that Saturday has arrived.

Tomorrow becomes today. And today, I compete in Primes.

I text May, pack up a few last-minute items, and then walk to her place super early. Most of my stuff is already at her house, where I left it after our makeup test. It's just safer that way. It's bright and warm—strange for October, but not unheard of. I stop at Starbucks for a breakfast of cold brew, texting May again to see if she wants anything. By the time I'm at her front door, she still isn't answering, and I'm getting annoyed. I ring the doorbell. Hard.

Her father answers.

"She said she was meeting up with a few people for breakfast near the con," he says, confused by my presence. He's used to seeing us together. I'm confused, too.

"Did she say who?"

"She said you knew them. Weren't you guys hanging out together last night?"

"We were," I assure him.

May knows we're competing today. Why would she go to the con without me? She knows we've got a strict schedule. Where could she be? Why wouldn't she tell me?

I breathe through my rising anxiety, telling myself it's okay. I *am* super early, after all. We have tons of time. We'll be able to get dressed, do makeup, and be ready for prejudging with no problem. Our time slot isn't until four thirty.

"Did she say when she'd be back?" I ask.

"Nope. Maybe soon? You can wait here if you want. We're heading to the Seaport later to see her, if you want a ride."

"What time?"

"Maybe in an hour? We're just finishing up breakfast. Want to come in? We made tots."

I love tots. Who would say no to tots? Plus, I'm still trying really hard to be reasonable and to relax. So I say yes, and I sit at May's kitchen table while her parents ask me about our latest cosplay and the strangeness that was yesterday. But then, a weird thing happens. I get a text from Inaya, but she's not the one who wrote it.

> This is Luca. I think you still have me blocked. Sorry for using Inaya's phone, but when are you getting here? Can we talk?

Luca is already at Controverse. So is Inaya. I'm sure they're already in their cosplays. Suddenly, sitting and chatting about cosplay while totting out feels like sitting in a grave and pulling dirt over myself. My anxiety crashes over me, and I stand up abruptly.

"Thanks for the tots," I say, running up to May's room. Our stuff is where I left it, all packed up and ready to go, but I unpack it again to make sure I have all that we'll need. Then I repack, seething the whole time.

If May isn't here to get ready, I'll bring the readiness to her. Today is maybe the biggest day of my life, and I can't waste time on patience and tater tots. What the hell was I thinking, sitting down?

I rush out of May's house and into a waiting Uber, and the first thing I do when the door closes is delete Luca's text.

◇ - - - ◇

It's an hour later, and all the deep breaths in the world couldn't calm the simmering panic pulsing through my brain. All semblance of reasonable Raffy has dissolved. I've had to wait in like three security lines to get this dumb suitcase and bulging tote into the con, then unpack everything for the prop checker and repack it, and still May has not responded to a single text. But I know where I'll find her. By the time I spot her through the crowd in the Art Mart, I've got the velocity and trajectory of a world-ending meteor.

"What are you *doing*?" I say to the side of her head, blowing apart whatever conversation she's in the middle of. May doesn't look at me right away, but I see the shock of my arrival in the tightness of her eyes.

"Sorry, one second," she says to the man she's talking to. He gives me a nervous glance, but I just pull May away, my bag catching someone's shoulder as I spin.

"Raffy, Jesus. What is going on with you?"

"What's going on with *you*? I had to bring all our stuff by myself today because you left without me."

May eyes the suitcase. "It's like ten o'clock in the morning. The competition isn't until this afternoon, I thought."

"Did you forget about prejudging? And what about building buzz? Luca and Inaya are probably already dressed, and we're not. I can't believe you'd just leave and not tell me!"

I don't get a chance to say any more, because May turns and walks back to the booths. She's shaking her head, heat emanating from her. Is she mad? *Why?* She has no right.

I chase after her, finally catching her at the head of the next aisle.

"I'm not letting you do this in front of these people," she says. Her face is flushed, her lips tight.

"Do what?"

"Reprimand me like I'm a kid. I'd never do this in front of *your* peers."

"What are you talking about?"

May folds her arms over her chest in a perfect imitation of my posture, and seeing this, I catch my first glimpse of how much of an ass I'm being. May whines in my voice: "Maaaaaay, you *know* how much this matters to *me*! I can't be-*lieve* you! How dare you do anything for *your*self when we're here to help *me* further *my* career? Heaven forbid you take a few *fucking* hours to network with other artists! Don't you know we *always* have to be in cosplay? Don't you know it's going to take"—she checks her phone, not breaking her mimicry—"six *fucking* hours to put on a goddamn costume?"

I'm stunned.

Something catches on my tote bag, and it rips open, spilling a cloud of bright pink tulle over my shoes. The people around us barely notice as they stomp across our outfits. I fall over the mess, dragging it together beneath me. I am frantic. This isn't just a costume to me. It's months of work. It's money. It's years of knowledge that I've pieced together by myself. Always by myself, until Luca came along. Until Inaya came along. And now they're gone, and I've only got May, and I feel like she's another tote bag that has just exploded. Another composite of time and memories and friendship unraveling, but I'm here on the ground, only able to fix one and not the other.

"Here," May says, handing me a shoe that has rolled away. We pick up the pieces together, and then, because I am kind of hiccup-sobbing, May leads me to the side of the room. She's silent as we refold the costume pieces, checking to make sure everything is properly accounted for before bundling it in the remains of the bag. When that's done, May folds her hands in her lap and looks at me.

We both apologize at the same time.

"No, listen," she cuts me off. "I was being an asshole. I know this matters and you're under a lot of pressure, but—"

"But nothing."

May's lips tighten, but I manage to keep going before her anger can return. "Don't apologize. I deserved all that. I deserve worse. You're right. Controverse is as much an opportunity for you as it is for me. And you're doing me a huge favor by competing with me. I'm sorry I was so mad. And I'm sorry I got in your face, especially here. I just get so focused, and when I'm angry, it's hard to snap myself out of it."

"Raffy, I know."

"That I get too mad about dumb shit?"

"No, I know the stakes are high. I know that if you have to choose between your art and anything else, you'll choose your art. It's part of who you are, and I admire the shit out of your determination."

I don't know why she is telling me this. I don't even think it's true. I feel like I am constantly chasing after time to work, choosing everything else and then getting mad at myself.

"But you're letting the competition get to you. You're taking this so seriously that you're not having any actual fun anymore. But you don't need to be so serious. You've got me to help you," May says. "I figured if I got here early enough, I could see the people I wanted to see. Then we could get ready together at my place, like we planned. I texted you last night, but maybe you missed it."

I pull out my phone, and sure enough, above all my frantic texts is a message from May, letting me know she'll be home around noon. I didn't even see it in my rush to get the day started.

"Didn't see it, did you?" she says.

I shake my head no. And then I grumble an agreement to her plan, which is pretty solid. I must have slept last night after all, and of course I managed to miss the one message that would have saved me a freak-out, a warpath, and a fight with my bestie on the con floor.

"Shit, I'm so sorry," I say again. "Usually I am prepared for anything. But after yesterday, I don't know what's coming."

"Have you ever considered that you can't be prepared for every future, but all the work you've ever done has prepared you for whatever happens in the present?"

I give her a quizzical look. "When did you get so wise?"

May smirks. "It's from *Cherry Cherry*, you idiot."

I have, of course, read every panel of May's comic. I have a few hung up in my room, blown up to poster size. I've got shirts and pins, too. Anything May makes, I buy.

I think about the quote, then say, "San Diego says that to March when March is freaking out about her future visions not being accurate, right?"

May's face blooms in surprise. "Yes! You remember!"

"Of course I remember. I love *Cherry Cherry*."

May helps me up. She takes the suitcase so I can carry the bundled tote in my arms. We walk slowly between the aisles of artists, picking out the things we like, saying hi to a few of May's new friends as we make the rounds. By the end of the next aisle, I'm feeling much better.

"So listen…" May starts slow. "Some of the people I'm trying to meet aren't going to be here until later, and—hey, don't panic, just let me finish, okay? I'll still compete with you. I promised I would, and I will, okay?"

She waits for me to say okay. I do.

"Okay, cool. But can you promise me that the second we're done on stage tonight, I'm free? There's a rumor that there will be a mandatory Craft Club photo shoot all day on Sunday for anyone who places. You said I could have Sunday to do art stuff, and I need you to promise you're not going to freak out if I take you up on that. Okay? Sunday is going to be, like, my only chance to meet up with some of these people, and I'm confirmed to do one of the drop-in amateur booths. I've been preparing stuff to sell all summer, and this is a huge chance for me, too. If

I wait until the end of the day to set up, no one is going to be here. Okay?"

May waits for me to panic, but I surprise her (and myself) by keeping it cool. I haven't told her about my impromptu trip with Evie on Sunday. I won't even be able to attend that photo shoot even if we do place.

"It's cool," I say. "Sunday is May day. No cosplay whatsoever."

"Really? You're really saying that?"

"I did promise, didn't I?"

At minimum, I owe May this reassurance. But, truth be told, I'm now pretty stressed by the realization that even if we do well, we may not be around to revel in the spoils of our success. But I tuck away the panic, knowing I should stress about this later when I'm by myself. May is right that part of being good at what you do is knowing you'll be able to handle yourself no matter what the present becomes, so I've got to be good right now, and I'll have to be good no matter what happens next.

"You got it. After tonight, you're free. It's a promise."

"Cool. And Raffy?"

"What?"

"There's a lot more to Controverse than just cosplay, remember? I think you'd really like some of the stuff on the floor this year. I know you're nervous, but maybe everything wouldn't feel unknown if you did a little exploring? I've got some time; we can hang out if you want. We used to just show up and talk to people, remember? No agenda, just fun."

"Yeah, I remember." I lift up my broken bag. "But I've got to do a few last-minute adjustments. And honestly, I've wasted enough of your day. I want you to make the most of this, too."

May's lips tighten again, and I know that I have answered wrong, though I don't get why. I thought she wanted to network. I thought she wanted to be free. I don't spend too long unpacking her expression, though, because I'm already thinking through everything I need to do to get ready for tonight. Suddenly, the con around us feels too loud, the air too thick. What would Evie say if she knew I was this close to triumph and decided to take a few hours off to…to what? Have fun?

"I'll meet you at your place later, okay?" I say, giving May a quick hug as I take the suitcase back. I can tell she's a little worried. "I'm sorry again. Enjoy your day."

I practically run off, my suitcase bumping into my heels the whole way.

FOURTEEN

It's a cloudy October morning the week before Halloween, and I'm worrying that Luca will dump me as soon as he figures out I've tricked him. It's Sunday, the last day of Controverse weekend, and I haven't seen Luca in ages. I've been finishing up Plasma Siren so that I could debut her on Saturday, showing her off on the floor in all her barnacled glory. And all in all, it went well! Especially considering I had to remake half the garment after my mom snipped it into a cocktail dress. Thank god she lost interest soon after that.

Anyway, now Siren is packed up and hidden in the back of my closet, and it's a new day. A day for Luca and Raffy. *Just* us.

Or at least that's the lie I told him. In a minute, when we get off of the red line at South Station instead of transferring to the green line at Park, he'll realize we're not going on a Fenway tour. I'm really banking on his love of surprises, which is a safe bet. We hit South Station, and I lead him off the train without him even raising an eyebrow.

So he knows something is up. But maybe not what? He'd probably be pissed if he knew. Luca likes it best when it's just him and me, holding hands in a dark theater or at the very back of a crowd. A secret, just the way Luca likes us. The art show was a fluke. Usually he gets distant when there are other people around, but when it's just him and me, he takes my hand first. And it's like time stops for just us, the rest of the world still and oblivious as we wander through it. It's like we exist in a loop, a reverie, a world that is created when our hands connect and disappears when we break apart.

I'm pretty sure he figures out where we're going when a mass of cosplayers passes by. He raises an eyebrow at me.

We walk across the channel bridge and into the Seaport, and all of a sudden we're at the convention center. Luca follows with a lazy smile on his face. He's got to know by now. And I'm relieved he's cool with it. Luca is the most adaptable person I know. He can be comfortable anywhere. He has a way of making the world vibrate like he is a magnet and no particle is immune to his pull. Everything—people, plants, pets—perks up when he walks by. It happens in every situation. So if I have to go without holding his hand for a day to introduce him to another part of my world, so be it. He'll thank me later.

We get closer to Controverse, and the crowds thicken,

costumed people everywhere. A band of cosplayers dressed in Zelda garb are busking out front, playing accordions.

Luca says, "I fucking knew it."

Suddenly, Inaya and May are jogging up to us, Starbucks in hand. They shove a drink at Luca.

"Sunday! Funday!" the girls chant together. Inaya thrusts a badge at Luca, who is looking at me with over-the-top fury.

"This is the surprise? We're going to your *nerd convention*?"

"It's not a nerd convention," Inaya snaps her badge at him. "It's a geekery gala. A comic book bacchanalia. A weeaboo Western."

"*Weeaboo Western* would make a great reality comic strip," May says. "Can I use that?"

"It's a NERD CONVENTION!" Luca shouts, and I think maybe I've really messed up. He's been good about not seeing me these past two weeks as I really buckled down and focused, and maybe he sees today as just another day lost to my cosplaying.

But then I see the anger is an act and the magic of Controverse is working on him. I wonder: Did he see this coming? Was he counting on it? Luca is watching the crowd with excitement now. Above us in the building, people pack into the windowed halls in all manner of cosplay and costume. The corners of Luca's mouth raise as he continues to gripe and argue in comedic protest. Protest just for the sake of putting up a fight. Grim yet excited resignation.

Oh, he's a goner. He's *so* into it.

Luca and I have talked about him coming to Controverse a bunch. For a long time, he flatly refused to believe that it could be any fun, so I had to show him compilation videos of all the super-intense cosplays. That got his interest, but he still refused to get a ticket. He kept saying, "If my dad ever saw that charge on my card, he'd know something was up right away. It'd be *done*. It'd be *over*."

So the girls and I pooled our money and got him a ticket, and I tricked him. I had to, to keep his plausible deniability intact. I feel bad about the betrayal, but as I see his eyes light up, I also feel something else. Victorious. Vindicated. I decide he *was* hoping for this all along.

I take the badge from his hand and slip the lanyard around his neck, pulling him toward me. Luca doesn't resist for once, fastening his hands around my waist. His face fills my vision as he closes in, lowering his voice to a playful and menacing whisper.

"You planned this? You got me a badge and everything?"

"Yeah."

"You must really want me here, huh?"

"Yeah."

"Then I'll go. But if I see someone I know, I'm running."

"I'll run with you."

"And"—he glances at Inaya, who is wearing a wig—"I'm not putting on any weird shit. I look good."

"You got it."

◇ - - - ◇

Con strategy is like a family mac 'n' cheese recipe. Everyone's got their own way of doing it, and everyone wants to talk about why they're right. For Inaya, May, and me, our strategy is informed by our schedules. Most cons are Friday, Saturday, and Sunday, with the big cosplay masquerade or competition on Saturday. This is why we try to do most of our shopping on Friday, when all the artists have the most stock, then spend Saturday in our best cosplay. Finally, Sunday involves casual cosplay meant for socializing. Networking. Saying hello to competitors, judges, and friends.

There was no way to get Luca to skip school with us on Friday, and bringing him on Saturday was a surefire way to overwhelm him with the weirdness of competitive cosplay. Sunday Funday was our best option, and I've got a plan for introducing him to this world.

You can't just walk someone through Controverse, or any con this big. It's brutal on the mind. It's prohibitively overwhelming. You've got to understand that they're seeing all this for the first time and let them see it. You go slow, lead by your curiosity, like hand-stitching embroidery instead of following the grid of a cross-stitch.

The atrium is packed, as usual, so we stick to the edges and enter the exhibits. All weekend, I've been keeping a list of places I think Luca will love, putting together a small treasure trail to follow once I've gotten him here. But as it turns out, we don't need to follow any trail. Luca is a shooting star, burning with excitement the second we're inside the exhibition room.

"Raffy, *look*!" He's got my arm in his hand, pulling me from a book booth to the glass shelves that display expertly painted models of monsters. He starts listing them for me as though I don't know them, as though they aren't labeled. I don't look at them, though—I look up at him, into his searching eyes. Each time he can name one, his eyes widen a fraction of a second before he speaks, and my heart jumps a little.

We make it into a few anime exhibits that Luca is more reserved in. One is a small house made to look like it's built out of waffles. People cram into the corners, taking pictures on top of large beanbag chairs that look like fat balls of butter and jam. Once it's our turn, Inaya and May throw themselves onto the nearest one.

"Take a picture!" they cry, their weight tipping the butter chair.

I take about a million photos. I stop when Luca taps my shoulder.

"Can we take a photo?"

I glance at him. "Are you sure?"

"Not to post. Just for us."

I smile. The girls untangle themselves, and it's my turn to be in front of the camera. I can't help but laugh when Luca just stands there, smiling, giving the camera a thumbs-up. I am almost positive this is how every photo of him ever must look. I let him take a few that way, and then, when the girls yell for him to change it up, I pull him down into the pillows with me. At first he's unsure, but then I've got my arm around his shoulder, my thigh across his, and he knows what to do.

The photos come out great, full of color and laughter,

chronicling the moment Luca went from being in my photos to me being in his. By the end of the shoot, all you can see are my feet, the shoe missing from one foot, as I roll over the back edge of the pillow pile. Luca remains on top, untouchable, smiling with a look of sheer demonic innocence.

The exhibits take up the morning, especially because Luca insists on taking a photo with everything he recognizes. Which is a lot. Because he's a complete nerd in denial.

"Where are you even gonna post these? Some private account?"

"You don't have to post everything, you know," he says, flipping between two nearly identical photos of him with a cosplayer dressed as slutty Hello Kitty.

"So that's for personal use?" I joke.

Luca zooms in on the muscles in his forearm, which are toned in a way that he knows I love. "Or maybe they're for *your* personal use, Raffy?"

I feign bashfulness. Luca keeps his eyes on me instead of looking back at his photos, waiting for me to notice the dreamy, questioning look on his perfect face.

"What?" I ask.

"You like that I'm here?"

"I love that you're here," I say.

We shop our way through the merchandise tents and then swing through the Art Mart. I take an especially long time looking at a print of Sailor Moon, her back to the viewer, her iconic pigtails flowing across a buttery sickle moon. I want it, but I've spent way too much this year already. At the next table, I look for Luca and catch him furtively whispering to May and Inaya. Something secret is happening, so I look away, giving them some privacy. Then May catches up to me.

"Look at these," she says, scooping up some bookmarks with puffy Pokémon rolling across them. I know she's distracting me, and I let her, amused that my friends think they can put anything anime-related in front of me and I'll focus on it. But then I see a bookmark with Jellicent on it. She's a Gen VI Pokémon, and she's got a male and female form. This artist has both. A totally rare find! We get into a discussion about it, and May's distraction works beautifully.

It's not until we sit down in the food court for a late lunch that I remember Luca and Inaya sneaking off. I'm so lost in my analysis of the cosplayers walking by that I don't even notice Luca handing me a large envelope until I'm already absently holding it.

"Open it, Raff." Luca nudges me.

I see the shape and size, and I know exactly what it is: the Sailor Moon print. I know better than to let on that I know, so I open it quickly to give the tears in my eyes a reason for falling.

"Saw you looking at it," Luca says, nudging me again. "I know how you like her. She'd look great on your wall."

"Luca." I don't know why I'm crying. Well, I do. It's the first time a guy has ever bought me something. And I always figured I'd get gifts of roses or chocolates someday, but Luca found something I wouldn't let myself have and gave it to me anyway. Not for my birthday, and not for Christmas. Just because he knew I wanted it.

"I love it," I tell him truthfully, slipping it back into the envelope so it doesn't get grease on it.

Luca glances around, determines that it's safe, and then gives me a quick kiss. When he pulls away, his eyes lock on something behind us.

"What's that?"

He doesn't wait for an answer. He just walks toward the crowd of people forming in the wide center of the food court. I leave our stuff with May and Inaya, who are going through photos, and catch up to Luca just as he burrows his way to the front of the cheering crowd.

We stand in a thick line of people at the edge of an invisible stage where six cosplayers are engaged in an intricate dance around one another. Their weapons swing and fly in slow motion, emulating the drama of battle with no actual impact. It's theatrical fighting, a scene from a game I recognize but haven't played. The people nearest to us are cheering the loudest. At their feet are speakers, blaring the music we heard from our table.

"What are they doing?" asks Luca, wonder in his voice.

"It's play fighting. It's not real," I say.

"I know. But why?"

I point out the cameras to Luca. Not just the phones people are using to record, but the handheld video equipment at the edges of the scene.

"People make videos for the cons featuring the big cosplayers," I say. "Some compete, but a lot do it to meet people. It's a social thing. Others come to photograph and make movies if they don't want to cosplay themselves. Usually a lot of the shoots happen out here."

Luca starts moving again, this time toward the escalators. I chase after him, jogging to his side as he hits the landing. Right before he reaches the photo shoot he's spotted, he stops short.

I see what's caught his eye. Christina Wynn, standing on a low wall, illuminated by multiple soft boxes as a string of photographers raise huge cameras up at her. They snap and swarm around her feet like fish wrestling for cast-off crumbs.

She is not actually flying, but from the angle she's being photographed, I can tell she will look like she's floating in the photos. The light perfectly catches each exquisite detail of her cosplay, but she could be swathed in shadow and I'd still know every groove and scale. She's wearing her *Dragon Sage* armor, which I watched her build over the last six months on Ion, and it's stunning in person.

"Who is that?"

"Christina Wynn. She's from Canada. She's 'Christina the Winner' on Ion."

"You know her?"

"No, she's a big cosplayer. She placed in Controverse Primes last night."

Luca barely hears me. He's looking around now, suddenly seeing the cosplayers that glow at the hearts of the mob. The focal points of affection, adoration, attention.

And something in his mind clicks. I can almost see his thoughts connect into a constellation of understanding.

"We're doing this," he tells me. "Next year, we're showing up to compete."

FIFTEEN

I wait at May's house, passing a heat gun over some foam armor to warm out the cracks and wrinkles I'm sure only I can see. I adjust May's wig and get started on my prosthetics and makeup early. I generally do a good job of finding minute things to worry about while the clock ticks toward noon.

May arrives home right on time, glowing with excitement. As we dress, she talks through the people she got to meet and the collabs she's going to get started on right away. She even got an offer to booth with another artist who likes her work, which is huge. *Huge!* The conversation eases me out of my own thoughts and micro-panics. I sink into my usual pensive efficiency as I listen, and before I know it, we're dressed. We look at ourselves in the mirror, the density of details almost too much for the small dimensions of May's room.

I am dressed as HIM, an iconic villain from the nineties animated show *The Powerpuff Girls*. HIM is a devilish, lithe figure in red, swathed in tufts of pink fuzz and thigh-high stilettos. And he has crab claws. Bizarre, I know, but easily recognizable by the judges, who are mostly millennials. Millennials love a good reference, and they *all* watched *PPG*. They'll know me in a second, and I know the reaction is going to be wild.

From head to toe, my skin is coated in cherry-red makeup that gleams with even the smallest movement. Prosthetics pull my nose and chin into devilish points, and I've ridged my cheekbones to give the illusion of my skull pushing up through my skin.

HIM is iconic for many reasons, and I've adapted all the core references—the red skin, the boots, the tutu and collar, and the claws—into a distinctly Elizabethan take. I have the ruffled, cotton candy–pink lace sewn into a bodice of fine, bloodred brocade, and an elaborate sash tied tightly around my waist. I even made an authentic codpiece, which might be cheeky, but I think the judges will like it. And of course, I have the boots. They're black, though not patent leather (it would clash), and they have gorgeous lacing up the back. They're what you might have found under Queen Elizabeth's many skirts if she were feeling nasty.

Best of all, though, are the gargantuan crab claws I've created. My claws are hyper-real and a startling, boiled red. They look torn off a monstrous crustacean, something thickly armored to survive the flaming depths of hell.

All in all, the look is very Lady Gaga meets Red Lobster, very Shakespeare in hades. I look fucking fantastic.

May looks even better.

She's dressed as another villain, also from *The Powerpuff Girls*: Princess Morbucks, a famously bratty rich bitch with puffy red hair, who uses her father's money to create armor that gives her all the abilities of the actually powerful Powerpuff Girls.

So basically, she's little girl Iron Man. And that's the joke of the costume. I've taken the rather overdone Iron Man armor and recreated its brilliant golds and chromes around May's much curvier body. And to tie it in with my HIM costume, I've designed the armor to look like that of an Elizabethan knight. May looks antiquated but new. Deadly but regal. I hope every single Tony Stark we run into literally power-jets out of her way when we strut onto the Controverse floor.

"Shit, Raff, we look awesome," May says. I'm adjusting the crimson puffs of hair that border her head, making sure the sculptured teasing I did will stay put. It will. I look at May, and I'm so happy she's the one here with me.

"We *do* look awesome, don't we?"

May's parents insist on taking photos of us as though we're going off to prom. They won't post them, which is a rule they know to respect, but they say they want to have them to look back on when May and I are famous artists. Their supportive statement makes my stomach twist the whole drive over to the Seaport, which I spend cradling my gargantuan claws. As the radio plays

WBUR, I drift back into my buzzing anxiety about all that could go wrong, but May pulls me out when she asks me to reach an itch on her shoulder, between the plates of her armor.

"Such a princess," I joke.

"That's *right*. A little higher, though. And can you use your claw?"

"Weirdo!"

"Whatever," she laughs.

Per the instructions in the email we got last night, we enter through the back of the convention center, where several clubbers are waiting to check us in. We're led through the same dark hallways until we are installed in the prejudging room from yesterday, where competitors await their turns in nervous pairs. There are only thirteen teams remaining, so I zero in on Luca and Inaya right away, then spend the rest of our waiting time pretending I cannot see them at all. I'm so quick to do this that I'm not even sure what they're wearing, and I convince myself I don't care. May and I are clearly causing a stir among the other competitors, and I just focus on making sure that stir ripples all the way out and ruffles Luca's perfectly coiffed hair.

Otherwise, things are kind of normal. Too normal.

"There are no cameras," May points out. She's right. No one is filming this.

I jump when I hear my phone go off in my bag. Our turn is coming up, so I rush to silence the ring before the prejudges get to us. Quickly, I shuck off one of my claws and carefully bend over, balancing on the high heels, but I nearly fall backward when I see who's calling. It's Evie. But why?

"Raffy, what are you doing?" May asks urgently.

"Hello?" I say into the phone.

Evie doesn't say hello back. She says, "Where are you?"

May snatches the phone from me, hangs it up, and tosses it behind us just as the prejudges circle in. A clubber is with them, tablet in hand, recording everything.

I pull my claw on. I pull myself together in general, and May and I begin our rehearsed explanations of our costumes. Behind me, someone goes, "Hey, did you drop your phone?"

I ignore them.

"HIM's armor was inspired by Elizabethan fashion, because I wanted to historically contextualize the ruffled collar and puffed sleeves alongside Princess Morbucks's golden knight armor. And also because the fabrics from that era are utterly fab to work with. Plus, HIM's theatrics have always felt distinctly Shakespearean to me, so it all kinda worked. And it doesn't hurt that the contrast with the claws is truly gruesome."

"Excuse me, is this yours?" the person behind me asks again. "Someone is trying to call you."

May snatches the phone away from them, silences it, and tosses it onto our stuff. One of the prejudges asks me for more details about my bodice.

I'm distracted. I barely manage to answer with, "It's a handmade corset."

May clears her throat, and I go on.

"I didn't use authentic whalebone, because it seemed bad to kill an entire whale just for one undergarment. I used zip ties instead for the structure of the corset, then reinforced the structure in the bodice, which is made using a brocade I found at Craft Club and updated with hand-embroidered black pearls. Everything was either handmade or updated by me in some way, including the lace for the ruff and the skirts. I didn't create it, but I did starch it. I also acid dyed it and then hand-pleated the skirt for the ruffled effect."

"And the shoes?"

I take May's hand so I can show the judges my carefully laced boot covers, but my eyes are drawn to my phone, lighting up again and again. What is going on? Does Evie know I'm here? She knows I'm not camping, and I totally forgot to give her another lie for today. I forgot. Shit. *Shit.*

I barely listen to myself as I attempt to explain how I made the boots. And I take so long to get it out that I don't get a chance to talk about anything else before our time is up.

The judges drift off to the next pair, leaving May standing over me with her hands on her hips, looking way too concerned for someone who isn't a principal or a police officer.

"Raffy, don't get mad, okay? You got a little lost, but I'm sure you gave them enough to work with. And just remember that winning doesn't have to be everything, okay?"

I start to take my claw off so I can grab my phone, but May snatches it away again.

"Don't. It's only going to make your anxiety worse," she warns.

"You're treating me like we've already lost."

"You're behaving like you want us to. You didn't even talk about your custom codpiece! Wasn't that, like, the whole *point* of wearing a codpiece?"

I take a few teetering steps back on my stilettos. "I thought you didn't care about any of this."

"Well, I care about *you*!" She can't fold her arms, but I can tell she wants to. She can't do much of anything with her armor on. Any onlooker would think we're having a very awkward, slow-motion fight.

"And I know this matters a lot to you, but the world isn't going to end if you don't get first place. You made it to Primes. You're for sure going to get an honorable mention at minimum. And we look *ah-ma-zing*. Can't that be enough?"

I'm forced to consider that word: *enough*. Is it enough? Am I?

Is second best enough for my followers? Maybe it would have been, if I'd been posting regularly leading up to this. They come to me to learn, to watch, but in the aftermath of Luca, I've barely been streaming on Ion. I've been too embarrassed, too furious to show my face. I've done it all alone. This was supposed to be my big, victorious reveal.

And what about Evie? Second best has never been enough for her. In fact, my very best has never been enough, either. I remember last year when she looked at my Plasma Siren cosplay, called it poetry, and then cut it up. So would these builds be enough for her? Would an honorable mention be enough? No, of course not. Inevitably, Evie is going to see me cosplaying one day, and if I'm not the best at it by then it's better that she never see me do it at all.

And nothing but winning will be enough for *me*. All that I do is measured against the person I am trying to become, and his standards are the highest of all. He is strong and unshakeable and kind and joyful. If I can become him, become *that*, I know the rest will fall into place.

But I'm not him yet. I'm me. Anxious, emotional, weak-ass me. No matter how much I reassure myself that I'm ready, that I can do this, a single missed call from Evie sets my anxiety off and reduces me to a babbling kid in a costume. I'm not enough to prove anyone's doubt wrong. The only thing I'm proving is that I'm still not ready to be the son Evie demands, or the person my dreams depend on.

"Don't think about her," May says, way too late.

I remove one of my claws and put out my hand. "Give me the phone."

May hands it to me, regret in every line on her face.

I take the phone and power it down, chucking it to the floor beside our stuff. I hope it gets stolen. The perfect excuse to never listen to any of Evie's voicemails.

"Screw her," I say.

"Screw her." May smiles. We hand-hug, since actual hugging would be deadly in these cosplays.

"We're here. And that's enough."

"We *are* here," she says, "And that's *everything*. You did this, Raffy. Now, you ready to win?" May says.

"I am." I grin.

Madeline enters the room, and she asks us all to listen as she reads off our next steps. We're told there will be cameras and that we aren't supposed to look directly into them. Then she reads some reminders about how Primes work. There will be the typical three categories for judging: armor, needlework, and FX (as in special effects). Each category will have a first, second, and third place. Then the judges will award best in show, runner-up, and second runner-up for the entire competition. Those are the big awards, the ones you want.

Looks are going to be judged individually at the category level, but pairs will be judged together for the best in show placements. May is in the armor category. I'm in needlework.

Then, like the most bizarre parade ever, we're led to the massive auditorium set up for Primes. Backstage, we're told to remain in our pairs as clubbers rush back and forth silently. It's hard to see much, but we can hear everything through the speakers as the hosts get the crowd hyped up. Ads for Craft Club's new line of wigs are played, along with some sponsored content for a few upcoming movies and games that are receiving a ton of focus this year. Then the judges—the *real* judges, Waldorf Waldorf and the others—are brought on, each with a grand introduction that lists their formidable skills, achievements, and points of expertise. They discuss how excited they are for all of Controverse to see our looks, and the thousand-strong eat it up.

The real show is about to begin. Usually they take the looks out by category, but this year they're having the couples walk together. We knew that much coming in, and May and I whisper-confirm our moves as the first few couples perform. We're totally aligned and ready to go.

"Raffy and May, you're on deck," Madeline whispers as we approach the curtain. My adrenaline begins to spike.

Then a familiar voice comes from the shadows.

"May, do you need help with your power pack?"

Inaya and Luca are behind her. The couple before us is called out.

"Thank you," May says as Inaya hides the pack in May's shoulder guard more securely.

"Don't touch that mic," Madeline whispers to Inaya, and then they're both fiddling with May's costume. I can't hear what they're saying because the crowd is cheering as the cosplayers before us finish. Which means we're about to be announced.

Stage fright, which has been prickling in my throat this whole time, is washed away by bright terror when I see exposed wires hanging out of May's back. In a flash, I move Madeline and Inaya to the side, gather the mic cord and the power pack, and put them in a pocket of space below May's shoulder.

"There," I say, just as our names boom through the speakers.

"Wait!" Luca thrusts something at May. Her cape, which I completely forgot about. May throws it on just in time.

"Thank you," I whisper to him and Inaya. And we're up.

We enter halfway through the intro I wrote, already behind.

"...known on Ion as *Crafty Rafty*, with entries in the armor and needlework categories," the announcer booms, and the clubber beside us draws back the curtain so we can walk.

I've watched this moment a million times from the audience, in person and through streams and in people's stories on socials. But as I step out before the crowd, I feel brand new in this space, in this time, in this look. I am not Raffy—I am HIM. May is nowhere. Princess Morbucks reigns besides me. And coursing through the cheers and cries is the narrative of our creation, broadcast from the dark sky as if by an omniscient god.

"HIM and Princess Morbucks have returned to annihilate those Powerpuff Girls for *good*," reads the host.

May and I hit center stage, and this is the big moment.

"HIM's claws are made to look sinisterly realistic, but they're all foam. Meanwhile, Princess Morbucks's power suit is fully equipped with working circuitry and LED lights. Only the best for Princess!"

That's May's cue. She hits her signature pose—hands on hips, bratty and imperious. A sensor in her hip connects to one on her hand, and the lights in her suit flare to life.

Or they should.

Right now, though? Nothing.

May hits the pose again, and still nothing happens. I'm sure it's due to that last-minute power pack fiddling, but there's no time to fix it. As a result, I miss my own pose, where I'm supposed to jab at the audience with my claws. I go for it too late, just as May sweeps her cape around herself, and suddenly we're fastened together as bundles of heavy velvet get caught in my crustacean grip.

May and I move to untangle ourselves at the same time, but only one of us is in stilettos. I feel the stage swing out from under me as I topple, and I try to catch myself before I remember my hands are literally gigantic crab claws. I land squarely on my chest, making a terrible grunting noise, and my hands fly out in front of me. The claws detach, sailing through the air, and the next thing I hear is a crash in the audience as they land among the camera crews.

The sound is horrible and distinctly that of many expensive things falling over, and there's even a small burst of sparks.

The host makes some sort of joke, and people are laughing. As I scramble to untangle myself and stand, I fall again on my pointy heels.

Someone dives into the mess to retrieve the crab claws. The stage lights go out as clubbers rush to help May and me up. We're barely halfway off the stage when the crowd begins chanting our names, but I don't see them. I can't see anything through the tears that are for sure about to ruin my makeup. We messed up in the worst possible way, and all I can see before me is our impending defeat.

The lights come back on, and the chants dissolve to cheers. I don't see any of it. My world stays dark, my future even darker.

Whatever enough is, this isn't it. I'm not it.

SIXTEEN

The holidays! A time of light, love, and for most families, hosting. We're no different when it comes to the hosting part, except it's never family. Instead, our guests are artists. People from my mother's world, curious people who seem to have dropped out of the sky with no way to climb back up into their clouds. They just show up, and they stay forever, and no matter how many signs I put on my bedroom door, they never ever knock before barging in.

It makes it hard to hide and to get work done, not that I have a ton of work to do. With Controverse behind me, I'm in my slow season, the season I usually spend working on my builds for spring and summer. So I should be designing, researching, and gathering materials, but picking a path just feels impossible this time. With

Luca in the picture, things are both exciting and terrifying, too fast and utterly slow.

Almost always, I work alone. I work for myself. I work for my vision. The sudden accommodation of two visions freezes me and quiets my hands and wipes my mind clean all at once. It's almost like I dread getting started now that I know the work won't be completely mine. And that doesn't quite make sense either, because at the same time, I'm completely ecstatic that Luca is going to cosplay with me.

Luca wants to cosplay! I can imagine how amazing it'll be when it's all done, but I can't bring myself to start.

My phone lights up with a few more texts from Luca. Whereas I have spent the past month since Controverse in some sort of craftless daze, Luca is fully spiraling into the world of DIY videos on Ion. Since I brought him to Controverse, he's changed in a wonderful way. He has turned his skepticism toward cosplay inside out to reveal the gleaming enthusiasm of the truly obsessed. Combined with his usual energy, it's hard to keep up with all his questions and ideas.

Maybe that's why I can't seem to pick a project? You'd have trouble too if your maybe-boyfriend sent you no fewer than six half-baked ideas a day, for weeks. And maybe that sounds annoying, but it's not. It's an opportunity.

Luca and I are built from very different materials. If Luca is lined with enthusiasm, I am insulated with ambition. If we were even a little more alike, the difference would hurt us, but our contrast is beautifully stark. Our clash is one of power. One I'm learning to not just trust, but believe in.

I can't stop thinking about how popular two young queer boys would be in the cosplay scene. I'm dreaming of the end. I'm fixated on it, and I can't help it. Luca is undeniably hot, and I'm undeniably talented. Together, we're going to be iconic.

Going to be.

That is, if I ever figure out how to start. Mostly I've just been playing video games, like I am right now, and telling myself it's "research."

Another text comes in from Luca, this time a link to a tutorial on prosthetic zombie makeup.

Zombie Bambi?

He's referencing one of my stranger couple cosplay ideas. An animal look designed around Bambi from the Disney movie and his mother, except in my interpretation, she's come back as a zombie, and she's bitten Bambi. Weird, I know, but for sure eye catching. And Luca loves any look that would show off his body. Can't say I mind that idea, either.

But the vision stops there. It's always just a glimpse of the glamour. This time, though, I'm able to look a little further into the future, and I realize something. All I can see are the moments of glory, but just past that is a darkness I can't shake. Not an evil darkness. A *nothing* darkness.

No matter how excited Luca is now, I know this is all going to end when he realizes what will happen when we step onto that con floor together in cosplay. People will assume. They'll ship us. Whether Luca likes it or not, the internet is going to out us as a couple before he's ready. From what I know about his deal with his parents and their attitudes toward comics, cons, and cosplay, this would be a nightmare scenario for Luca. The second he realizes his new dream will have to coincide with coming out, that dream is going to die. My dream will, too, I guess. I should put us both out of our misery and spell it out for him, but I'm too scared even to do that.

The truth of this layers over me like chilled, wet wool. It slows me down and I die in my video game. I become slow all over, except in my heart, which flutters like it's got hiccups. Maybe I can't start because I know this can't end well. Maybe it's hardest to begin the things we know will bring about ends.

Luca texts me again.

> I'm kidding. I'm not dressing up as a deer. Not even for you, sicko. ;)

I cast away my controller and swing my legs over the side of my bed. Then I'm standing and stretching, suddenly itching to make something.

For a long time, I've been careful with Luca. Worried that the strange relationship we have would come apart in my hands. But

Luca keeps outsmarting my fears. He keeps surprising me, like at the art show, like right now as he continues to send me ideas. I need to give him—and us—a chance, right? If this is just my anxiety derailing another good thing, I'll never forgive myself.

If Luca is ready, I can be ready, too. I won't let my fear of the future define my behavior in the present. Luca has finally, *finally* entered my world, and I'm not going to make him leave it just because I'm afraid.

The doorbell rings, barely audible over the music (presently Dolly Parton). It rings again a minute later, then a third time. I run to get the door and barely notice the several adults (Evie included) lying on the living room floor in a circle as they roll through some sort of chemical bliss. Blech. Old artists are so needy.

Right as the bell rings again, I get to the door and find a delivery girl with no fewer than eight giant bags of food. I sign for them and gather the bags into my arms, annoyed on the delivery person's behalf. I'm carrying the last bag into the living room when Evie sits up, her bob a bit askew, and says, "Raphael, what is this commotion?"

"I'm guessing it's your dinner?"

"So it is," she says pensively. She's for sure high. Probably doesn't remember ordering all this Indian food. I turn to go, but she's up in a flash, tearing bags open.

"Come, sit, eat with us, Raphael. You spend too much time in that room looking at screens. Come look at faces. Screens can't smile or cry or ask questions."

That's the point, I think.

I glance at the other adults. They're all in a state of delirium. Their faces are splotchy and surprised, then intrigued as the food fills the house with the aromas of naan and curry. One person picks up a plastic container and shakes it, listening to the contents splat about.

"I'm going to get plates," I say, but out of nowhere, several other guests float in from the kitchen, plates and utensils in their arms. Like Evie, they're all swathed in a sort of space-like pajamas, like the night shift of the Starship Enterprise. I don't know why. I don't care why. If it's not space pajamas, it's some other weird thing. Some of them I know from past parties, and others are indescribably similar to the ones I've already met. Soon, they're all arranged around the living room, trading stories in their unusual languid fashion.

"And then they opened that Panera Bread," one of them is saying as though delivering a eulogy. "And that's when I knew it—that's when I knew the town was dying. And so I thought: stay. Stay, Margaret, and paint the death. Face the death. Say 'death' and see how it tastes."

The two people Margaret is eulogizing to moan, "*Deaaaathhh*."

"Tastes like French onion soup," Margaret concludes. "So I did a series on bread bowls. I called it *Carb-e Diem*. Seize the bread."

And so on like this for half an hour. I get through a plate of food without anyone noticing me, thank god. My mistake is trying to leave quietly right after.

"Raphael, you're what, fifteen now?"

I sit back down, turning to the man who knows my name. He and my mom share a haircut. It's distressing.

"I'm seventeen."

"Ah, nearly out of high school, right? What's next?"

"The wooooorld," intones Evie, whom I hadn't realized was paying attention. There's a joke in the way she elongates the word. Sarcasm, I guess. Like I think I can handle it but can't, and she knows it.

"Your mother says you've got some nascent talent when it comes to a sewing machine. Have you thought about apprenticing?"

"Nope," Evie blurts. "I can't get him to sit with anyone unless it's in a class. He wants to do *more* school."

"Oh, why be so practical? You're so young," asks a very tall lady named Rocky. Rocky is trans; she did a series of found object sculptures last year that chronicled her transition. She's one of the few artists I actually like.

I make a point of looking at Evie when I answer, "I want to learn as much as I can as I figure out my artistic perspective. I'm not sure what I want to do yet or what I want to say, so I'll do everything until I know more."

"Oh, he's smart, Evie," Rocky says, but she says it as a scold, like Evie has told her otherwise, and recently.

"What do you like to make right now?" Rocky asks.

When I don't answer right away, Evie says, "He's very crafty. Tell them about your *school project*, Raphael."

And I know she knows it wasn't just a school project, which makes the fact that she cut it up all the worse. Maybe because she's high or maybe because she just feels like being cruel, she steeples her fingers and announces, "Raphael likes to play dress-up."

Rocky brightens. "Drag?"

"No, no." Evie hurries past the topic of drag, like she doesn't want the noble art of drag to see our dirty little conversation. "Like cartoons. Little characters."

Somehow, I manage to say, "Cosplay."

"Yes, yes, my son, the *cosplayer*."

If the others know what cosplay is, they don't admit it. If they don't know, they're not about to ask. Evie has her knives out, and anything that moves might get stabbed.

Rocky is the bravest. "My nephew does that," she says warmly, like she can sense I'm gonna bolt. "He likes to dress up like a fox."

"A fox?"

"Yes, he has a fox suit. He tells me the community is quite active. Just all *sorts* of animals. They're very accepting."

"That's something else," I say. "I design and build costumes from movies, comics, and video games."

"I've seen a fox in a movie," says the man who thought I was fifteen. "I'm sure of it."

"Focus, Boris," Evie says. "This is serious. It's arts and crafts. Raphael is *very* crafty."

"Oh, have you been to Craft Club? My nephew loves that place," Rocky says unhelpfully.

"Have you, Raphael?" Evie says pointedly. "When Boris and I were setting up the loft, I found *several* Craft Club bags stuffed in the linen closet."

I give Rocky an anguished look, and she returns it with a stunned, apologetic horror. She's trying to help me, but what I really need is to leave. Evie can make fun of Craft Club for hours.

"Evie, you're too elitist. Craft Club is very cute," says Rocky.

"Yes. Cute." Evie sighs, long and powerfully disappointed.

I have a lot to say. The words spool in my mouth, threads of fury coiling at the back of my teeth. I swallow them down, and they knot tighter in my gut. I've never seen my ambitions and my crafting as being in conflict, but Evie sees assured mutual destruction. Media that cannot be mixed. I know I could argue that they are one and the same to me, but it's not worth it. Or it's not possible.

I don't take the bait. The conversation moves on. I try to stay and listen to show that I haven't just been flayed alive, but my mind has already escaped upstairs. It's in my room, where my phone is on my charger, slowly filling with messages from the boy I'm falling for.

Who wants to cosplay.

With me.

I guess we're both pursuing dreams in spite of our realities. Between Luca and me, I wonder who is going to be forced to wake up first.

I'm still feeling dreadful about the way Evie talked to me, and it's days later. I haven't done any work at all. Well, I've done school-work, I guess. But nothing with my hands. It sucks.

It's also December. Which normally I love because it's a great excuse to be inside all the time, but it's been super mild. This is why, when I'm leaving school that Wednesday, I'm not surprised to get a text from Luca that reads:

> Come to the fields. Meet me under the bleachers.

I have been living in Boston forever, but I never knew about any of the fields in the area until Luca. Now I know about most of them, and I know he means the ones near Magoun Square in Somerville. Even so, I have no clear idea of where the bleachers are, much less how to get under them. But as I pull up, I figure it out, wondering the whole time what Luca is up to. I shoot May a quick text letting her know to wait for me at Donut, Jonut! (a *Rocky Horror*–themed doughnut shop in Davis Square that we love).

I pause as I near the fields. Luca is out there with some of his friends, passing a ball back and forth. He sees me but doesn't stop, which is normal. Some of Luca's friends know about him, but most don't, and we do what we can to keep it that way. I keep my gaze on the middle distance and walk past the game. Any onlooker watching would see nothing between us, no tension, no connection at all.

Then I'm under the bleachers. I'm not waiting long before Luca swoops in next to me, pulling me into a sweaty hug.

"You're so *damp*."

"Now you are, too! Wanna play?"

"Like you'd ever let me play."

Luca scrunches up his eyebrows. "Like you'd ever *want* to."

I shrug under my backpack straps. "What's up? Is something wrong?"

Luca drops to the grass, cross-legged, indicating I should join him. I kneel, because I don't want to get dirt on my jeans. He has his backpack, too, and from it he grabs a notebook that reads PHYSICS on the front. He flips through pages of notes until the dense numbers disappear, and suddenly I'm looking at full-page drawings.

"I've been thinking about what we're gonna do, and I figured it out: Phobos and Deimos from *Pantheon Oblivia*."

It takes me a second to realize that he's talking about a potential cosplay, and then another second to swallow back the panic.

But to Luca, there's nothing potential about this. After the hundreds of ideas he has sent me, most of which I haven't had time to respond to before the next idea showed up, he has decided on this one. I can see it in the way his whole body is focused on showing me he's serious.

I think again about that awful realization I had, and the details of that realization smudge into a blurry bruise that I won't let myself consider now. So I don't react. I just keep us moving forward, saying, "The twin crow gods?"

"Yeah, with the wings. I envision these huge wings that open and close. And they've got crazy-cool armor. Not huge or bulky, but super detailed. And—"

"Luca, wait—why them?"

I know why, but I want him to say it. And he says, "They're perfect, Raff. I swear to god. I've thought through it, and they're gonna kick ass as a double look. They've got cool coordinated armor, and they look like us. Deimos has that pleated mage tunic you'd look so cute in, and Phobos has, like…"

"He's nearly naked," I provide.

"Well, yeah, except for the chest plate and the…I think it's called a codpiece?"

"So you want to be a sexy crow god, and I get to be the pudgy wizard pigeon sidekick?"

"They're supposed to be *equals*, Raffy."

"Luca, we're not…"

Do I want to say *equals*? We're so different, it's hard to see where we even align. I expect Luca to look down at my body, which is certainly not his body, but he doesn't. Just looks at me and shrugs. "I don't see the issue."

Which is the issue, I think. Artistically, at least. There's a second, bigger issue, though: This is a very, very gay costume. Maybe it's Evie's spooky intervention, or maybe I'm just a grumpy person when I'm not working, but the urge to blurt this out to Luca lurches in my throat, threatening to break me open.

I press it down. The boy next to me is full of light and wind and electricity, a static storm building around a fantasy. And to ask him if he knows what he's doing would be to ask him to turn it all off, to never let it start because of how it'll all end.

I shrug. "I'm in. Show me what you've got."

He thrusts the drawing at me and starts to explain it. "I think we can use plumbing equipment to attach the wings to our backs, but I don't know how we're going to drill through cloth. Do drills work on cloth?"

I lean in, looking at his work. The drawings are blocky, but I immediately see what he has in mind, and my own brain starts working through the problem he's getting at.

"Look at this part here," I say, tapping the back of the costume. "If we cross these two straps, we can put a support band between the top and bottom, and then fasten a board to the whole thing."

"What? How? Show me." Luca hands me a pen. I cannot imagine ever asking anyone to tamper with my sketches, but he doesn't care. I quickly outline what I mean.

"I get it, but where are we going to get these parts?" he asks.

"My house?" I say.

"I should have known. Can we go now?"

"What about soccer?"

"Oh, the boys will understand." Luca waves them away. "Are you free, though?"

"I'm supposed to meet up with May and Inaya for doughnuts."

Luca whistles. "Is Donut, Jonut! a ticketed event now?"

I glance around, and then inch closer. I've still got my fears, but I choose to live in these past few minutes.

"Stick with me," I say. "I know the bouncer."

If anyone were watching us walk along the fields, they'd see two boys, hardly a gap of air between their bumping shoulders yet an entire world between them all the same.

◇ - - - - ◇

The bliss lasts until we actually need to get to work.

Luca is wide-eyed as we stroll into Craft Club on a Saturday afternoon. I'm still a brittle, brooding ball of pins after what Evie said to me about Craft Club being cute, but he doesn't seem to notice. He's golden with wonder right now. It coats him, sweet and glowing, trailing from his fingertips as he rushes to touch every texture Craft Club has to offer.

I try to feel that wonder, too, but the truth is that I'm feeling a bit frantic as I approach both a brand-new build *and* the Herculean task of guiding Luca through the process. If it were just me here right now, I'd be in and out. But with Luca, we're not shopping for materials. We're shopping for ideas. I get inspired by supplies, too, but Luca takes it to a whole new level, entirely new cosplay concepts cascading from him as we walk through the aisles.

"This place is freaking awesome," Luca says as he slow dances with a giant Santa Claus. "I barely got a chance to look around last

time, before you caught me in the aisle with all those gems and...
those sparkle-dot things."

"Sequins."

"Sequence?"

"See-*quins*."

"See Quinn's *what*?"

"Luca, I swear to god."

"Relax, Raff, I know what sequins are. I'm just messing with
you." Luca moves on to the knitting aisle, immediately locating the
extra-large yarn. Someone has unraveled a bit of it from its bundle,
and Luca makes me close my eyes as he does something with it.

"Okay, open."

When I open my eyes, Luca is fully sprawled on the Craft
Club floor, one arm crushed beneath him, the other clutching the
stomach of his shirt, which bulges terribly. Out from under the
pushed-up hem explodes a mess of yarn, like spilled guts.

And I laugh. It surprises me. I forget I'm supposed to be
brooding and snap a photo while he rolls around and makes pitiful
dying noises. He keeps the joke going for a few seconds too long,
and a family stops at the end of the aisle, sees him, and decides not
to shop for yarn today.

"Raffy," he whispers. "I'm weak. Come closer. It's so dark."

If it were anyone else, I'd walk away. No, run. But it's Luca,
who I am convinced was designed in a secret lab to teach me
how to go with the flow. So maybe this process won't be perfectly
efficient, but does it have to be if we get to do it together? I relent,

taking a knee beside him. His shaking hands find mine as though it won't be long now.

"Raffy," he says through pitiful coughs. "Take my yarn intestines. I want you to have them."

"And do what?"

"Knit a sweater. For my mother."

"Oh my god, Luca."

"She looks great in salmon."

"Luca, this is gross."

He looks right into my eyes, his grip fierce now. "Tell her she looks great in salmon. Not pink. Not peach. Salmon! Promise me!"

I wait a beat. "Are you done?"

Luca cracks a smile. Then he shoves the yarn back into the bin as best he can with one hand, because he's still holding my hand. I pull him up and away.

"You're never making the Avengers," he says.

After hours at Craft Club and hours more working with Luca in the studio, I'm finally by myself again. All the guests are gone, too, so I'm changing out the linens and towels in the loft. I will undoubtedly resume sleeping here, maybe in the next few minutes, even. I'm exhausted. Working on a build is one thing, but working with Luca is like its own separate project. His focus comes undone at the slightest provocation; his resolve to be serious is bound with the least tacky glue. Even after I finally got him out of Craft Club, getting him to actually sit down and start working with me this afternoon was nearly impossible. He wouldn't stop draping armfuls of fabric over his head, imitating flowing hair, and asking me if he should get bangs.

"Are you in crisis?"

"No."

"Then no. Bangs are for people in crisis."

We got nothing done, yet I'm spent.

But I'm smiling. I try not to overthink it.

Like all my projects, I figure I'll document this one on Ion. But this time, I get to document Luca's work. Or, rather, his whimsical inability to do any work. I smile as I flip through my photos until I reach the first one I uploaded. It's the photo of Luca with the yarn, and I cackle remembering the moment's ridiculousness. When I threw it up to my Ion feed, I captioned it, "Last words: Yarn it all," which I think is very funny. I check the views and comments on today's other photos—some reposts of Plasma Siren and a close-up of her makeup. My usual ritual, like tending a small garden plot. I'm up to nearly ten thousand followers, which feels like a major achievement.

Luca, of course, gains me a ton of views. He's a new person on my feed, and he's cute as hell. I've got a bunch of comments from cosplay friends asking me who the new boy is. A cousin? A friend?

I respond to all of them with mysterious, coy deflection, which I think is a clear indication that we're dating. This somehow fills me with energy, and I finally detach myself from the couch. I'm extra careful cleaning up this time, and it's not until after I'm back in the house and freshly showered that I check my phone.

I have sixteen missed calls from Luca. A seventeenth call sets my phone vibrating in my hands.

"Take it down," Luca says when I answer.

"What? The photo?"

"All of the photos. Take them down."

"What's wrong?"

"My brother saw one and told my mom. Take it down."

"Okay, I will, hold on."

I delete the photos from my feed. All the comments and coyness are swept away, too.

"It's done," I tell Luca. My chest is tight. I feel terrible, but I also feel angry. I've never compromised so automatically for anyone. But it's Luca, and I get it. I have to get it if I'm going to be with him.

But if he can't deal with this, how will he deal with the cosplay, or with us?

I focus back on Luca. The rage in his voice is not at me and not for me to respond to. It's despair. Desperation.

"I'm sorry," I say. I can't help it.

"It's fine. I gotta go."

The call ends, and my screen fills with the emptiness of the photos I've just deleted, my gallery showing an error. It reads: Hmmm. Sorry! There's nothing here.

I sit down on my floor in just a towel, and the wonder of the day yellows like rotting paper. I feel, once again, the impossible balance that holds me together. They were just photos. How does Luca expect me to balance his new fascination with cosplay against his own secrecy?

My anger smolders in me. Ion is my place where I don't have to hide any part of myself. That Luca's problems have somehow found a way into that space feels so unfair. And I feel guilty even thinking that, knowing I'm not the real victim here. Still, I feel defensive. Almost territorial.

No, I tell myself. Don't think that way. No project is automatically easy. You have to think outside of your circumstances, not think deeper into them. You've got to design your way forward. Relationships are real. They aren't always just fun and games. They aren't always cute.

Cute. Like Evie said. I hate that word.

I'm not cute. I'm real. I'm Raffy, and if anyone can find a way to make this work, it's me.

SEVENTEEN

- - - - - - - - - - - - NOW- - - - - - - - - - -

For the final announcement of Primes, the judges gather all the competitors onstage. I don't cry. I don't even frown. Not because I don't feel like it, but because I can't. I'm floating outside myself. All my rage, all my disappointment, lingers in the hot air of the auditorium, buoyant on the swells of cheering and laughter from the crowd. From a distance, I am going to watch myself lose. From afar, I watch May drag my stiff, empty body to a spot marked with glowing tape. We're placed near the end of the stage, almost completely out of the spotlights. Probably at the request of the poor camera operators I nearly killed.

"My, my, *my*," growls the host. "Now *that* is what I call a competition worthy of Controverse! Give it up again for our cosplayers!"

The crowd booms and claps as we're led in a final strut across the stage. I stumble my way through, unable to see where I'm going as I continue to watch myself on the monitors all around the auditorium. Then we're back in the shadows, and I'm thankful I can't feel anything.

Did Inaya really sabotage us? Did Luca, by handing May the cape? I circle these thoughts without fully thinking them, because I know that the broken LEDs weren't the problem. The performance was. The fall was all May and me. No one pushed us. No one had to. If I let myself feel even a fifth of my failure in this moment, it'd melt the costume right off my body.

Maybe my mother was right. I wince, remembering her calls. As if tonight isn't bad enough, I'll get to deal with her after.

"Thirteen teams competed in Controverse Primes. As with previous years, winners in each of the categories will be individual, but this year's best in show, runner-up, and second runner-up will be team pairs. This year, we're also letting the audience's voice be heard for the first time in Controverse history, using the voting mode on the app. Final scores are determined by the judges, but audience participation will definitely come into play. You just wait and see. Now, are we ready to find out our winners?"

The crowd goes nuts. Armor awards are first. May's name doesn't come up. Needlework is next, and I'm ignored. FX is last, and I don't even bother listening.

"Now it's time for the big moment. We're going to bring our four top-scoring teams to the front. Are you ready?"

Now the crowd is hushed.

"Luca and Inaya, please step forward.

"Team Satoh Twins Cosplay, please step forward.

"Team Christina the Winner, please step forward."

My mind is a hundred miles away, on a plane with my mother, careening toward a career in fashion. My cute little hobby forgotten.

"And Team Crafty Rafty, please step forward."

May and I nearly miss it, but one of the clubbers is right there to lead us forward, thank god. We exchange a baffled look before managing to smile for the cheering audience. I'm shocked we've ranked high enough to crack the top four, but my hope is squashed by the realization that there's no way we're going to gain enough points with audience votes to break second or first.

The other teams drift backward, conceding the stage to us. I want to run after them, join them in their misery instead of being forced to stay up here, so close to my goal, forced to watch someone else win my dreams. It seems so cruel.

I stare at Luca on the monitors broadcasting our faces in HD all around the auditorium. For the first time I take in what he's wearing. He's costumed as Raiden from *Metal Gear*, inky-black armor snugly fastened to his muscular body from toe to chin, his hair drawn into perfectly sculpted, gray spikes. Next to him, Inaya is in something totally different: an intricately embroidered blue dress with a slit that goes nearly up to her hip bone, a cloud-white cape, and…is she wearing a straw harvester's hat? The pairing makes no sense until she tips back her head to laugh, and I see her glowing, blue eyes—some sort of prosthetic mask?—and I get it.

Raiden from *Metal Gear*, and Raiden from *Mortal Kombat*. Fucking genius.

Luca and Inaya look confident. Playful. Waving at the crowd and posing for photos. Luca catches the camera broadcasting to the monitors and gives the world a big thumbs-up. I think of how far he's come. I think of how it should have been us up here together.

All of a sudden, Irma Worthy walks right in front of us. I didn't even hear her introduction. She's got a microphone now, smiling out from under her fluffy dirty-blond hair. Her bracelets and rings clink and jingle as she sweeps an arm across the crowd.

The crowd gasps as they realize who's taken the stage. Luca and Inaya look at each other in surprise. May elbows me and points into the dark aisles of the auditorium, and I see the shining lenses of the cameras panning across the crowd to capture their awed expressions.

"Something is happening," she whispers.

Irma shushes the crowd. The monitors go from showing our shocked faces to showing the Craft Club logo, which means we are all basking in the glow of Elizabeth Worthy's smile.

"Here at the Controverse Championship of Cosplay, we honor ingenuity in all its forms," Irma says, winking. "Year after year, this stage sees incredible costumes, astonishing performances, and, dare I say, a few well-planned surprises." Here she turns to stage full of cosplayers, like she wants to drink in our reactions to what she says next.

"And now it's time for one final surprise. Tonight, there will be no winners."

The crowd gasps.

I gasp. Not a regular gasp. A *gay* gasp. A *theatre* gay, gasp.

"At Craft Club, we believe in the power of creativity and the fun of creation for creation's sake. That's why this year, Craft Club is sponsoring a special final round of the Controverse Championships of Cosplay. As we speak, an arena is being set up in the central hall of the convention center, outfitted with an entire Craft Club worth of fabrics, supplies, tools, and gadgets. Everything you could possibly need to create your next, best cosplay."

As she speaks, the monitors transition to footage of crews setting up shelves of supplies in a section of the hall, curious onlookers held back by clear partitions forming a huge semicircle. Four large tables have been set up like piano keys, each with two sewing machines, two glue guns, scissors, and bolts of fabric.

She turns to us.

"This new third round is a televised, final crafting challenge in which our top four teams will have to create one brand-new cosplay per team. From nothing to something to champions. The final round will take place tomorrow. Those who accept the challenge will have twelve hours to complete a single build with their chosen partner, working under the pressure of a time limit, while the entire world watches."

Around me, the other cosplayers are whispering with confusion. Some seem excited. Some seem terrified. Inaya looks pissed.

Cameras are creeping onto the stage, capturing our reactions. I can feel them zooming in on my face. I don't know what I look like. I don't know what to feel in this moment. And then my ambition begins to smolder, then glow. All of a sudden, I return to myself, and I'm smiling.

Coordinators appear onstage, sporting plush cushions in four different colors. Upon each cushion sits a glimmering crystal of the same color.

"Teams, now is your chance to accept this challenge or give up. If one or both members of a team forfeit, the next-highest-scoring team will be eligible. If one member of a team is unable to compete, another can be selected. Finalists may also form new teams." As Irma's eyes pass over me, I swear I see a flash of evil.

"Now, step forward if you accept this challenge."

The stones wink at us.

We can't do this. I promised May she could have Sunday, and I've got a trip with Evie planned.

We can't.

The Satoh twins move first, taking one of the tokens. I turn to May.

"We can't," I tell her.

May marches forward and swipes a token from its cushion, and I join her a moment later. She leans in, her puffs of hair blocking our faces so she can whisper, "We'll figure it out. Talk after."

We turn to see what's taking the other teams so long. Luca is looking at Inaya with shock as she says something to him.

Then Inaya crosses the stage to one of the other competitors. Christina the Winner, an all-star cosplayer from last year. The two girls join hands and whisper to each other. As the crowd makes noises of confusion, they approach the third token, lifting it up together.

"Could it be? Have two competitors dissolved their teams to form a new powerhouse cosplay couple?"

The resulting gasp from the crowd is so loud and so powerful, I nearly feel myself dragged forward into their awe. Christina's partner storms off stage left. Luca is left alone onstage, blinking at Inaya, who is too busy posing for photos with Christina to care.

I look at the crowd, then at Irma Worthy. She's got a smug smile on her face, like she knew this was going to happen. I suddenly wonder if my conversation with her wasn't the only private meeting she held with competitors as she put together her show. If she wanted drama, she certainly got it by letting Luca and me stay. This upheaval also feels like it's covered in her artistic fingerprints.

It takes a bit longer to figure out who earned the last token. Turns out the next-highest-scoring team is a pair of seamstresses who both competed in the needlework category. They're dressed in ballgowns made to look like fast food—one of them is Taco Belle (from *Beauty and the Beast*), and the other is Snow White Castle (Snow White, obviously). They cry and hold hands as they take the last token.

"See you tomorrow morning, cosplayers!" Irma Worthy is

beaming at us. I swear her eyes linger on me, locking me into the promise I gave her yesterday. For better or for worse, there will be a show.

"See you in the morning, my beloved Controverse," she says to the crowd. And the house lights come up behind us as we're led offstage.

EIGHTEEN

Luca and I are in the studio on a rare Saturday afternoon when we're both free, a week into February. The awkwardness of the photo I posted has come and gone. Luca isn't one for big apologies, but he did apologize the next day. The day after that, too. And then he got me a Christmas gift that was apology themed, and finally I told him to cut it out. His parents' squeamishness with cosplay isn't his fault, even if his reaction to the photos I posted felt harsh. And Blitz Con is coming up in May. Blitz is sort of like a preview for Controverse, where all the major players show up and show out for the first time in the season, and we've got tons to do to get our own builds ready. I'd rather have him here with me, helping, than afraid to be with me at all.

"This is beyond weird," Luca tells me as I encase him in clear plastic wrap.

I just say, "Keep turning. I've got to get it around your whole torso."

Luca obliges, stiffly spinning as I draw the wrap over his stomach, over his ribs, over the shallow valley between his shoulder blades. Then I start applying duct tape over the wrap.

"The tape will give us a flexible mold of your body. We use the plastic wrap so that we don't tear off your nipples," I explain. Luca considers this as I create a cocoon of tape around his torso.

"I'm not going to be able to get out of this," he whines. "It's too tight, Raff."

"We have scissors."

"If you're going to cut it up, what's the point of doing this in the first place?"

"You'll see. Just trust me."

Luca stops spinning. He does that thing where he stares at me quietly until I look back. I hold out a few seconds longer than usual before obliging him with a kiss on his clenched jaw. He smiles and keeps spinning. Minutes of silence go by as I finish taping over his entire torso, even his shoulders. Then I grab a marker and start drawing on the outline of the armor, using a blown-up photo of Phobos as a reference.

"You know," Luca says into the silence of my focus. "Everyone always says this, but I really did think quicksand would be a much bigger deal in life. You know?"

"What?"

"It's just…" He drifts from me to take a swig from his water bottle, and it's a very awkward movement given how limiting the duct tape corset is. "You know how when we were kids, people in shows were always getting trapped in mud, or tar, or quicksand? I swore to myself I'd never get trapped that way. But, like…" Luca gestures around at the sunlit studio, then brushes a droplet of water from his chin. "Where's the quicksand, Raff? Where is it?"

I know Inaya would ignore this attempt at distraction. May would laugh. But I think about it. I get what he means.

"Whirlpools," I say.

"What about whirlpools?"

I sit down on the floor, where I've got sheets of foam laid out, the shapes of feathers traced onto them so that I can give Luca something to do. We have to get the feathers cut out so we can shape and prime them tonight, then leave them out tomorrow to dry. Evie is gone this week, and I need to make the most of it.

"Whirlpools make no sense," I say after a long pause. Luca is used to my pauses by now. He teeters over to me, watching me trace more feathers as he attempts another sip of water.

"It's like your quicksand. Whirlpools used to scare the crap out of me as a kid. I never wanted to be on open water."

"Huh." Luca gives me one of those slow, lazy grins of his. I forget what I'm saying, because at this moment the low winter sun is behind him, nestled against the soft curve where his neck turns into his shoulder. As usual, he's in these little soccer shorts. The sun shows every hair on his legs. It collects behind his ears, ember red. It glows on the fuzz of his jaw.

"Why do whirlpools make no sense to you, Raffy?"

I trace, flip my pattern over, trace again.

"Pirates were always getting sucked into these massive whirlpools out in the ocean, right? Firstly, that's horrifying. And secondly, are we expected to believe that the ocean just…like… opens up like that? Just forms a big hole? I mean, whirlpools are all suction, right? But they've got to be sucking things *to* somewhere. Like, where is all that water being drained off to? Where do the pirates end up? I can hold my breath for a long time. I'd be okay with getting sucked into a whirlpool if I knew where it went. Like some sort of Oz, but underwater."

"Like Atlantis?"

"Yes! Like that. But it's never specified. How much would that blow? To get sucked into a whirlpool and just, like…be pooped out a zillion miles underwater?"

Luca considers this. "You'd be crushed." He puts down his bottle and swipes the marker from where I left it on the table. I get the hint and take it from him, trading my tracing for sketching atop the duct tape encasing him. I'm sure it can't be super comfortable being wrapped in plastic. Probably he's a sweaty mess. Up close, by the light of the sun, I can see every articulated muscle in his forearm. I resist the urge to push him elsewhere in the studio, where the light can't touch him like that.

"Crushed for sure," I say. I think for a few minutes longer about the unfathomable depth of the ocean, and past all the darkness, a further, denser darkness of the earth. Always shifting. Always coming together and breaking apart. I think about what sort of mysterious, terrible crack might open in the ocean floor, swallowing everything above it in a roaring and inescapable whirl.

Luca's fingers pull at my hair, gliding down my cheek and tilting my chin so that I'm looking directly up at him. "Still thinking about all that suction?"

I let out a laugh, but a stifled one. I am careful not to move an inch, desperate to keep the square millimeter of connection between Luca's knuckle and my chin.

"Come on, keep drawing," Luca says, pinching me. I do, suddenly bashful. Usually it's me reminding *him* to get back to work. The reversal feels awkward and causes me to start rambling.

"I'm almost done. Then we'll snip this off you, just a single cut before we cut out the individual shapes to make a pattern. I think I'll probably use neoprene to make the basic shape of the costume, and then we can make the bulkier pieces out of foam. And for the ornamental pieces, we'll of course use the Worbla, but I'm not sure which Worbla. I kind of want to check out a few Worbla armor tutorials before—"

"Worbla! If I hear one more word about that thermos plastic—"

"Thermoplastic."

"Whatever. I'm not touching the heat gun."

Luca hates the gun, and I don't blame him. There's a small crescent right in the middle of his (perfect, unfathomably perfect) right butt cheek from a few weeks ago, when he sat on it. Or I guess rolled onto it. We were both rolling. That was at the point in our crafting session when neither of us was wearing much or working that hard. Luca was the one using the heat gun before he started kissing me. He's also the one who left it out, but he has yet to forgive me for what's going to be a (cute, unfathomably cute) scar.

"Oh, I meant to ask," I say with a mischievous grin as I slide the tip of the scissors under the edge of the duct tape, careful not to nick skin. "How's your ass?"

"I've never had any complaints," he says.

"Shut up. I mean the burn."

Luca looks down at me, one sly eyebrow raised.

"Ask it yourself," he says, wiggling his eyebrows.

I'm about to go back to cutting when, sensing my fraying focus, Luca goes, "Wait! Wait. Take a break. Look at me."

I pause, not trusting myself to look away and cut at the same time. I look at him, and now the sun has drawn neon seams upon his shoulders and hair.

He smiles. "You never let me distract you on the first try," he says.

"I know you won't get back to work until you get what you want," I say.

"Ah, so you figure there's no point in delaying the inevitable?"

"I figure..." I trail off, slowly putting the scissors down. "I figure I might as well give you what you want."

"What I want?" Luca asks. It's soft, but because his hand has again wound into my hair, the tug on my scalp suggests un-soft intentions.

I straighten my shoulders, pushing into the tug. "I mean, isn't that what you want?"

I see a few things flicker in Luca's eyes. Lust, but also a flitting hesitance. And a dot of fear, too.

"I have condoms," I say simply. "If you want to wrap other parts of you in plastic, I mean."

Nothing about Luca's expression changes. Or maybe the dot of fear grows into a blot.

"Wait, wait," I backtrack. Did I get this totally wrong? "We don't have to. Sorry. I thought. I just...you're always trying to distract me, and I thought..."

In a whirl, Luca is down beside me, strong arms pulling me close so that his own body comes into focus in all of my senses at once. He has a way of filling me up, captivating me completely. Even dressed in tape, he does it now, and we're kissing. I rise into the kiss, heartbroken when it ends so he can speak.

"Your mom isn't back until Monday night, right?"

I nod.

"So we have all day?"

"And all night," I say. "And tomorrow. And tomorrow night, too."

Luca leans in, and his lips are soft on the ridges of my ear as he whispers, "I could take you to bed right now. We could do whatever you want. Everything, maybe. But your mind would still be in the studio working. So don't you think it'd be a good idea to get as much done as we can now? And fool around later?"

I blink at him, shocked. He leans closer to whisper something else.

"And besides, you give shitty head when you're distracted."

I push him back. He's laughing as he clumsily stands in the tape corset, adjusting his shorts. I have to do the same, but I'm not as cool about it. I'm blushing, scandalized. Being this close to a guy this often is very new to me. Luca is usually the one pursuing, and I'm the one delaying. But this time, he's turned it around on me.

Smugly, Luca hands me the scissors, and I resume snipping this stupid pattern off him.

"Told you," he says.

"Told me *what*?"

"That I'm serious about this. I'm not just a looker, you know."

I don't dignify this with a response. Then, softer, Luca adds, "Though it is good to know you still want to hook up with me."

"What? Obviously. Are you actually insecure about that?"

"Nah," he says, but there's still something there, waiting to be asked. Maybe he's toying with me? I finally snip to his armpit, and the duct tape encasement hisses open. I help him out of it, and he scratches his chest.

"I guess I do wonder," he finally admits, and now there's a distinct uneasiness to him. Just a hint of it, but it's clear to me he's been saving up these words for a moment like this. "You're always working, or you're wanting to work. It's nice to know I can still distract you. That sometimes you want me more than you want to work. I know it's probably annoying, but I can't help it. You're cute when you focus."

I beg myself not to prove him right, but without thinking, my hands have already found their way back to the foam feathers. I freeze, staring at Luca. I have no idea what to say, and maybe he knows that, because he just sits down next to me, takes the pencil from my hand, and resumes tracing.

"We gotta get these done so we can texture them with the Dremel tool," he says. "And then we should use that wood coat stuff. It takes a long time to dry, but if we do a round now, we can do another round before we fall asleep tonight." He glances at me. "If that's what you want, I mean. I can also head home if you think you'd get more done by yourself. I don't want to stress you out."

I sit still, looking at Luca until he finally looks back, and I make him watch as I leave my work behind. Working with him is chaotic and slow, but it's fun and amazing, too. He brings a joy to this whole process that I've come to depend on. To love, even. I'm not sure I've ever told him that, but I want him to know it now.

A hint of unease wobbles in his stare like a low candle flame. I lean in, and I kiss him with force and full focus. I sense the flame blow out briefly as Luca pulls back. "We can keep working," he reiterates. "I'm serious. I don't want to make you choose."

It's what I need to hear. That I don't have to choose. With this comes a surge of bliss, of relief. For once, my anxiety lets me relax in the moment.

I lean closer to him, away from the foam and duct tape, the pencils and the blades. My work can wait a few minutes longer, but suddenly I can't. I push Luca down, easing over him so that we're bundled together in a jungle of foam and drawings and craft supplies.

I surprise us both when I finally say, "I love you."

Luca sits up so quickly we nearly knock skulls. Then he's standing, and because he's the most athletic guy ever, he pulls me up with him. I'm sitting on the table before I know it.

"You *do*?"

I'm getting bashful now. "Sorry, that just slipped out."

Luca spins from me, leaving my legs swinging. He raises his fists in the air and lets out a wild, "WOOO!" like he does at his soccer games. I don't get what's happening until I see the relief on his face.

"Raffy, I've loved you for, like, *months*. And I wasn't sure if you felt the same way. But you *do*."

I must look very confused, because he gets close and starts talking in his game-play voice, the one he uses to explain complex anime plots to me.

"Okay, our relationship is like this. First, I basically stalked you, and you caught me, so like, not a great start for me. But then we finally hung out, and it turned out everything about your life is cool. Your mom is famous, and you have this studio and cool art friends, and you go to cool art shows and wear cool clothing that you *make yourself*. And besides all that, you're, like, a genius artist. Like, I've never seen you do a bad job at anything. And meanwhile,

I can barely make, like, macaroni art, but for some reason you don't care. And *then* we start making a cosplay together, and I'm *sure* you're going to hate it because I'm slow and needy and distract you, but somehow you find a way to teach me stuff and don't hate it. Instead, suddenly you *love* me?"

Luca lets out another whoop, and I'm laughing as he pulls me into a bear hug. I finally free myself and clarify.

"It's not sudden. I just didn't know when to say it."

"Well, Jesus, Raff, you had me ready to run. I thought you were, like, barely tolerating me."

"Nope." I smile. I can feel the blush on my neck and face. It's the same feeling I had the night Luca dressed up for Inaya's show and sang anime theme songs. The feeling of being shown love. The feeling of being *so* enough for someone that my anxiety can't convince me otherwise. At least not right this minute.

Luca sits on the table beside me. It's the same table where we had our first kiss.

"Look at them," Luca says about our reflections in the glass cabinets.

We make faces at ourselves. Luca bumps me with his shoulder.

"I love them."

I bump him back.

"I love them, too."

"Wanna get back to work?" he offers.

"Nah," I say, impersonating him. "You do shitty crafting when you're distracted."

"Okay. Harsh. But true. You have something else in mind, then?" he asks slyly.

"A few things," I say, my hand gliding up his thigh, into those little soccer shorts.

It's time for a break, anyway.

NINETEEN

May and I sit among the shells of our costumes on her floor. She keeps yawning, and though I'm exhausted, I don't let myself feel it. A half-eaten pizza sits in its box in front of us. I'm using makeup wipes to get the last traces of red off my skin and out from behind my ears. The various Ion recaps of today's Controverse antics play from her laptop, but I for one cannot stomach the footage, since it's mostly us toppling over on repeat with explosion sound effects.

"Raffy, I've thought about it, and it's too big of an opportunity to pass up—"

"Stop."

"Come on. I'm serious. I'll do it with you."

"I know you will, which is why I'm telling you to stop."

May has offered several times now to participate in the

crafting challenge tomorrow. I have said no several times and in several different ways.

"So, what?" she asks. "You're really giving up?"

I've thought about it for a long time. Or, actually, I only thought about it for a few seconds in the breathless moments after Irma's announcement, and I've been rationalizing my decision ever since. I'm not giving up. I'm growing up. Moving on.

"I have to," I say, shrugging. "I promised I wouldn't make you do cosplay stuff on Sunday, and I'm keeping my promise. Plus, Evie and I are going to New York to meet with her fashion colleague. She left me like six messages about it while we were on stage."

Most of Evie's messages were just her demanding I call her back and tell her my shoe size or shirt size or something else clothing related. Evidently, she doesn't trust me to dress myself, so she was out shopping. That's how I know she's nervous about tomorrow. She never shops for me.

May slides closer to me. "I don't feel like I'm talking to Raffy. Raffy never gives up."

I shrug. "We basically lost already, didn't we? Christina and Inaya make a powerhouse team. There's no way we can compete against that."

"Maybe not you and me, but what about you and—"

"Don't you dare."

May smirks. She makes a show of starting Luca's name, but I tackle her. Laughing, we come close to rolling into the pizza box.

"May, I *swear* to god, if you suggest what you're about to suggest..."

"Fine. Fiiiiine," she whines, squirming away. "But I figured if anything could get you two to talk, it'd be the chance to outshine Inaya. I mean, just think of the boost it'd mean for the *Crafty Rafty* brand."

I wince at that. I don't want to think about Luca, sad and abandoned by Inaya in the spotlight. And I certainly don't want to think about streams or clout or followers. But I'm not quite ready to say goodbye to all those dreams forever. Not my crafting dreams, and maybe not my dreams of fixing things with Luca, either. I don't know what to do, though, with the flight to NYC only hours away. I just know that I'm feeling tired and cynical and I can't wait to never wear high heels again.

"I'm sure Irma told Christina and Inaya to team up. She was smirking. It's just a plot for Craft Club," I say, going back to scrubbing at my skin. "Just a way for them to make money. The more drama, the more viewers."

"We should still do it," May says, curling in on herself. "Or at least you should. I bet they'd let you compete on your own."

"What?"

May yawns. "You're better than anyone I know. You could do it on your own, if you wanted to."

I...haven't thought of this. I wish May hadn't said it. The second she does, I feel my old ambition sparkle alive in my bloodstream. Could I do this all on my own? Should I try?

That's the last thing I think about as I fall asleep next to her on the floor.

◇ - - - ◇

In the morning, May borrows her dad's car to give me a ride to Controverse, even though it's so early that all the street lights are still on and the day is only a deep-blue smudge along the black horizon. We don't talk. It's too early to talk. It should be too early for the anxiety clattering through me, but I'm nervous about what comes next.

When we arrive at the convention center, there are film crews and coordinators ready to film our entrance. As the sun rises, we park where they tell us to, grab our things, and march into the convention center for the final day of Controverse.

May hugs me goodbye.

"Thank you," she says, "for not making me make a hard choice. I'm still your ride-or-die, number-one fan, though. I'll be cheering you on the whole way."

"If they even let me compete," I add.

"Want me to stay until you know?" May asks.

"It's better if you don't."

The convention center is desolate at this hour; it's not opening to the general public until eight o'clock. We were told via email that we'd have some prep time, an orientation, and a mic test. Then filming will start right at eight. Alone, I walk up to the coordinators that circle Irma Worthy. She's giving instructions. When she sees me by myself, she frowns.

"Raphael, welcome back. Where is May? She needs to be here in the next twenty minutes."

"She's…" I resist the urge to look out the doors after her. "She's not coming."

The corners of Irma's eyes crinkle.

"She had her opportunity to give up last night onstage. She committed to the challenge. Don't tell me she got cold feet."

"I'm sorry, but—"

"You know how many people will watch this, right? You can't really be thinking about giving up now, just as we're about to begin. Do you understand the preparation that has gone into this? Do you understand the work we've put into getting this ready for you? And now you show up with minutes to go and claim you couldn't convince your friend to *want* this for herself?"

Irma circles me. Politely, her staff turns away. I can't look at her. All the warmth I saw in her the other day is gone, replaced by the cool determination of a businesswoman. She notes the way I'm avoiding her eyes and says, "I'm surprised. I thought we were on the same page when I gave you that second chance. I thought you wanted this."

"I do want this," I say. "More than anything. I'd be willing to compete by myself."

Irma shakes her head, causing her massive hair to shake, too.

"Controverse is a team sport. You know that. Perhaps there's someone else who would be willing to work with you? A certain boy, abandoned onstage last night?"

"I'm not calling Luca," I say bitterly. "Please. Just let me work alone."

"And why would I do that? If you want a future in this world, you're going to need to learn to work with others. You can't do everything alone. You certainly can't do this alone."

I draw back as Irma leans in close. It's weird that she's smiling. It's weird that she's still giving a glossy performance, like she's back on the stage. "I'm going to let you think about this, mm-kay? Find a teammate, or forfeit. You're here because I wanted you here, but I can't convince you to do what it takes to stay. That's up to you."

She leaves me in the care of Madeline, who is busily dialing numbers on her phone. Probably calling other backup contestants.

I clutch my phone, too. I know that if I called May right now, she would come through for me. But it would break our trust. After today, what would become of our friendship?

It's time to give up. It's time to move on. There's a suitcase waiting for me to pack it up at home, to zip myself into a new life where I am chic and focused, having left the messiness of crafting behind forever.

"Ten minutes," Madeline says between voicemails.

I turn my phone over in my hands. Maybe I should call Luca? Maybe I gave up on him too quickly. What's stopping me from calling him now? It could be pride; it could be fear. Whatever it is, I just stand there as my chance slips away.

"Two minutes."

It's too late. Time has made the decision for me.

"Raffy!"

Cool air blasts my back as the doors rush open, followed by the warmth of an arm over my shoulder. He looks tired, like he hasn't slept at all. "I heard you could use a partner."

I stare at Luca like he's not even real.

"Did May call you? What are you *doing* here?"

"Saving your career. We'll talk later," he whispers to me. Then he throws a prizewinning smile at Madeline and says, "We're ready for our second chance."

There's an exchange between the clubbers and Irma, who looks beyond self-satisfied with this development.

"Superb work," she says to me, a thickly ringed hand on my shoulder. "I knew you'd choose right."

I let her believe that.

We're pushed through security and into the makeshift Craft Club. They've brought jerseys for us to wear over our clothes, and they tell us to put our stuff in a private curtained area. For a moment, we're silent, each of us watching the other.

"Luca, why are you doing this?" I ask.

"I want to do this."

"But after everything that happened, you said—"

"I know what I said."

"No talking," the coordinator commands. "Hurry up."

We're led into the main area, where the rest of the teams are already waiting. Inaya sees me first, then sees Luca, and her face goes from surprised to amused. I shove down my usual jealousy toward her. Inaya is the most focused person I know, and right now, I need to be focused, too.

"We'll film Irma explaining the rules in a moment, but first some housekeeping items before we start rolling."

The coordinator explains that cameras have been set up all over the arena with live feeds that'll be shown on Ion. On the *home page* of Ion, actually. We'll be filmed for the entire twelve hours, followed by judging at the end. Teams only need to create one outfit each, but they must be fully completed. We're allowed to take breaks by ourselves outside of the filmed area, but never with our teammates, and talking to other teams off camera is also forbidden. There's a single bathroom off to the side, and each team has a changing room near their station that can be used for getting into costume.

"This is going to be in front of the whole world," I tell Luca.

"I know."

"Do your parents know you're doing this?"

Luca lifts just one eyebrow. "Does Evie?"

Fair point. I forged her signature on all the forms. I guess Luca did the same with his parents. It's just like old times, the two of us hiding with one another. But that's about to change for sure.

The clubbers come around with a bin to collect our phones. Before they take mine, I type a quick message to my mother.

Something came up. I can't go with
you to NYC. I'm sorry.

I don't bother telling her anything else. Not that I'm at Controverse. Not that I'm excited. Certainly not that I'm about to be on TV. It won't matter.

Then I hand over my phone, and the clubber disappears as Irma is prepped for her entrance. The cosplayers are marched back behind the shelves, and we're told that we'll come out one team at a time. I try to listen to the directions, but I can't stop thinking about Luca's shoulder pressed to mine.

The camera crew leave us for a minute, and suddenly we're all alone.

"So, my favorite boys are back together," Inaya says to Luca, sarcastic.

"Get lost, Inaya," Luca says. "That was pretty brutal, what you did last night."

"Sorry," she laughs. "But I told you I was going to do whatever it took to win, didn't I? You can't say I didn't warn you."

Luca crosses his arms. "Whatever. I'm on Raffy's team now."

Inaya laughs. I'm reminded of our lost friendship, and I wonder if I ever really understood it—or Inaya—at all. I was always so captivated by her and her talent, but were we ever actually close? There was mutual respect, but our relationship always felt mostly work-based. Cosplay, crafting, and then little to no contact after Blitz Con was over. Inaya chose Luca, and now she has chosen Christina. Maybe this is just the way she works.

"You should give up now," Inaya says playfully. "Unless you just really love hanging out in last place."

"Please, you're just scared of Raffy," Luca says.

Inaya shrugs. "Maybe, but there's only one of Raffy on your team. Christina and I have been scheming all night. This is a competition for serious crafters. No offense, Luca, but I'm not sure how far you're gonna make it once we actually have to do, you know, hard work."

I don't laugh. Luca and I have a lot of history between us, but Inaya's comment feels outright cruel. I know she's just speaking her mind, but I see Luca dim a bit.

"It's a show, Inaya," he says. "All of this is a show. You could do the best work, but if no one wants to watch you, I don't think Irma's going to care."

"And why would people want to watch the two of you more than the two of us?"

At that, Luca strips off his shirt, alarming everyone. He untangles his jersey and pulls just that on. It's tiny on him, originally meant for May, and the result is a very taut view of his chest and abs beneath the thin material. His exposed arms bulge as he flexes.

"Well, for starters, I've got this going on," he says.

I take Luca's side. "Yeah, for starters, he's hot."

Inaya rolls her eyes. "You're using sex appeal? In a crafting competition?"

"I'm using sex appeal in a *cosplay* competition," Luca corrects. "You of all people ought to know that a bit of skin can go a long way. Isn't that why you teamed up with me in the first place?"

Inaya lets out a small laugh. "You've got me there."

The coordinators return, shushing us. The audio guys finish hooking up our mics, and the lights are up on the arena floor. It's time for introductions.

The first two teams are called in.

"You nervous?" Luca asks me.

I am. I have no idea what we're about to walk into. We've prepared nothing. Schemed not at all. Luca and I have barely even talked these last few months, and there's so much to talk about. But the clock is ticking, and everyone is getting ready, so where do I even start?

"I'm really glad you're here," I tell him.

Luca looks down at me.

"You are?"

I nod. It's the truth. When he walked through those doors, I felt relief. It's the first time I've seen him in a long time without feeling sad, or angry, or annoyed.

The next team is told to enter. We're walking in last.

"I know it's bad timing, but I really want to talk about what happened," Luca says. "I even wrote out what I'd say, but it never felt like enough for you. Nothing ever did, to be honest."

That doesn't sound like me. It sounds like Evie.

"Do you ever think about trying again?" he asks.

"All the time," I admit.

"Bet you didn't think it'd be here and now. Sounds like everyone's counting on us to fall apart again," Luca says.

"Don't worry, we won't. We'll figure it out," I tell him as they call for us to enter.

"Yeah, we will," he says.

I'm talking about the work, but as usual, Luca is talking about us. He takes my hand, and that's how we enter the arena. Two boys, fingers locked, ready to face anything.

TWENTY

- - - - - - - - - - - - - *THEN* - - - - - - - - - - - -

SEVEN MONTHS AGO

The truth is, I had no idea what would happen if I told Luca that I loved him. Saying it was as scary as cutting into new cloth. I always measure, I always trace, I always know the shape of what I *want* to create. But I never know exactly how it'll turn out. *I love you* was the plunge. The slice. The commitment to that final shape, whatever it may be.

So much about Luca and me has happened without words—has *had* to happen without words. No names, no definitions. The time spent between two boys, sometimes painting, sometimes gluing, sometimes sewing, but always touching? I have a name for that, but Luca doesn't. And I've always known that namelessness was important to him.

It's not bad if it's not named. But if it's love? If it's love, it's something, and if it's something, it can't be nothing. It can't just go away when it's hard.

I didn't know what would come after the moment. But I knew I had to find out if there would be an "after" at all. So I said it. I made the cut.

It turned out that what came after was a lot of kissing. At least in this situation, my measurements and my careful tracing and my pained planning paid off.

In the wise words of Luca: *WOO!*

Luca and I walk through Craft Club hand in hand on a Sunday afternoon. Evie's home right now, so we're taking a break from the studio. It feels weird not to be working and weirder to be holding hands in public, but I'm strangely at ease. Maybe it's because I'm exhausted, or because I'm hitting the bottom of my iced coffee from Jurassic Perk. Or maybe I'm learning to enjoy breaks. I don't know. I don't feel anxious for the first time in…ever? And since I'm not on the verge of panicking, I don't mind that Luca is leading us toward whatever catches his eye. Sure, I made a list—I am in love, but I am still Raphael Odom—but Luca has changed the way I approach projects, and I think it's for the better. Right now, my top priority isn't progress. It's watching Luca get inspired.

"I was thinking we could get, like, studs or something? I saw a video where this girl glued studs onto her collar," Luca is saying, picking through packets of geometric studs in brass, silver, and chrome. "We need a copper color, though. I guess we could use that buff stuff you got?"

He's talking about Rub 'n Buff. You use it to buff on a worn look, and he's exactly right. I was thinking that, too.

"Where would we put the studs?" I ask.

"The hilts of the weapons. And maybe on the straps?"

Luca's ideas are becoming less whimsical and more strategic. Ideas I can work with. Good ideas, actually.

"We can use glue for the flat-backed ones on the weapons, but that won't hold for the straps," I say. "We should get ones we can use on flexible material."

"Do they make those?"

"Luca, it's Craft Club. They make everything."

He squeezes my hand, pushing a warm kiss into my hairline.

"Okay. Here's the plan," he says, knowing I love nothing more than a good plan. Luca's plans are very simple—really just next steps—but whatever. It's the effort to stay organized that counts. I pull on a serious planning expression, salute him, and await orders.

"You go grab the fabric. I don't know how to do that. I will go ask about Rub 'n Buff and sew-on studs."

"Look for rivet studs specifically. Check the leatherwork aisle."

"Right. Rivets. Studs. Leather. I like where this is going."

Another kiss, and he's off. I march to the back of the store, where the bolts of fabric form a jungle of patterns and colors. I review the list in my build book. I'm looking for neoprene, or a scuba-suit-like fabric that has a matte finish. You won't see much of it under the armor, but it provides a very workable surface for affixing the lightweight foam pieces. I'm also looking for a knit fabric for Deimos's shawl. Which reminds me to grab magnets—the key to a durable cosplay is having intentional break points so that things like capes just snap off if they get caught. I add that to the list of stuff we'll grab at the hardware store after this.

I take my time, for once. I feel each texture, waiting for inspiration to spark in my palm as it drifts over the right bolt. I locate the neoprene I want, then the knit, but I keep exploring. I find a roll of soft pleather scored with scales. Without thinking about it, I mentally dress Luca instead of myself. This fabric would fit him like a second skin. Maybe I could make a full-body suit and dress him as a heartless from *Kingdom Hearts*. Something slinky but athletic. Lithe, dark, dangerous.

I find a second fabric that could work for that: a bolt of slick patent leather. It's super stretchy, more like a Lycra. Even better.

"Can I help you with anything?"

I turn to the clubber, their magenta vest rousing me from my daydream of dark cloth and skintight armor.

"Yes, actually. Can I get cuts of this and this?" I pull out the cloth I actually came here for, writing out the yardages. Then I wait by the cutting table as the clubbers help the people before me. I fiddle with my phone. Absently, I swipe through Ion. My recommended feed is full of people getting ready for Blitz.

One video is titled "Final Touches for Blitz!" Another is labeled "Blitz Makeup Test Number 2."

The lazy vibe of my day dies, just like that. Here I am, just now getting my fabrics cut, and people are already nearly done? Before

I can stop myself, I'm fast-forwarding through other videos, checking out photos and bingeing on updates that make me feel worse and worse. Then I'm looking at my calendar, counting the days until Blitz.

Not to be dramatic, but mathematically, we are *fucked*.

I try to do the whole *deep breaths* thing. I have to calm down before Luca finds me, or else I'll ruin both of our days. But I can't calm down, and suddenly I can't be in Craft Club. I leave my fabrics behind and race to the doors, scrambling outside before the sheer abundance of the store overwhelms me.

Do I usually shake like this? Do I usually shiver? I pace around the plaza until a cool voice cuts through my racing thoughts.

"Raphael?"

I look up. I'm in front of Jurassic Perk. There are only a few people seated outside in the cool, March day. One of them is a man I vaguely recognize, maybe someone Evie knows? But then he moves, and the person with him comes into focus. It's Evie herself, staring at me like I've just fallen out of the sky.

"Hi," I say.

"Oh, so *this* is the young Odom that Evie keeps hidden away," the man says playfully. Evie gives him a pained smile, hiding her own surprise just in time. I'm guessing this is a gallery colleague. Probably not the person she wants finding out about me and my dirty little habit of cosplaying.

"Were you in Craft Club just now?" the man goes on, filling the silence between Evie and me. "What are you working on? I'll admit, I'm more than curious to see what the offspring of the great Evie Odom gets up to in his spare time."

"I'm making—" I begin.

Evie snaps out of her daze. "Oh, Raphael is very private. Let's respect his process and not pry, Marc."

Marc shrugs. Evie stands. "Excuse us for a minute, will you?" Marc shrugs again as Evie sweeps me away. I throw him a Mayday look, but he's on his phone.

Evie stops in front of Craft Club. The doors slide open, but we don't enter. She just looks at me, arms crossed, like she's brought me to the scene of a crime she knows I committed.

"Don't you dare," she says.

"Dare *what*?"

"Try to embarrass me in front of one of my colleagues. You were going to tell him the truth. I could sense it."

Evie takes advantage of my shock by snatching my notebook from my hand. She flips through my sketches and diagrams, her disgust deepening with each page.

"It's not embarrassing," I say meekly.

"Oh, no, it is," she quips. "I looked up all this *cosplaying*, you know. I thought maybe I was wrong after Rocky talked to me about it over Christmas. But my instincts, as always, were right. It's dress-up. Not even drag. Just dressing up as cartoons."

I mean, yes, it is, but in the same way that painting is just smearing shit on paper. I don't say this. I still can't find my own voice.

The doors try to close, but jerk back open because we're still blocking them. A small family carrying bright pink bags stops short of our argument as they try to exit, then awkwardly passes through it. Evie flaps her hands at them like they can't see or hear her.

"You couldn't have picked a more spiteful hobby, Raphael. I mean, seriously. Cosplay, from what I've seen, is nothing but the cheap mimicry of someone else's design. I thought if I surrounded a talented child with originality, they'd covet the divine singularity of what they alone could create. But no, here I find you at home in a store for *hobbyists*, presumably to rip off some other artist's work and play heroes and villains. I could scream, Raphael, I could just scream."

And because this is Evie Odom and I don't trust her *not* to scream, I finally speak up.

"Stop, please," I beg. "It's not stupid. I'm good at it, and I take it seriously, and thousands of people—"

"Seriously?" Evie raps a knuckle against my build book. "All I've ever wanted was for you to take your art *seriously*, Raphael. This isn't serious. This is trash. To think what you could create and don't. It's a waste."

I have heard Evie's speech about art a million times. Those million times plus this one finally condense into a rich and dark resentment that spills out of me.

"How come my art isn't serious unless I do it like you want me to? How come I can't just make stuff for myself? How come art doesn't matter to you unless it fits your narrow criteria for what you'd put in a show? Maybe that's not what I want. Maybe that's not what I do. Maybe what I make is not up to you, and maybe you don't get to control it."

Evie's face sours into a pinched, frozen thing as I ramble. We're both shouting now. A small crowd of onlookers has formed on either side of the Craft Club entryway.

"It's not control. It's direction, Raphael. The house, the studio, your schooling—your whole world is made from what I've earned helping artists become the best versions of themselves. You create costumes, I create careers. And I am good at it, and I won't apologize for being good to you. Asking you to take yourself seriously enough to create *real* art is *not* the abuse you're making it out to be. It's just called being your mother."

Abuse. I've often wondered about my relationship with my mother, and the word *abuse* sometimes floats into my mind. It doesn't seem to fit my experience quite right, but I haven't let the word go, either.

Evie sniffs. She looks around, and the various people watching all look away from her flinty stare. If she's self-conscious, she doesn't show it. She just sighs and hands me my notebook.

"Here. Go. I need to get back to my meeting. We'll talk about this later."

I know we won't. We don't talk about the things we hate in our house. I take back my notes, or I try. Evie holds on for a moment too long, like she's testing me.

"No more studio," she says lightly. "That space is for artists. You can use it once you get over this plagiaristic bullshit."

Evie leaves me to sort out my reaction in front of a crowd she created. For once, I can't form a plan or even devise a next step. I consider just toppling over, which is pretty much how I feel, but then a hand takes mine, and Luca is leading me back into Craft Club. We stop in a random aisle, and he hugs me.

It takes a second for my emotions to find their way through my shock. I feel, first and foremost, fury. But I also feel humiliation. I don't know how much of that Luca heard, but I have to assume it was a lot by the way he rubs my back and doesn't say a word.

"So," I mutter into his chest, "that's Evie."

"She's…" Luca trails off. "She's a lot, isn't she."

"Oh yeah."

"May was right. She's a scary lady."

"Oh, the scariest."

From behind us, someone clears their throat. For a moment, I'm afraid it's Evie again, but it's a clubber. They hold out a shopping bag, and in it I see the fabrics I picked out, all cut and folded.

"Here, Raffy. Compliments of the Club," the clubber says. They smile sympathetically, and I gather they saw what happened. I take the bag, managing a breathless *thank you*. Their charity stings. In a good way, but in an overwhelming way. All at once, the tears I've been holding back spring from me, and I hide my face in my hands. The clubber vanishes, and it's just Luca and me again.

Evie brought so much down upon me just now—scoldings and accusations and drama—but atop all of that is the cavalier meanness she throws around. It's so sharp when she wants it to be. I'm crying because of her, but also because of this kind act from these craft store employees, who are so much more supportive of me than my own mom. And I don't even know their names.

Luca doesn't let me go until the worst is over. Then he grabs something from the shelf.

"Hey, hey, look," Luca says. "Sea Foam Dream, number six."

He's holding a bag of tiny faceted rhinestones. I realize we're in the bedazzling aisle. For some reason, this anchors me. I swipe my tears away with the heels of my hands.

"I just want to make stuff," I say. I sound miserable.

Luca kisses my head again and again. "You're good at making stuff. The best."

"Evie says we can't use the studio."

"I'm not worried," he murmurs. "We'll figure it out. We'll fix this. You know that, right?"

I look at him. I don't know that, but he seems to.

I nod, standing up a bit straighter in his embrace.

"We'll fix it," I say back.

TWENTY-ONE

- - - - - - - - - - - - - NOW - - - - - - - - - - - - -

Luca and I stand before our table. We don't touch, but the air between us buzzes. Literally. Cameras mounted on drones sweep over us as the crew takes establishing shots of the competitors. I'm told to keep my eyes forward and a look of determination on my face, but I sneak glances at the coordinators. They are pointing at Luca, frowning. They're staring at his arms and too-small jersey, but we've already started, and now it's too late to reshoot our entrance. They'll have to let him compete as is. And Luca, as is, is eye-catching.

I stop the smile right before it reaches my lips, pursing them in a self-satisfied pout instead. The nerves I was feeling before are still here, still threading through me in neon coils, but I'm floating in a fantasy now. Off beyond the reality of my usual sorrow. I think I've finally snapped. I think I've finally reached a point of no return.

The camera drone flutters away, and the crews move on to filming Irma Worthy giving an introduction to the rules as she slowly walks through the aisles of supplies. While they do that, coordinators come over to turn on and test our microphones. One of them gives Luca a dirty look, pointedly placing his discarded shirt on our table.

Luca winks at them. Then he catches my eye and shrugs.

I shrug back.

We take turns shrugging.

"Cut it out," a clubber whispers.

Irma must have finished her intro, because the camera crew sweeps toward us at our individual tables. A clubber named Ginger has us stand side by side, and then she launches into questions.

"Can you talk about your decision to change teams? Was this always the plan?" Ginger thrusts a puffy microphone into our faces.

I have no idea what to do, or even really how a mouth works anymore, but Luca is ready to go.

"Inaya and Christina are a powerful duo, but Raffy and I have worked together before, and we're excited to create something incredible today. You won't be disappointed."

After a pause, Ginger asks, "What is the nature of your relationship history?"

"We've worked together before on cosplays," Luca says with a smile.

"And what is the nature of your relationship now? Not just collaborators, are we?"

"We are…" Luca trails off, looking at me. He laughs. It's his nervous laugh.

"We are going to win," I answer.

"Well, okay, then!" Ginger says. "I can already sense the heat from these two! Let's go see what some of the other teams are up to."

She moves on, and Luca gives me a thankful nudge.

"Good save," he whispers, reaching over me to grab a tablet.

"What are we even doing here?" I ask him.

"I came here so you could compete, so we could beat Inaya."

"Why, though? Until Friday, I thought you guys were a thing."

"What? Like, *together*?"

"Well, maybe not *together* together. But you have all those videos and posts, and you hang out a lot now."

"Those are photos, Raff. Of characters. That's not real. That's cosplay. Inaya and I have only ever kept it professional. I was just her model. She never even let me make stuff."

I feel my old anger flare to life. "So why did you stick around?"

Luca taps on the tablet, waiting for a nearby camera to pan away.

"We made a good team. I let her dress me up, and she let me tag along to cons and stuff. My parents like her a lot. If I'm going to do this geeky shit, she's the person they want me doing it with."

"They like that she's a girl, you mean?"

Luca nods. This sucks to hear out loud. I've always known this, but now I know for certain. It makes me feel worse.

"So if you guys make such a good team, why did she ditch you?"

Luca's smile is sad as he stares across the workroom to where Christina and Inaya are already launching into sketches.

"Christina is the best of the best. And Inaya is serious about being better than even the best. She's ambitious, just like you. And I'm just…"

He looks at me, then looks away quickly, like he wants to let his sentence die.

"What?" I prompt.

"Dead weight."

Luca does look at me now. It feels like he's apologizing to me, not for our past, but for being who he is. My heart clenches, and I find myself racing to defend him from himself.

"You're not dead weight. You're…"

"Pretty? That's what Inaya always says. She said it was good for her metrics every time my pretty face showed up."

"You're *charismatic*," I correct. "You've got something no one can craft. People are drawn to you. It's impressive and important. Don't let yourself feel down about it."

Luca glances around, then bumps me with his shoulder. Like he used to.

"Sorry, couldn't help it," he mumbles, playing it off. A camera drifts closer, and we have to stop talking. Really talking, I mean.

"Shall we start?" Luca says easily.

I scan the room. The other teams are conferencing, too, except

Inaya and Christina. They're running for the stacks of supplies, grabbing fistfuls of fabric from the bolts on the wall. They've clearly got a plan. The other teams are also probably way more prepared than us. All Luca and I have is a blank page and a whole lot to talk about.

"You up for modeling whatever we make?" I ask.

"Yeah, but what do we make?" Luca asks me. "What *can* we make?"

I've been asking myself that question since we teamed up. I wish I had known he was going to be here. If I'd had even an hour to plan, I could have put together a build. I could have assigned him jobs. But now, every second I spend thinking and planning is a second we don't have for construction. This game is for players who have been planning since last night. It's not for two boys who have barely spoken to each other in four months.

We can't make any mistakes. We can't experiment. We can't guess. Can't even wonder. We have to know what we're making. We have to make it better than anything else we've ever done. And we only have twelve hours. Less, since I've been sitting here and hyperventilating.

I push my emotions out of my mental work area. It's time to start.

"We need something simple we can embellish," I say. It's barely a plan, but I think it's the right philosophy. "Something conceptual, maybe. If we create something that no one is expecting, we can get points for creativity to make up for what we can't do with construction."

Luca is nodding, but in the way that boys nod when they're not listening at all. He's got a stylus in his hand, drawing on the tablet as I ramble about options. Ginger circles in on us after some cue from a cameraman.

"The other teams have already begun supplying their builds. What's the holdup, boys?"

"We've just got a ton of ideas," I tell her. I can't stop looking into the cameras, even though they told us to keep our eyes on Ginger.

"A lot of ideas? Looks like you've got a sketch there—have you decided on what you'll be building today?"

I look at Luca, who is clutching the tablet to his chest. With a devious smile, he flips his drawing around, showing the camera a figure adorned with sweeping wings.

"We're doing a combined Phobos and Deimos look from *Pantheon Oblivia*. The bird gods, merged into their final form."

TWENTY-TWO

I am, as they say in the old tongue, fucking stressing the fuck out.

I don't know, maybe I'm being dramatic. I haven't really relaxed since Evie yelled at me outside Craft Club. She's away again, but Luca and I are keeping out of the studio, just in case. We've moved everything up into my room. It's much worse than the studio, but my door locks, and at least when I pass out mid-work, I'm only a few feet from my bed. Not that I'm really using it. Blitz Con is only three weeks away, and we are so behind. I refuse to spend precious minutes on sleep.

But I do fantasize about sleeping, usually with Luca. Not sex. Literally sleeping. Nestled together in a warm bed, in a cozy cabin somewhere wintry and unnamed, with a fresh day's light cast sideways through closed blinds. A deep sleep. A great sleep.

Anyway, I'm a mess.

"But you're my mess," Luca says, massaging my hands.

"Sorry, I didn't realize I was saying that out loud."

My hands are stiff with fatigue, like overworked clay left out to dry by accident. We're sitting on my floor, *Demon Slayer* playing on my laptop as we work. I've been hand-embroidering a pattern onto Deimos's cowl. Luca is…I'm not sure what Luca is doing. Probably I gave him a task, and instead of doing it, he's watching *Demon Slayer* and finding small excuses to put his skin against mine. Which I like. But I would also like to be done with this build so I can sleep.

"Give me your other hand," he says, and I do.

A familiar compulsion captures my attention. When I get this frayed, I have to make lists.

"Okay, so what's left? The wings need to be reshaped and then probably touched up with the airbrush; your armor is mostly set, but we should do a fitting; and then this godforsaken cape I'm working on. I think I'm going to do a muslin first just to make sure I get the shoulders right. But don't worry, you don't have to measure anything. I can set it up on my dress form."

"What's your dress form? I'm afraid to ask."

"No, don't worry, it's not, like, a form I take in which I'm suddenly in a dress. It's that limbless, headless mannequin you keep slow dancing with. It's just a torso on a pole."

"You're so much more than a torso on a pole to me, Raffy."

"Shut up. Okay, so once we have the muslin done, we can see where we need to dart—"

"The Muslim?"

"*Muslin.* With an *n.*"

"But Muslim has an *m.*"

"Luca, please, I'm trying to think."

I feel his smile as his lips graze my knuckles. I raise my other hand so he can press his cheek into my cupped palms. My back is sore from hunching over my work, and it pops and crackles as I stretch.

"The sewing shouldn't take long because the garments themselves are pretty simple, but the tailoring needs to be perfect, or else they'll bunch weird beneath the armor."

"When do we do the armor?"

"I was thinking you could start that while I sew."

I feel Luca shift, unsure.

"Like, do the armor by myself?" he asks.

"Not all of it. Just get it started. I can show you what to prepare."

He groans. "But I've already cut out so much stuuuuuuff."

"Okay. Fine. You sew."

"I can't sew. You won't show me how to."

"I don't have *time* to show you how."

Luca slumps to the floor next to me, and he's a little angry when he says, "*We* don't have time."

I look at him, and he's a bit blurry in my tired stare.

"Luca. That's my point. That's why I sew and you cut. I don't get what the problem is."

"The problem is…" Luca starts, but then he stops. I feel a prickle of heat in my throat. Anger? Fear? What did he almost just say?

Luca's own throat seems to have sealed shut as he decides not to say whatever he is thinking. I can almost see him swallowing it down. And I know I should pry open his mouth and whisper it out of him, ask for it nicely so that it doesn't plant itself inside of him and grow into resentment. The stuff that breaks people up.

But I don't have time for whispering. For talking *or* for fighting. I don't even have time for sleep. Now more than ever, I'm aware of the vastness of what I'm trying to accomplish and of how hard it is to accomplish much with Luca as my partner. Though I've been clinging to the idea of us succeeding together, in moments like these, I feel like I will succeed in spite of Luca. He's resisting a process he himself began, and it's putting me in an impossible situation. It would be twice as much work to do all of this alone, but it would still almost be easier.

It doesn't help that he complains. Like, a lot. The creative labor is one thing, but that's not what's breaking me. If I crack, if I buckle, it'll be because of the emotional labor of carrying two people.

And who will pick up my pieces if I break? Who will put me back together? Will he resent that task, too? This is why I work alone. This is why I *should* work alone.

I turn away from this spiral.

"The problem is that I'm exhausted," I say to him. These bad thoughts are trademark Tired Raffy. They're not what I want to think or who I want to be. "We both are. It doesn't help that we lost the studio. That's on Evie, not us."

I remind myself often that this is her fault, not Luca's. It helps me reframe all the extra work I won't be able to do on these costumes; we're only barely going to finish them, if we're lucky. It won't be my usual high-octane detail work. And that's okay. We'll be recognizable. The quality will be good. There's no glory in an awesome cosplay if you're too exhausted to actually feel glorious.

"Has she said anything else to you since that day?" Luca asks.

"Nope."

"Is that good or bad?"

I don't know, so I don't answer. Luca plays with my fingers. "It interesting how neither of our parents like cosplay, but for different reasons. Evie thinks it's too common, and my parents think it's too weird."

It probably doesn't help that Luca's parents are sort of right to be scared. After all, their fear of cosplays and cons is more about their son's bisexuality, and here he is, creating a cosplay for a con with his secret lover who is a guy. And neither of us have pants on.

Poor Luca Vitale. Just another pantsless youth, corrupted by arts and crafts.

Luca stands up and stretches. My thoughts derail completely when I see a sliver of his stomach beneath his bunched-up shirt. Catching me staring, he grabs the shirt's hem and pulls it over my head, smothering me as we tumble to the floor. He gasps, laughing. My doubt is forgotten as I wrestle back. He's stronger and definitely heavier, but he acts like I'm made of pure gold as he lets me pin him. Still under his shirt, I find the loose collar of his tank top and push my head through it so we become a two-necked, two-headed monster. I spread my arms out through the sleeve openings, too, curling my hands into his. I adjust so that my forehead falls in the gap between his ear and his shoulder, my breath loud in my own ears as I exhale into his neck.

"Raffy, what are you even doing?"

"Honestly? No idea. It just seemed funny."

"Wow. You really are exhausted."

"What do you mean?"

"You never let me just hold you. You always have to be doing stuff."

Someone has to do the stuff, I almost say, but the bitterness is gone. It's melting as the heat from Luca's skin pushes through my own shirt, through my own skin. I'm so, so tired. I've done so much. Maybe I've done enough for today and it's okay to take a break. He makes me want to take a break.

"All I want is this," I say.

"I think you want a lot more," Luca observes. An onlooker might think he means something physical, but I know better.

I sigh. "I want a lot more, yeah, but sometimes I also want just this."

I sink a bit further into our joined warmth. Maybe it's the exhaustion, but I never knew Luca was so comfortable to lie on. My sewing is forgotten. The muslin can wait a little while longer.

"Just this?" Luca asks.

Just us, I think. I wait to say it. I wait a long time. I fall asleep waiting, and Luca lets me.

TWENTY-THREE

I'm used to working in front of a camera. On Ion, I used to do it all the time. I worked, I talked, I joked. I should be okay with the televised round of Trip-C, but of course everything changes beneath the bright lights of Controverse. First of all, there's more than one camera. There are a dozen. And instead of just talking to myself, I'm talking to everyone. It's the most public process you can imagine. Creation as consumption. It messy, and fast, and real, and scary. And as Luca and I get underway, I realize something.

I fucking miss this.

This. *This.* Just…making stuff. Just picking up things, putting them together, and creating something without second-guessing every choice. Being free. When Luca and I first met, I remember feeling this way. He changed the way I created for the better. And now the joy of creation is back, ironically, in the most competitive setting yet. I think it has to do with Luca, who always saw the magic in what I could do. Right now, as we navigate our new challenge, I begin to feel that magic again.

Controverse wakes up around us, crowds pressing against the transparent barriers to gawk at the massive camera contraptions sweeping over us. People call out our team names, begging the cameras to zoom in on what we're up to so they can see it on the screens above us. When I do allow myself to glance at the crowd, I see that Luca and I have quite the audience. I throw them a shy smile, and they wave. Luca waves back, and they go wild.

Mostly, though, we work. We work like our history isn't sitting between us. Or we work like only history sits between us, the fabric of the past slicing apart as we work, turning into scraps of material that we sew back together to form something new, something strange, something so much better. Because of the cameras, we can't talk. We can only focus on what's happening right now, and work together at creating something incredible.

And I feel that magic, that joy, that excitement, that I'd let myself forget in the months leading up to Controverse. It's intoxicating to feel like myself again. Is it Luca? Is it the lack of Evie? Is it the lack of sleep?

I don't know. I don't think too hard about it. It's time for my hands to think instead. I just keep working, keep making, hoping I don't lose it. Besides me, Luca keeps me planted in the present. I give him instructions as we go, the adaptations of our old process coming together in my mind as the cosplay forms before us.

"Since we're doing a look that combines features from both, we'll do the base with neutrals," I tell him as we finish tracing out the feathers. "That way, we don't have to paint all of the foam, just the colorful accents. We can do most of the detail work with Dremeling and airbrushing."

"So the final thing will be black and white?"

"We'll use the light gray and the matte black, but then we can add blues and whites for more depth. Pass me the cutter."

I alter the wing shape to be more symmetrical, knowing we won't have time to correct for anything that accidentally gets traced backward. I quickly sketch out the major shapes I want, referring to the sketch as I hand them to Luca.

"Sixteen of these, eight of these, twenty of these. One set in black, one set in gray."

"Really?"

"I know it's a lot, but I think my math is right."

"No, I mean, you're cool with me cutting it all out? You're not afraid I'll mess it up?"

I know what Luca is saying. *You trust me?* And the way he says it puts an uncomfortable warmth on some old wounds. Was I always so exacting, so demanding?

"Just do your best," I tell him.

"I'm trying. So hard. I don't want to let you down again," he says.

We are not talking about a bird costume. We're talking about us.

A camera pans over our work. I keep my voice low. "You won't. You can't. You showed up, didn't you?"

"I didn't want you to work alone. I should have shown up so much earlier, Raff. I'm sorry I haven't always shown up when it mattered."

My nose tickles. Am I going to cry? I'm *not* going to cry. I deflect, motioning at the crowd of people. The world outside of competitive cosplay and this layered conversation. "You had stuff going on. People who needed you to be someone else."

Watching Luca and Inaya team up broke my heart, but a part of me always understood why they did what they did. It was just a means to an end so they could both do what they love. I shouldn't blame Luca for leveraging the easiness of a straight-looking partnership. I should blame homophobic people for demanding that kind of act in the first place. Still, I wish it had all been different.

"But I'm here now," Luca says urgently. "I'm here. For us."

I look at the plans in my hands—in his hands, too, because we're both unwilling to let go of these stupid designs. My breath shakes as I pull it into my lungs. My heart skips, my pulse scatters.

"Can I trust you with this?" I'm not talking about arts and crafts.

"I'd love it if you could try," he says. He's also not taking about arts and crafts.

And then, just like it used to, time stops for just us. I don't hear the crowd or see the cameras or feel the chill of the arena as Luca says something that forces everything else to fade away:

"I want to kiss you."

I let go of the designs, and Luca tosses them onto our table without looking away from my eyes. Would he kiss me in front of all these people? He must catch the question in my stare, because a defiance flashes in his eyes. Before I can stop him, he leans in and plants a kiss right on my cheek. More toward my jaw, just under my earlobe. He's taller than me and has to bend down, so for a moment, we're curled into each other.

I hear a whoop go up from the crowd. Luca hears it, too, and I can feel his lips pull into a grin on the skin of my neck. He gives me a warm nuzzle, and the cheering spreads. Then we're apart and back to working, and a new energy threads through everything. The crowd has a new focus on us. The cameras rush over, looking for any trace of the intimacy we just displayed.

"All eyes on you," Luca whispers, pushing me forward as he takes up the task of cutting foam like nothing just happened. The cameras reach us, but instead of a kiss, they get me rambling about our process.

"We want the feathers to be pliant, to give a drifting look when the cosplayer moves, and so we're creating the effect with high-density thin foam that we'll shape, treat, and lightly airbrush." I catch Luca grinning as he listens to me talk.

"What about the kiss?" a crewman inquires. "Can we get another—"

I interrupt. "We also want to keep the ornate filigree detailing that so many illustrators love rendering when they paint Phobos and Deimos, so while Luca cuts out the wings, I'm going to work on a pattern we can use to stamp on, sort of like a texture transfer. It'll look great from afar, and it'll really wow up close."

Ginger catches up. She nods along as though she's listening, but I know she's twitching for a chance to ask about Luca and me again. I don't give her the opportunity. This is about showing up and showing off, not gay antics. Or actually, it might all be gay antics? I'm not sure. But I don't give myself time to doubt, and I don't give Ginger time to ask.

"For the main part of the outfit, I would typically do a lot of armor plating, but with the time constraints, we can't mold, sand, paint, buff, and fit a ton of armor. So instead, we'll do a sort of stripped-down armor over fabric."

"Stripped-down, you say?"

"Yes. Over fabric, as in over clothes. I'm pretty good with patterns, and I know Luca's measurements well enough to create a pattern, but it'll be faster to drape."

Ginger gives me a wink. "Does that mean you have measured each other up before?"

"It means we're trying to work, or are the hints too subtle for you, Ginger?" Luca butts in. He gives me a playful nudge, too. Ginger lights up at this, even though he's shut her down, and I realize that they're doing an entire performance that I haven't even been tracking. Somehow, Luca has both ended the conversation and appeased Ginger's inquisitiveness all at once, and she beams at him with a note of excitement and…gratitude? I don't quite get it until she turns to the cameras and says, "You heard it here, folks!

These two are up to all sorts of shenanigans. Sparks are flying in the arena, and from the comments, it looks like people are dying to know what's going to happen next. So don't you dare look away, Controverse! Thanks, boys, for *all* the tips."

She gives the cameras another smarmy wink, and I get it. She's trying to create intrigue and excitement around people who are mostly keeping their noses down, working. Luca gave her just enough to create a story.

But I don't understand why Luca did this. This is the last story the old Luca would want to tell. For a moment, I can't move as I think about what he's given away and why.

He kissed me. In front of everyone.

My first instinct is always to worry, of course. Is he going to be angry with me? Will this hurt him? But Luca looks delighted. As Ginger skims over to the other groups, he bounces with a lightness I haven't seen in a long time. He's dancing a little bit as he slices through the thin foam, humming to himself. When he looks at me, his eyes don't betray any regret.

"Are you sure?"

"About what?"

"About that. You know she's going to lean into that story, right?"

"What story?"

"That you and I have a thing."

"Don't we?" He grins.

"Do we?" I ask sincerely.

"We could. If you wanted."

My pulse speeds up, pinging against the underside of my skin, making me hot all over. I don't know. I return Luca's unasked question with an unintentional grin. Then I get back to work, which makes much more sense than my confused emotions.

Soon the wings are all cut out, and it's time to shape and glue them. Together, we press them into their new form, and gradually our hard work becomes something remarkable.

"I'll go grab the PVC pipe," I say. This isn't typically found in a craft store, but it is a very useful material in cosplay construction, so they've got a whole bunch of pipes lined up against one wall like a slanting, bone-white forest. While I wait for a clubber to cut the lengths I've requested, Inaya joins me. For a moment it's just us, without the cameras.

"Having fun with our dearest Luca?" she asks.

"Yeah, actually."

"I figured you'd be at each other's throats by now," she says absently. "Not *down* them."

I feel myself blushing. "It was just a kiss."

"Just a kiss. Hmmm." Inaya turns her back as she scans a shelf of screws and fasteners, like she's really shopping. "I'm not sure it's ever just a kiss, Raffy. Especially not to Luca or his family."

"What are you getting at, Inaya?"

She turns, facing me. A mysterious, cunning aura emanates off her, same as always. "Nothing," she says lightly. "I've always seen you as competition, Raffy. I was excited to compete with you for real this year for the first time. When I heard you might drop out for May, I was mad. I'm glad Luca came through for you."

"May called him," I say.

"Actually, May called me, and *I* called Luca," Inaya says.

I nearly step backward into the stacked pipes. They groan as I brace myself on them. "What? *You* did? Why?"

Inaya crosses her arms, looking me up and down. "I want to be the best. And to be the best, I want to win against the best. And that's you."

I'm speechless. I craft because I love to create. Inaya crafts because she loves to achieve. I tried to be like that, and it made me miserable. Clearly, she feels differently.

"I'm glad he showed up for you. Just don't let him bring you down," she says, putting one finger in my face and pointing toward the workstations with the other hand. "Luca has a way of distracting you. Don't let him stop you from doing your best."

The clubber returns with the lengths of pipe I requested.

"Anything else?" he asks.

"No, I'm good," I say, taking the chance to edge away from Inaya. She gives me a coy wave, then starts giving the clubber her own list of measurements.

I dawdle on my way back to the table, trying to think. Inaya's words snake through my head, pulling my thoughts into strange, bendy patterns. *Don't let him stop you from doing your best,* she said. My best, according to Inaya, happens in spite of Luca. She must have dealt with same the frustrations I did, trying to teach someone so new. Clearly, her way around it was excluding Luca entirely, and she's telling me to do the same.

A familiar tightness takes over my heart. The cold fury, the blistering drive. It feels wrong and invasive after the elation of this morning, like the sudden onset of an infection.

No. I'm not choosing, because there is no choice to make. I can do my best *and* I can let myself feel what I feel. I won't cut Luca out because it's easy to be alone. He's risking a lot to be himself here with me. I'm not going to shut him out of something he's fighting so hard to be part of. It would be wrong, and it wouldn't make me a better competitor. It would only make me ruthless. Like Inaya. Maybe that works for her, but after being with Luca, I've realized it's not for me.

I grab a heat gun and a few other things as I hurry back to the station. When I'm close, a sudden commotion fills the arena. Cameras push in to get my reaction to what I now realize is some sort of disturbance in the crowd near our station. The rest of the cameras are pointed at Luca, who is blushing so hard that even the tops of his shoulders are red. He's facing down the clear barrier, behind which a small lady has captured the audience's attention. She is wide-eyed, her breath fogging the partition. She is speaking rapidly and shaking her head over and over.

I know who she is.

This is Luca's mother.

TWENTY-FOUR

It's late on Monday—like, midnight late—and I'm about to clean up my makeshift workstation when I realize Luca never showed up for our session.

I've been so focused on what I was doing that I didn't even realize he wasn't here. I got so much done tonight on the props, and I might even have time to insert some LEDs at the rate I'm going. I'm in a great mood, feeling more accomplished than I have in weeks. I didn't even notice Luca had ditched me until I look at my phone and see a single text from him:

sorry, something came up tonight.

You okay?

Luca doesn't text me back that night or the next morning. I can sense something is off, but I'm not sure how to ask about it. If he were mad, he'd tell me, right? Or maybe he wouldn't. But why would he be mad? The last time I saw him, I was bundled up in his shirt, snoring into his collarbone. It was, as he said in a text right after leaving, Mind-Blowingly Cute.

I've never been called cute in my life. That I become cute when I am on the brink of exhaustion and collapse should be a concern, but I was too tired to acknowledge that. The text made me feel warm. Hugged in his absence. Now I feel a creeping cold. It gnaws at the edges of my haze, trying to break through and tell me something. But what? What did I miss? What have I done wrong?

I think about this for most of the school day. When I see Luca, his eyes seem to slide right over me. I text him when we're in class together and watch him ignore it, which is possibly the most horrible thing anyone has ever done to me. As far as my anxiety goes, that's the equivalent of pulling a pin out of a grenade. I'm just waiting for the explosion.

Instead of exploding, I do what I always do: I make stuff. In precalc, where we're supposed to be doing independent work, I peel strips of paper from my notebook, each about an inch wide. I fold and roll the strips, turning them into strands, and then I braid them into a chunky band. By precalc's end, I have a new woven bracelet.

It doesn't help.

By the end of the day, Luca still hasn't texted me back. I know he's got a game today, so after the last bell rings, I head to the buses that pick up the athletic teams and bring them to their rivals. At first I don't see him, because I'm looking for his lone figure off to the side, moping about whatever's got him down. But he's actually right in the thick of the team, engaged in some sort of game with his friends. It's his laugh that grabs my attention. Bright and careless, it has nothing to do with the version of him I imagined.

And the laugh cuts off right as our eyes meet.

I don't understand what I'm feeling, just that it's bad. I turn away, looking for a place to aim myself, because suddenly I know I made a mistake in coming here. I end up ducking in between the busses, finding one with a door open and hurrying up the steps just as the first tear blurs my vision. I don't get why I'm crying. I know I'm tired. I know I'm being a little unreasonable.

The bus driver gives me a second to compose myself and then says, "You on the soccer team?"

I'm on the soccer team bus? Oh, awesome. Lovely. I curl into a seat on the far side of the bus where the other boys can't see me, getting ready for my escape. I could climb out the window, maybe? Or bribe the driver to drive away.

"Raffy."

I look up. Luca stands at the front of the bus. He nods at the driver—they're friends, of course—and then joins me in my hiding spot.

"Why are you crying?"

"I don't know."

Which is the truth, but also not really the truth. So I add, "Because you're ignoring me."

Luca takes almost a minute to respond. At first, I think it's because he's thinking of an apology, but then halfway through the silence, I see the way his jaw is clenched. His shoulders are hunched. He's angry.

"You didn't even notice," he says. His voice surprises me after the silence, and I almost don't hear what he says next. "When I didn't show up, I thought you would be worried, or at least mad, but you didn't even notice I was gone last night. I don't know what's worse: that you probably loved working alone and didn't want to ruin it by checking in, or that I'm such a small part of your world that you didn't even realize I was missing."

"Wait," I say. "*What?*"

"You'd be mad, too, if *your* boyfriend would rather be doing arts and crafts alone than with you."

"Wait," I say again. "We're boyfriends?"

"I don't know, Raff. Are we?"

Rationally, now is not the time to moon over Luca admitting that we are maybe boyfriends. Later, I will feel the threat of his unsureness, and that will matter more, but for the few seconds after the word enters the air between us, I can't help but feel reassured. If we're fighting, there's something to fight about. What we have is worth fighting for. I needed to know that, especially today after thinking Luca was ignoring me. It makes me smile, which is a huge mistake.

I wipe the smile away and check to see if Luca saw. He didn't. He's focused on the vinyl of the seat in front of us.

"You haven't even asked what I was doing last night."

Once again, I have become distracted by the details. It didn't even cross my mind that there might be a bad reason for Luca's absence. I'm still unraveling the day's anxiety and stitching it into a less selfish point of view.

I feel so, so dumb when I repeat his question to him: "What were you doing last night?"

I expect something soccer-related. I don't expect what Luca says, which is:

"Being screamed at."

"By who?"

"My mom."

I give Luca a chance to say more, knowing he doesn't like it when I overwhelm him with questions he's not really ready to answer. But then the next big surprise comes.

"My parents want me to stop seeing you."

"Wait, what? They know about us?"

Luca makes me wait as he picks at the peeling vinyl, probably knowing what he said has set off a hurricane of questions in me.

"They don't know everything, but they figured out enough. They must have caught on that I wasn't always hanging out with the boys, like I told them. And then they put together the rest from those photos from a while ago. They know who you are, and my mom watched a bunch of your streams. She made me show her all the pictures I took at Controverse."

"Jesus, Luca, I'm so sorry. Were they mad?"

He tilts his head back against the seat. "They were mad about *eeeeeeverything*. They made me tell them about you and explain the cosplaying. And then they went through my Netflix history and made me explain what each show was about. Have you ever had to explain *Evangelion* to a Catholic Italian mom? The second I said the heroes have to defeat angels, I knew I was doomed. Like, *doomed* doomed. Anyway, after that, I got lectured about lying and about the importance of family for another two hours. We didn't even eat dinner. That's how I know they were mad. And not just mad. Big mad. Big Italian mad."

It's my turn to lean back. I swallow my questions, unsure how I can fix any of this.

"Want to know the worst part?" Luca asks. "They didn't even bring up the whole bisexuality thing. The whole time, I was just waiting for that to be the climax, and I was even a little relieved because we were finally going to talk about it. Finally, I could be out to them, no matter the repercussions. And I could tell that's what they were really mad about, but they refused to even mention it. It's the same as always. Maybe worse. I can't go over to your house anymore. I'm not even supposed to be talking to you."

Whatever anger I had, whatever has kept me moving today, is gone now. I don't even feel sorrow. Just a spreading numbness.

I jump as the bus kicks to life. A hand slaps the window, and I can see Luca's teammates taking turns jumping, trying to get his attention. He waves them away with an easy smile.

"They saw us talking," I say. "Are you going to get in trouble?"

"Nah, they have my back. That's what it means to be on a team. If I got grounded, I'd be out of practices and games, and they wouldn't be able to function without me."

He stands, gesturing for me to get up too with a sweep of his arm.

"Unlike some people," he says to the back of my head.

"Luca, come on, I'm sorry—"

Luca whistles, getting the bus driver's attention. They exchange some sort of hand signal, ending in a thumbs-up. Then Luca leans on the back door's hinge, and it pops open just wide enough for me to slip through. The driver returns the thumbs-up.

"Here, so you don't have to walk by everyone," Luca says, indicating it's time for me to go. I'm too scared to just jump, so I sit on the ledge and scoot out onto the pavement. I turn to look up at Luca, expecting him to slam the door in my face, but he's watching me. Waiting for me to say something.

"I'll figure this out. You don't have to choose," I say. It's what Luca told me once, and it got me to admit that I love him.

"You still don't get it, do you?" Luca says. He kneels down so that we're level, just me and him blocked from view in a gridlock of idling buses. For the first time since we started talking, a real smile plays at the edge of his lips. "*We'll* figure something out. Come here."

Relief sweeps through me as I step forward between his knees, his lips pressing to my hair as his arms collapse over my shoulders.

"We work together, okay?" he says. "I'm not giving up."

"I'm not giving up, either," I whisper.

Luca picks up my wrist, playing with the little paper bracelet I made in precalc.

"You made this today?"

I nod.

"Aww, you must have been real nervous if you made something," he says.

I shrug.

"Can I wear it? For my game?"

I suppress a smile. "It's all yours."

He tilts my chin up. The air is thick with the fumes from the buses, and it's noisy, but everything feels romantic as he slips the crude bracelet from my wrist and winds it between our locked fingers. His kiss lands light and quick on my cheekbone, fast as a dragonfly.

"Boyfriends?" he asks.

"Definitely," I say.

"Cool."

Luca winks. He stands and eases the door closed, and almost immediately, the bus rocks with commotion as the team climbs aboard. I slip away, keeping my head down, a plan already forming in my mind.

TWENTY-FIVE

Luca is looking at his mom. She is red-faced, too, as though she is suddenly aware of everyone watching. But her focus is on him, her emotions unreadable except for the steam that condenses on the partition. She's breathing heavily, like she got here in a rush. Like maybe she's mad.

"And it looks like we've got a parent on the sidelines, but she doesn't look pleased! Could it be that she didn't know this is what Luca needed her signature for?"

It's a moment before I register that this question has been aimed at me, and Ginger's microphone is in my face. I push it away and get closer to Luca's mom. When I glance at Luca, there is a shadow in his eyes that I've seen before. Shame.

My heart breaks for him. It is unfair that he has to navigate this. It is even worse that he has to do it here, in front of all these people. People looking for a show. And I'm sure Irma meant for this to happen. Luca's mom has a lanyard on, and she's trailed by a clubber, as though she's a special guest brought in just to create this moment.

The crowd's murmuring bubbles up as people notice there's something bad happening. The excitement snuffs out all at once as Luca's mom says, "Luca, what is this? Why wouldn't you tell me about this?"

Luca's shoulders are hunched. Whispers swarm through the arena. Nervous laughter, too.

"I've been calling you. Why is your phone off? Why didn't you tell me you were on TV? What is all of this? How come I had to hear about it from your *cousins*?"

"I'm sorry. I didn't want you to worry. It's not that big of a deal," Luca pleads.

"Not a big deal? You think not telling me about something means I can't worry? I worry even more when I feel like I don't know my son. And *this*?"

She slaps her phone against the partition. It's a blurry screenshot of Luca kissing me. We are the terrible thing that dragged a mother through an entire convention center to confirm with her own eyes.

"*This* is no big deal?" she says. "I have to learn *this* from your cousin? From the internet?"

"Ma, I'm sorry. I can't talk about it right now, okay? Just go home, and I'll explain everything later. Okay?"

Luca is practically begging. I've never heard the word *okay* said with such emotion.

His mom crosses her arms. Luca crosses his arms. They reflect one another, except Luca is about a foot taller.

"You're staying?" she asks.

"Yeah."

"You want to be here?"

"Yeah, Ma."

"This matters to you? He matters to you?"

Luca swallows. "Yeah, it does. He does, too."

Controverse never goes silent, but in this moment, I swear it comes close. Luca's mom purses her lips, thinking about his answers. If she's conscious that an entire show, a dozen cameras, and countless production staff have started watching *her*, she doesn't show it. But I think she's seen the energy and attention and the love assembled around her son. I can't be sure, but I feel like I see something shake loose in her rigid expression.

"Then I'm staying, too," she announces. "I never missed a game in your life, and I'm not missing this," she says. "I'm your mother, and I cheer you on. No matter what. Okay?"

The silence is broken by the collective sound of every pair of lungs in a one-mile radius gasping. *Theatre* gay gasping.

Luca is surprised, but his smile is already breaking through. "Okay, okay," he says.

His mom grins, too, looking just like him once again.

"This makes you happy?"

Luca nods.

"Then you should do your best. You're a Vitale, and we always do our best. And…" She looks at me, then looks away shyly. "And he…?"

"He makes me happy, too."

"Then you bring him over for dinner after, okay? Don't eat the food here. It looks like poison."

From Luca's face, it looks like she's given him the best possible blessing in the world. And then his mom looks to me, and I find myself nodding obediently. Yes, of course I will come over for dinner. No questions asked. She gives me an approving smile.

Luca puts his hand on the partition. His mom presses her palm to the other side.

"Make us proud," she says.

Somewhere, someone starts to clap, and it breathes movement back into the silent arena. The crowd gathers around Luca's mom, rocking her with their cheers.

"Let's get back to work." Luca pulls me back to our station, and the cameras find other things to focus on, other plots, and we're left alone to work.

"Luca, that was—"

"Let's just work, maybe? If that's okay?" he says. He's trying not to smile. He's trying not to let the world know how relieved he is, and I get that. It's easy to go from relieved to suddenly crying, and there's no stopping tears like those. So we just get back to work to the sounds of the crowd cheering us on. Now, Luca's mom is among our supporters, and she cheers the loudest of all.

◇ - - - - ◇

The cameras stay close on our hands for the next few hours. Luca and I fall into a rhythm, and gradually, the accumulated materials merge together to become a chest plate, shoulder armor, a helmet, and even wings. We barely talk at all, only when we need to figure out what's next. I end up moving on to pattern-making for the more complex garments while Luca transitions to props. He's better with foam than I remember. Like, actually skilled. And that leaves me time to sit with my fabrics and sewing machine and think.

And think. And think.

I lose nearly an hour trying to put together a pattern. I can't decide on anything. Can't commit to anything. What if I make the wrong choice? What if I make the right choice but don't have time to execute it because I've spent so long sitting here worrying? What if I get everything done, but it doesn't matter because Evie figures out where I am and send assassins to take me out the next time I go to pee?

Arms encircle me from behind. I'm so lost in my thoughts that I barely register the crowd going *awwwwwww* as Luca says, "You're thinking too hard. Let's go for a walk."

"Where?"

"Just come."

Luca leads me away from our station, past the people pressed to the glass, and over to the aisles of craft supplies. We stop in front of the shelves of fabrics. Unceremoniously, he takes my hand and shoves it between the rolls.

"I don't get it," I confess.

"Whenever we used to go fabric shopping, I swear you would touch every single fabric before making a decision. It was like your hands were thinking for you. So if you're going to think, you might as well think with the right part of you. Here, like this."

Luca drags my hand across the rolls. We're in a section of quilted fabrics in blacks and gray, like futuristic insulation. Something you could use for a regal space uniform, maybe? I picture heavy coats that barely shift in the wintery winds of a distant planet. The other textures give me other visions, like the cloth is falling over invisible ideas and revealing their hidden shapes.

I see Luca's point.

"Good," he says, like he can see my doubts releasing me, my creativity coming back to life. "Now do your thing."

So I do as Luca says and let my hands think for me. As my mind sheds its inertia, a design forms in my head. The materials fill in like a paint by numbers, and soon I've got several options piled up in my arms as I waddle to the cutting table. Breathlessly, I tell the attendant what lengths I need, and then I go back for more. What was I thinking, taking this long to explore? I'm in my favorite place in the world with no budget. Now is the time to go as wild as I want. Now is the time to let the fabrics do the work for me.

I walk away with a luscious, soft leather (fake, but convincing), which I'm going to use to make a fitted crop top and high-waisted slacks. It'll be a lot of work, but the fabric has some stretch, and I know Luca's measurements already. I also find a gorgeous bulky knit that I want to use for the Deimos cape. I can distress it to give it some personality.

My scissors fly through the material, raining ribbons onto the floor as I cut out the sections I need. The panels pool together with barely a moment to settle before I'm gathering them together, needle and thread driven through their pinned edges. The pants come together, rough and quick, and I toss them to Luca.

"Try them on," I demand. He doesn't even bother going to the changing room. He's in his briefs in a second, then in the pants a second after that. I look up, take note of where I need to adjust them, and then pin a few darts in. I mark the darts, slip out the pins, and Luca's half naked again. I know the crowd must be having some sort of reaction to this, but I don't bother looking. I'm tailoring now, and I need to focus.

The top is a bit easier. I don't do sleeves. Sleeves are a nightmare, and I don't have time to wait for the strange magic that only sometimes shows up when you create them. Besides, Luca will protest if I cover up his triceps.

The cape is the easiest part. I coil and sculpt the bunched

material around the neck of the dress form, finding the exact right balance before I hand-stitch it into place.

"ONE HOUR!" announces Ginger. I take a breath and look around. The other teams' projects are in similar states of half completion. I see that Inaya is dressed in a gorgeously tailored leotard of white silk. She's fastening on a skirt, a pleated affair in three layers, made from rich jewel-toned fabric. She catches my eye and throws me a thumbs-up, but behind her, Christina is watching me, too, with a decidedly less encouraging vibe.

I turn away. I saw what I needed to see. They're doing Sailor Moon. A super popular cosplay and an anime icon. Except just plain Sailor Moon would be too easy. Christina and Inaya have reached for the heavens and brought down the most powerful version of the icon: Eternal Sailor Moon from the *Stars* season.

I get back to work. Our cosplay looks good but plain. And then it hits me—I know what we need to do. I dash into the aisles and return to Luca with arms spilling over with jewels.

"Bedazzling? Really?"

"Really."

I've chosen a panoply of metallics, golds, and coppers.

I bedazzle like my life depends on it. Luca joins me, following the pattern I've started, replicating it perfectly and symmetrically upon the chest of the armor. We've created a bird of metal and power, wings spread wide. Then we're fingers deep in Rub 'n Buff, dotting it on, taking care to avoid the black armor beneath.

"Hey, look at me," Luca whispers.

I do.

He dots some of the metallic finish on my cheekbone. I'm about to return the favor when I see the cameras zoom in on us.

"Remember when you put highlighter on me at Inaya's show?" Luca says.

"Yeah."

"I think about that all the time. I want you to do it again."

I stand on my toes, and he bends down so that our cheeks touch. When I step back, a streak of brass runs up his cheek, the cut of his cheekbone glowing. It brings back the memory of Inaya's show, but also the memory of seeing Luca in the art room more than a year ago, gold spray paint soaking into his skin.

Thinking that far back gives me a sudden nostalgic vertigo. Staring at Luca, I feel the past and present collide in me. For a long time I was lost. Angry. But right now I feel excited. It's been forever since I've had this much fun making something. Spring Keeper and the Pinehorn were complex and mind-bending. HIM and Princess were intimidating and stressful. All of those builds were created furiously, leaving me tired and weak and barely alive enough to enjoy wearing them.

But with this shitty bird costume that Luca and I have thrown together in eleven hours under high stress as the world cheered us on? It's an entirely different feeling of accomplishment. It's creation, bright and fast and real, and though I am tired, I feel whole again. Pieces of me that had long since drifted out of alignment have joined back together, and I'm a new machine. A new

Raffy. I remember my heart, and within it, I finally find the energy to let go of the grudge that's been keeping it going all this time.

"Think we'll win?" Luca asks.

"Honestly? I don't even care," I say, and it's the truth. "I'm just happy we made it to the end."

Luca gives me a curious look. "You sure you're Raffy?"

"I'm sure." I smile.

I'm halfway through suiting Luca up when I realize I never created shoes or any sort of arm armor, like bracers or even gauntlets. But Luca surprises me with two claw-footed boots, his actual shoes trapped beneath layers of foam and glue. And he's made bracers, too. They're thick, but expertly proportioned with the rest of the costume.

"I didn't have time for the bow and quiver," Luca says as he shows me the rest of his work. "So I made a spear."

It's simple, but the metal illusion is perfect. I find some scraps of leather, and a minute later, the spear has a real handle. It takes a few minutes more to glue on some extra studs, and suddenly the weapon looks camera ready.

"Nice," Luca breathes.

I stand back, and I'm looking at a demon bird warrior. I don't see the flaws. I only see the magic.

The timer goes off a minute later, bright and shrill, and all hands go up.

We did it.

We actually finished.

TWENTY-SIX

Inaya is a saint. A god. A legend. A savior. Not only does she let Luca and me move our half-built cosplays into her basement workshop, she even helps us finish them. We pay her in pizza, but half the time, she doesn't even touch it. It's like she just wants to have a project to advise on more than anything else. And her parents, whom I hadn't met until now, are probably the nicest people ever. They welcome Luca and me into their home in a way neither of us is completely ready for.

"They're just happy I'm hanging out with other humans," Inaya explains. "They support the cosplay stuff, but they still think it's pretty weird. I'm sure seeing you guys here with me is a relief. For a while, I think they believed you were made up."

Somehow, with her help, we get the weaponry done. We get the

LEDs installed so that the blades shift between purple and white. As the week draws to a close, I'm standing by myself in front of Inaya's bedroom mirror, looking at our work. I'm unrecognizable.

I'm a myth. A terror. An angel. The wings have a gorgeous sweep to them, each feather bending just slightly as I move around. The harnesses we made are comfortable and totally hidden beneath our armor. The metalwork gleams with polish, and you can even make out Inaya's signature detailing on the plates. She added that as a surprise, pushing me to let her embellish. It hurt me a bit, but giving up complete ownership of every piece was something I should have done long ago. With her there, everything moved faster, and Luca became much more productive. As I take in the cosplay, I see evidence of his work everywhere. In a good way. The design itself is much more heightened, much more extravagant than something I would normally do. I'm dressed in his ambition, created with my skill, and finished with Inaya's genius. It's a prize-winning build that's sure to get us tons of photo ops.

Downstairs, I hear Inaya and Luca laughing. They're on FaceTime with Luca's parents, who call out of the blue a lot. Luca told them he and Inaya study together, and they believe him. Inaya is gorgeous, of course, and a girl, and they always make sure no crafts are in the background. As a result, Luca's parents seem satisfied. Even better, they're traveling to Connecticut the weekend of Blitz Con, so Luca doesn't even need to think of an excuse.

I sigh as more laughter rings through the upstairs hallway. It seems I'm always envious of what Inaya can create just by being herself.

By the time Luca and Inaya enter the bedroom, I'm all smiles again.

"Damn, Raff," Luca says. "You look awesome. Can I try mine on, too?"

"Of course," I say. "In fact, you'd better. Tonight's our last chance to make changes before we head out tomorrow. Inaya, are you still okay to drive?"

She gives a double thumbs-up. "But we're splitting parking."

Luca beams, then vanishes back downstairs to get dressed.

"I'd better help him," I say, edging toward the door. It's hard to maneuver with these wings.

"Don't," Inaya says. "I'll make sure everything fits. And I'll help him pack up. I want to see your face when he reveals the cosplay tomorrow at the con. It'll be like a first look video."

"You mean like from a wedding photo shoot?"

"Exactly," she says, and she dashes after Luca.

I catch myself grinning in the mirror. I know why, but I won't let myself admit it. Reluctantly, I start to change back into my normal clothes. Tomorrow is a big day. The biggest, maybe. I couldn't be more excited.

◇ - - - ◇

Shockingly, we make it out to Providence okay. The drive takes us two hours, which is twice as long as it should, but Inaya and Luca want to stop for fries. Twice. So we roll up to our hotel pretty late on Friday night. It's raining a little, but it's warm, and the whole world is painted in fuzzy neons.

"It's cool that Inaya's parents are so chill," Luca says as we wait for our room keys in the lobby. "I can't believe they just let her do all this stuff."

"Yeah, well, they get that she's a big deal in this world, and they want to support her. They just don't want to come to all the events, if they can avoid it."

"Yeah," Luca says wistfully.

I get what Luca is feeling. Must be nice to be Inaya.

By the time we're upstairs, I'm wired with excitement. Inaya and I sprawl out on the beds, then jump back and forth between them as Luca checks out the bathroom, then the view from the window. He's restless. I'm not sure how he explained the overnight to his parents, or if he even told them he was leaving Boston, and I do my best not to ask. Things between us haven't thawed completely since he got in trouble. And he's risking everything by being here with me now. I don't want to remind him that I'm a liability, if I can help it. Good vibes only from me.

"I brought face masks," Inaya says as she unpacks. She tosses them onto one of the beds. They're designed to look like masks from famous scary movies, which is very Inaya. "But first, let's hang everything up. I want to steam a few things tonight."

Inaya helps me unpack Phobos and Deimos, laying the harnesses out first and then the wings. We hang the caul in the closet, which is very funny to only me. Then I help Inaya hang up her dress on the back of the bathroom door. As she runs the steamer over the fabric, I peel open one of the face masks and apply it. I am Freddy Krueger tonight. As I smooth down the cool edges, I realize Luca is gone.

"He's on the phone, I think," Inaya says.

I slip past her and out of the hotel room, still wearing the mask. I find Luca at the end of the hallway.

I catch only the very end of his conversation. When he turns to me, his face is flushed. Splotchy. He asks, "What are you wearing?"

"A mask."

"Why?"

"For healthy, glowing skin. Who was that?"

"My dad," he says. His phone starts ringing again, but he sends it to voicemail. "My dumbass brother was supposed to cover for me, but he's being a dick. Don't worry, though, I'll handle it."

"Wait, do your parents know you're here?"

"No, it's cool. Can we not talk about it?"

"Luca—"

"Please? Can you just trust me?"

I want to know more, to help if I can, but I'm not sure what I could even do. In the moment, the only thing that feels right is saying, "I trust you."

Luca takes my arm in his. When we get to the room, he pushes me against the wall right next to the door, and then very carefully kisses just my lips. I smile, and the mask droops a bit.

"Careful, now," he says, pushing it back into place. "Or I might just find out your secret identity under there."

"Don't worry, I have my glasses in my backpack."

"So the mystery continues." He winks.

From the room comes a small bang, and we hear Inaya swear.

"Let's help her out?" I offer.

Luca's phone begins to ring again, but he powers it down. My chest tightens, but he throws me a rebellious smile.

"Let's!" he says, but the usual enthusiasm in his voice feels forced. Something is for sure wrong, and with every missed call, I can feel it going from bad to worse.

TWENTY-SEVEN

The final judging takes place on a makeshift stage that the clubbers have put up in the fake studio, reorganizing the supplies behind it so they form a bright and textured backdrop. The judges sit at a long, narrow table on an opposing stage. The partitions are removed, and the Controverse crowd surges forward, filling the space in between the tables and workstations like tumbling beads.

For the first time, we're allowed to interact with the people who have been cheering for us. And absolutely everyone wants a photo. I last in the chaos for about ten minutes before I manage to escape and hide out in a nook. I linger there, watching Luca from afar, just enjoying his inexhaustible energy when it comes to entertainment.

And then, from seemingly out of nowhere, May appears. She pulls me into a tight hug, and we nearly topple over into a shelf of embroidery hoops.

"You did it, Raffy, you did it! You made it through! How the hell do you feel?"

I'm beat. My fingers prickle with burns from the glue gun, pokes from the sewing needle, and scrapes from god knows what else. I'm sore all over, but I kinda like it. It's evidence of a day spent trying my best.

"I feel awesome," I say.

"You guys did *great*. I really thought maybe you'd kill each other, but wow! You just…figured it out."

I give her a benevolent curtsy, like I'm some sort of relationship saint. Then I ask, "How was the Art Mart?"

"Good. Great, actually. But I'll tell you later. I think you need to be onstage soon?"

May is right. The judges have taken their seats, and Luca is waving me over. May squeezes my arm and wishes me luck, and then I'm racing behind the shelves as Waldorf Waldorf announces, "Let the Controverse Championship of Cosplay grand finale begin!"

Taco Belle and Snow White Castle go first. Snow is the one in cosplay, and it's a Bo Peep–style dress with an exaggerated hoopskirt. She sweeps onto the stage like she's in a royal dressing room and not a makeshift craft store, and the dome of her dress swivels at her hips. It's absolutely huge, the shape nearly a perfect sphere beneath her cinched waist, and it looks pink until she stops moving and we see the skirt is actually red with large white dots. The edges are piped in thick white tubes, and pronged teeth poke out from the bottom of the hem, flicking against her pink-stockinged legs. In contrast, her upper body is wrapped in leafy green, and on her head is the strangest item of all: a felted hat that looks like a flowerpot.

"Oh, I get it," Luca says. I get it a second later, along with everyone else, when Taco Belle gets on the stage and helps Snow White Castle into a headstand. The skirt shifts, the bell of it yawning open to form a toothy mouth, and she brings her stockinged legs together like a wagging tongue.

"It's the Piranha Plant from Mario!" says Waldorf Waldorf, and the crowd claps appreciatively at the bizarre transformation. Then Snow tries to get fancy and wave her arms (which are sleeved to look like leaves), and she falls out of the headstand. Snow and Belle roll together in a frantic tangle until finally a clubber rushes onstage to help them.

The crowd loves this. I dare say it's even better than me catapulting my crab claws into the crowd during Primes. I finally relax, taking refuge in their misfortune.

The Satoh twins go next. They've created an incredibly recognizable Jack Sparrow cosplay. I am sure the look is a hit with ladies between the ages of thirty and forty-five.

And then Luca is up. There's no real pretense to his performance, no canon-certified poses or self-serious acting. It's just him and his crowd, and they adore him. Who wouldn't? His performance is pure camp. There's flexing, there's power, and then, as the crowd reaches a fever pitch, Luca drops into a split.

It happens quick enough that the wings billow up, settling

back down around Luca as he raises his arms, victorious. Then he makes a show of not being able to get out of the split, and before I know it, I'm being shoved onstage to help him. There's no denying the increase in cheers when I show up. At first I'm nervous, but then I'm not. I find Luca's smile, half-hidden beneath his askew helmet, and it gives me the focus I need to keep the show going. I don't drop into a split with him—I'm not trying to die today. Instead, I go behind Luca, pulling the wings out to their full span so we make a bizarre, Vegas-like tableau. It's goofy and probably looks not half as glorious as it feels, but whatever.

Luca and I run from the stage and back to the other teams, laughing the whole way. Then it's time for Inaya and Christina, who have vanished into the aisles. I don't understand why until music booms through the speakers.

"Sailor Moooooon," goes a familiar chorus. It's the song she uses in the classic anime to transform. And that transformation is usually an iconic explosion of ribbons and gymnastics. It's such a recognizable thing for lifelong anime fans that several people in the crowd start crying, realizing what they're about to see.

A figure takes the stage. Inaya, but she's quick-changed her outfit. Now, she is dressed in a tight pink sheath, just head-to-toe coated in Pepto Bismol pink. Even her face—upon which anime eyes have been painted—and hair—in two iconic buns and pigtails—have been wrapped in fabric. The bodysuit has been airbrushed and bedazzled to iridescence, flashing as Inaya spins and poses.

Christina appears, handing Inaya a large heart-shaped pillow, which I'm sure is meant to represent Sailor Moon's iconic brooch. She holds the pillow aloft like it really is magic until Christina pulls some sort of string and the pillow explodes into confetti and ribbons. They pour over Inaya, creating a beautiful mess on the stage, and Christina does her best to gather up the excess and throws it into the air. It's bafflingly silly. It's amazing.

And then, the finale. On a musical cue, Inaya hits the front of the stage. Christina gets behind her, grabbing hold of the back of the pink costume. She pulls, and a seam along the chest pops open, revealing white underneath. She pulls harder, and all at once, the pink suit tears from Inaya, revealing the costume I first saw her in. Eternal Sailor Moon, who wears a simple white leotard and multi-colored skirt. There's no wind, no light show, no special effects, but in that moment, we are all standing before the moon princess herself, enchanted. Breathless. Chanting along as she transforms before our eyes.

And it's not over. Christina produces sleeves, which she slides onto Sailor Moon's arms. Then she ducks down to pick up something from the back of the stage—giant white wings—and I see it before she does. It'll be impossible to get both wings into the rigs at the same time, like she wants.

I race onto the stage to help, reaching Christina just as she reaches Sailor Moon. At first she's surprised, and then she's angry. But *then* she sees what I'm helping her do, and she passes me a wing. Together, we spin toward Sailor Moon, sliding the wings into the rig at the exact same time as the music's big finish. And Sailor Moon—or Inaya, lost in her character—seems weightless as she sweeps across the stage, as though the wings have released her from gravity's grip. I clap as loud as anyone else, proud to be part of something so epic.

We're asked to return to the stage in pairs, and the judges ask questions about what we've built, why, and how. It's not like the barbed exchanges of Quals, though. It's friendlier. More celebratory. I find myself actually listening to the other teams instead of rehearsing my own explanations and defenses.

When it's our turn, Marcus the Master starts our judging with a standing ovation.

"You boys did that in twelve hours? I'm blown away," he bellows. "The detail alone gave me chills. But the wings? Awesome work."

Waldorf Waldorf takes over. "Luca, Raffy, this is quite the ambitious build. Did the two of you plan this out ahead of time?"

"Nope," Luca says. "We didn't even know we were a team until this morning."

"But you worked so well together," adds Yvonne. "Did you know each other coming into this?"

"Something like that," Luca says with a smirk.

"How did you meet, then? School?"

"Actually, bedazzling," I say. "We met bedazzling."

There's a rolling laugh in the crowd that doubles when neither Luca nor I indicate that this is in any way a joke. Luca takes my hand, riding the wave of excitement, and plants a kiss on my hairline. Camera flashes go off, and I have the distinct memory of seeing Luca for the first time a year ago at Craft Club with a wall of gems flashing before us as his smile changed my life.

When Waldorf Waldorf gets the crowd back down to a simmer, we're asked questions about how we did what we did. Luca nudges me. "Tell them."

I do.

"We split up the work. The wings promised to take the longest, and they needed time to dry, so we started with the feathers. It's all done in foam, with a bone base of PVC pipe that slides into some plumbing equipment on a board in the back. The rig is made from a sheet of thick plastic, some nails, and those bendy U-shaped things you use to fasten pipes to…other things."

Luca turns, and I point at the parts as I talk. Belatedly, I recall the name: "A two-hole strap!"

Luca does a scandalized gasp. "My name is Luca, thank you very much."

I go red. Not blush-red, but candy-apple red. Heat-coil red. Magma red. I am amazed my skin stays grafted to my radiating bones. The crowd, of course, loves this. The judges politely pretend they don't get the joke, which is fair. I have no idea what this show is rated, but whatever it is, I'm sure Luca just changed that rating.

I rush to slide off the wings, taking the reins back from Luca so I can show how easily the costume breaks down.

"Well." Marcus sits back. "I think we know who the crowd favorite is."

"But this isn't about favorites," Waldorf Waldorf interjects. "It's about crafting and creation and, of course, overall cosplay. We've got a tough decision ahead of us, don't we?"

There are nods across the panel. It's time for the judges to deliberate, so we're led into the crowd for up-close-and-personal photos with the fans. While a reverent line of selfie-wanters waits for Luca, Ginger grabs me for an interview. She brings me to the beading and bedazzling section of the fake store, framing the shot so that I'm surrounded by a wall of gilded strands and glitzy baubles.

"Ready?" she asks.

I nod. Ginger stands next to me and cues the camera. There's a pause, and then the cameraman counts her off.

"I'm backstage with Raffy Odom," Ginger says. I plaster on a smile and wave. It's very similar to streaming in the sense that no one waves back.

"Raffy, you've just shown us what you can do in just twelve hours. That's both a long time and no time at all. How do you feel?"

"Proud," I say right away. "Most builds take fifty-plus hours at least. There's a ton more we could have done for this look, but we wanted to make sure we'd have something to present. I can't even believe we managed to finish an entire look."

"You sure did! You and Luca worked very well together. Is it true that you didn't form a team until right before today's competition began?"

"That's right. I actually arrived thinking I was going to compete alone."

"Why?"

"My original partner, May, has a booth in the Art Mart today. She's a super-awesome artist. Her comic, *Cherry Cherry*, is going to be big."

Ginger gives a dumbfounded gasp. "Big enough to give up a chance to compete live, on Ion, for the title of Controverse Champion of Cosplay?"

"Some of us have lives, Ginger," I shoot back.

"Cannot relate, my dear, *cannot*. Though I guess we can't *all* be beloved arts and crafts prodigies! Speaking of lives outside of Controverse, I was talking with some people in the crowd while you were working. There seems to be a rumor going around."

I don't let my face show it, but a bolt of panic travels up my spine.

Ginger's eyes glint, like she knows she's spooking me. But instead of putting up my wall, I breathe out and tell myself to loosen up. I can handle whatever she's got coming. And because I'm paying close attention, I see the playful edge to her grin.

"Some of the spectators say that you and Luca have great chemistry. You knew him before this, right?"

My panic subsides, but it leaves me no time to think of anything clever to say. I end up going with the truth: "I thought I did."

"What does that mean?"

"It means…"

What do I mean? Why did today with Luca feel so familiar, yet so foreign? I feel that same vertigo again, like I'm watching myself from the past. And it's past Raffy that I address with my answer.

"People can surprise you," I say. "I've known Luca for a while, but I learned a lot about him today. I learned a lot about myself, too, actually. I guess we just needed to be put in the right situation to…"

"To what?"

"To make it all work," I say definitively.

Ginger laughs. A wide-eyed, shocked laugh. "Well, that's quite the statement, coming from a master creator such as yourself. Is there anything you can't make? Don't answer that—we need to save some content for our VIP subscribers. I have a feeling this isn't the last collab we'll see between Raffy, Luca, and Craft Club! But I do have one last burning question before you go. What's next for the two of you?"

How can I answer this? How could I know? I used to think I always knew what came next. I used to think that my plans were as good as destiny, but that's never been true. I've just always been determined, and lucky, and determined to be lucky. But you can't design a future and expect it to just happen. Like art, you can only start with intent. Your hands build the rest.

What's next for the two of you?

I've been asking myself this, too, in the very back of my mind.

But I know better than to try to answer it for Ginger, or for myself. This whole time, I've been focusing on the broken pieces of my world, the shreds and scraps that fell away when Luca and I couldn't figure things out. I've lived in that ruin for a long time. Only now am I seeing a new truth: that sometimes the broken bits are just the pieces you need to create something new, something better, something remarkable.

I have my intent. I have my hands. I just have to get to work.

Ginger is still waiting for my answer.

What's next for the two of you?

"I don't know," I say, which is honest. "But if I know Luca, probably pizza."

The joke is the right way to button off the interview, and Ginger beams with energy as she wraps up. She knows my social media well enough to rattle it off, and I throw a thumbs-up to the viewers.

"Keep an eye on this one, folks," Ginger implores. "Maybe two eyes, if you've got 'em."

The camera dips. We're done.

"Good work," she says. She gives me a hug. "We'll reach out soon. Don't quote me, but I wouldn't be surprised if powers that be at Craft Club ask you for some follow-up content. Paid, of course. Keep an eye on that inbox, okay? And good luck."

I barely feel the ground beneath my feet as I'm led back to Luca and the other competitors, who are being arranged onstage for the final scoring.

"Hey," Luca says as he takes my hand. "You good?"

I give his hand a squeeze. I'm so far beyond good, it's not even funny. "Want to get pizza after this?"

"Can't," he says. "You can't either. We've got dinner waiting at my place, remember?"

I totally forgot about my silent vow to Luca's mom. My nervousness must show, because Luca shakes my arm a bit and says, "Don't worry. We got all the newness out of the way. After this, you're basically going to be treated like family."

The judges take their seats. Silence—or as close to silence as a convention hall ever gets—falls over the massive room. When the judges speak, their voices are amplified through the speakers, filling the vast heights with reverb as they tell us that we've each done a great job.

There is, of course, plenty of obligatory plugging for Craft Club. Irma is onstage with us now, too, holding a set of massive checks facing toward her so that we can't see the names.

"Now, Controverse, I present to you your winners," says Waldorf Waldorf. "In third place, we have Stacy and Liv with the Piranha Plant dress!"

Taco Belle and Snow White Castle, who I guess are named Stacy and Liv, jump up and down. I clap for them, because that dress was incredible (and that failed headstand? Chef's kiss).

The room goes quiet in anticipation of second place being announced. It could go any way. It could be anyone. I hope it isn't us, that we've pulled through to first. I cross every finger I have and a few toes, too. I want this. Badly. I want it for Luca, who gave so much just to compete. I want it for May, who's screaming her face off in the crowd. I want it for Evie, who understands so little about me. And I guess I want it for me, too. I want it because I deserve it, because I'm a damn good cosplayer and crafter.

"In second place…"

Please, I pray.

Please.

"Raffy and Luca with *Pantheon Oblivia!*"

And just like that, we lose.

TWENTY-EIGHT

- - - - - - - - - - - - - THEN - - - - - - - - - - - - -
FIVE MONTHS AGO

The morning of Blitz Con, I wake up from my first real sleep in ages. It should feel awesome, but the moment I'm conscious, I know something is off. The room is too bright and too quiet. How long did I sleep? Why did no one get me up? And why am I alone?

Pillows form a puffy crown around where Luca was asleep beside me. Inaya's bed is empty, too, the covers peeled back precisely. Her little Totoro slippers are present, but not her.

"Guys?" I call out. Nothing. I check the bathroom, and it's dark and cool, containing just the telltale humidity of an early-morning shower.

Who raptured Inaya and Luca? This is what I wonder as I try not to freak out, which is to say that I begin to freak out despite my best efforts. I text them both a bunch of question marks. I brush my teeth, because it feels like the normal thing to do. I watch my phone the entire time, jumping through the roof when it finally buzzes.

It's just a calendar notification, letting me know that today is Blitz Con.

"Thanks, I know."

I sit on the bed. I stand up. I sit down, this time on Inaya's bed. That's when I see the note. In sloppy, rushed handwriting on hotel stationery, Inaya has written: *Breakfast.*

The note was shoved under my phone. I just didn't see it in my worrying.

I immediately feel relief, but then I reread the note.

Breakfast. With a period.

And why not just text me? Why are we suddenly in a period piece from the eighties?

The momentary relief has recalibrated me enough that instead of feeling panic, I feel intrigue. I dress quickly—not in cosplay, because the con won't start for another hour or so—and put on my shoes. Then I make sure I have my key before ducking into the quiet hotel hallway and riding the elevator down to the lobby, where I know I'll find Luca and Inaya sprawled out on the lobby couches, surrounded by a buffet of Dunkin' Donuts.

Except I don't. There are many people I can identify as con-goers in the lobby—they have absolutely no reservations about sitting on floors, it's very funny—but not *my* con-goers.

I check the Dunkin' Donuts. It's busy, but they're not in there.

I check the lobby again. I sit on the couches for a while. I send them another text on our group thread. Restless, I walk toward the con. Maybe they went for a walk, too? It's a cool morning, but still warm enough to be in short sleeves, and Providence's wide blue sky promises a beautiful day. My eyes seek out every potential hiding spot around me.

I make it to the Providence Convention Center, where crowds of people are already gathering against the barriers, their badges around their necks. I'm not wearing my own badge, and I'm directed toward the check-in booth for pick-up. I don't protest, because an open spot is calling to me, and my con persona kicks in. I march up, unshowered with messy hair, and hand over my ID. I make small talk with the lady giving out badges. When she hands me mine, I ask, "Can you tell me if my friends are already checked in? They're from Canada, and their phones don't work in the U.S., and I don't have Wi-Fi."

She gives me a pitying smile, then glances to her coworker on her right.

"We can't," says the coworker, who I'm guessing is some sort of manager. "There's an official meeting spot designated on the floor map, though. If they have a guide, that'll be where they end up. Or at the Dunkin' Donuts, god only knows why."

"It's the cinnamon sugar pumpkin spice latte," says the person who checked me in helpfully. "It's addictive."

I thank them and wind toward the crowd. Just as I get there, the con must open, because a roar goes up, and everyone races through the barriers as they're peeled back by smiling staff. Shit. My controlled crowd of two hundred people quickly disperses into the booths and the floor, and I'm lost in a sea of excitement, clutching my badge. I haven't even put it on.

I walk around for as long as it takes me to convince myself I'm allowed to freak out. As I call Inaya, I realize I have already freaked out. I have freaked right out of our hotel, into the con, in civilian clothes and bedhead.

She doesn't pick up. Luca doesn't pick up, either. Inaya doesn't pick up *again*, and this time I'm sent right to voicemail.

That's about when I lose it, right near the beanbag chair booth. A worker offers me a free "sit" on a beanbag, and I accept the flyer and plunge into the pillowed interior of one of the chairs. I stare at my phone and commit to spiraling.

Something is wrong. So wrong. I was right. It was too much to imagine that everything could come together, that I could hold it all together and get us through this con. All the tension that's risen up between Luca and me, all the disaster that's come from our relationship and our partnership, is here to collect. I can't hold it back any longer, and it found us in the night.

No, I realize, it found us yesterday. That call Luca had with his dad. I rewind to that exact moment and remember Luca hanging up quickly in the hotel hallway. He smiled too fast, trying to stamp out the frustration that was overtaking him. Trying to show me he wasn't mad. A trick.

I push myself out of the chair and leave the booth, ignoring the person trying to sell me the chair. Anger thrums in me, because I know I messed up. I let myself be convinced everything was okay, that we'd get away with this, and now Luca is missing, and Inaya is missing, and I've been abandoned on the con floor. I had a chance to fix this, and I didn't take it. I let my guard down.

I'm outside the con in seconds. Then I'm back at the hotel like I've teleported. Minutes have passed without my detection, lost in my fury. I ignore the chatty teens around me as I slam the elevator button.

My phone buzzes. A text from Luca.

> Where are you? I'm in the room.

I expect it to vanish, but the letters stay. I stare at them as I stumble out of the elevator and down the hall. I feel like a totally different person by the time I reach the door of our room. My anger fades beneath startling relief, and I realize that once again, my anxiety has been showing me a lowlight reel of what the future could be. Anxiety is awful like that; it shows you only the worst, and all at once.

I give myself a minute to recover before going in. I want to calm down as much as I can. I realize now that there are about a million possible explanations for where Luca and Inaya might have gone and why they've been ignoring me. Maybe they didn't even know they were ignoring me.

Then I get another text from Luca.

> We need to talk.

I die on the inside. All of me dies, all at once. I'm at the door, but I don't go in. My fear propels me backward, past the elevators, to the little room where you can get ice. There's a vending machine, and I hide myself behind it.

I text Luca back.

> Hey! What's up?

And he calls me right away. The second I pick up, he's talking.

"Raffy. I'm sorry. I have to go."

"What? What's wrong?"

"Nothing. Actually, everything. My family is asking all these questions, and my parents are mad. Like, *mad* mad. They know I'm not home."

I slide to the floor, my head tapping against the warm vibrating side of the vending machine. No, not this. Anything but this.

"Please don't go," I say. "We came all this way. Just tell them you'll be home tonight."

"You don't understand," Luca says. "It's not about where I am, it's about what I'm doing. And who I'm with."

I hear a suitcase being zipped in the background.

I can't help but beg. "Come on, Luca, *please* don't do this. Just say you're with Inaya. They love Inaya. You don't even need to tell them about me. We can just pretend we came separately. Or that I don't even exist."

"Raffy, *stop*."

I stop.

"I don't know what I was thinking," he says. "I can't risk dressing up with you. If my family sees even one photo of us, it's going to prove them right about all the shit they believe."

"We won't take photos. I won't even post that I'm here," I blurt.

"You'd be happy with that?" Luca says grimly. "Now I'm making you hide, too? Be honest, Raffy. You want someone you can dress up with and create with and be out with. Someone at your level. I'm not that person, and I'm never going to be. I made a mistake thinking I could do this. Any of this."

I suck in a breath. "Any of this?"

"Yeah," he sighs. "You, the art shows, cosplaying. It's just... too much for me. I'm sorry. I'm sorry I'm fucking everything up. I know how seriously you take all this, and I wanted to be part of it, but I can't. I have to go. They're calling me."

I try to talk, but tears get the better of me.

"Don't cry. Don't fucking cry," Luca demands. It's cold. And mean. But at the edge of his voice, I hear him breaking, too.

"I can't help it," I say. I push the tears away with my shaking fingers. "Please. Just stay. We'll figure it out together, remember?"

"I was wrong, Raffy. *We* can't figure it out, because *we* are the problem."

I'm the problem here. Not cosplay, not sneaking out. Me. Raffy.

"I gotta go," Luca says. He sniffs, recovers. His voice is stern now. "I'm sorry, Raff. Please don't hate me forever. I promise I'll make it right one day. Just...just give me some time, okay?"

I'm the one who hangs up, because I can't even attempt an answer. I just give myself over to seismic sobs that quake through me, so forceful that I don't make a sound. I try to stand and can't. I am confused and scared, and nothing feels real. Not the wall, not the vending machine, not even my phone, clutched in my hand as it rings again and again.

I block Luca's number.

I hear a door open down the hall, and a suitcase drags over the carpet. I hear a sniff, then another. Luca. Or maybe someone else. I nearly jump out from where I've hidden myself, but fear pins me in place. I wait in the silence as whoever it is slams the button for the elevators, and I don't move until they've descended. Then I'm racing for the door, convinced it wasn't Luca, that I'll find him unpacking. He'll hug me, and we'll cry together, and then we'll figure it out.

But the room is empty. Luca is gone.

And I let him go.

◇ - - - ◇

I stand in the hotel room for a long time, trying to breathe in the quiet. I don't know the extent of what I just lost, but it feels like I've lost everything all at once. Luca left. He left minutes before we were supposed to get dressed and have the best day ever.

I don't text him. I don't call. I don't cry. I don't really know how to do any of that stuff right now. I have spent my entire morning reacting to an imagined crisis that has suddenly, horribly become real. I know I didn't cause this, but I feel like I must have.

Fury flashes through me as I look at our builds, diligently laid out last night. I cannot imagine being this close to showing up, only to deny all your hard work and run away. These cosplays took so much time. They took so much life. And, because of it, they're magically alive. This armor is made of dreams and effort, and now it's being abandoned, just like me.

I hate looking at these costumes. They humiliate me. In this moment, they are the awful evidence of how stupid I was to let Luca work alongside me. Now no one will get to see them. They will be wasted. I was so proud of them, proud of myself for creating them while also creating a structure to hold together this confused relationship. But the relationship was also a waste. A distraction. I'm furious with myself for being so stupid for so long.

I hate the way these costumes look at me. And I hate the idea that Luca walked away from them so easily, as though they'd always be there to take him back.

Before I can stop myself, I'm breaking them. The first thing I break is my own armor, for all the good it did protecting me. The pieces aren't real, just foam and glue slapped together in ugly imitation. Flimsiness shaped like artistry. I crush the helmet next, driving my entire fist through it. A flash of pain reminds me too late of the wire I used to give the helmet structure, and suddenly there's blood spilling over the rent foam and unglued gore. The sight awakens me to what I'm doing, and I step away abruptly.

"Fuck this," I say.

I clean myself up as best I can, using supplies from my emergency craft kit to tape tissues to my cut-up hand. I should try to clean up the mess I've made, but I'm afraid if I lay hands on what's left of the cosplays, I won't be able to keep myself from tearing everything else apart. So instead, I grab all my other things—my civilian clothes, my charger, my overnight bag—and I leave. Just like Luca, I make a run for it, unable to spend one more second amid the evidence of all my mistakes.

I don't stop moving until I'm far away from the convention center, near the train station. I don't let myself look at my phone until I'm seated on a train back to Boston. I have a bunch of missed calls and texts from Inaya.

> I tried to talk him out of leaving.

> He said you'd understand.

She's still texting me.

> Where are you? Are you okay??? There's blood in the room.

I let her know I'm fine. She calls right away, but I don't pick up. I text her instead.

I'm on the train. I'm fine. Physically. Sorry. Do you mind bringing Phobos and Deimos back? You can throw out the stuff I ruined.

You did this? Wtf???

Sorry

I was mad.

I'm still mad. I'm ashamed of my reaction, too.

It's cool. I'm going to get dressed. You sure you don't want to come back? I'm texting Luca, too.

Good luck with that.

I turn my phone off, press my forehead to the glass, and watch the south shore roll by as I leave Blitz Con, and Luca, behind.

TWENTY-NINE

Losing sucks. Like, we all know this, right? No matter what you do to prepare for it, no matter how much you downplay your chance of winning, it sucks to lose. People who tell you that it's okay are just used to it—sorry if that's you, no offense. And sure, there's the upside of having even tried. It's the journey, it's the climb, blah blah. I believe all that, but it doesn't change the fact that no matter what, it sucks to lose.

So why am I jumping up and down, ecstatic, as we lose?

The moment we get second, I turn to Luca. It stings, but from the way he looks at me, it's clear he feels only excitement. And as he pulls me into a hug in front of everyone, I feel the same. It's hard to feel like I've lost anything at all when I've gained so much back in such a short period of time. A few months ago, I was crying on the commuter rail, devastated by the outcome of the relationship Luca and I tried to build around our many shaky secrets. Right now, we stand here in the glory of a second chance that we were brave enough to take. And that makes it feel like we've won something bigger than any Controverse cosplay competition.

We move forward to accept our silver trophies. Luca takes my hand and raises it up into the air, so high that I have to stand on my toes to keep from lifting off the stage. Any higher, and we'd be spinning above the crowd, elevated by their elation.

A clubber appears with a giant check for two thousand (*two thousand?*) dollars. Another has medals. They swoop them around our necks and then line us up for photos with the judges. We nestle among them, everyone smiling as the crowd starts chanting our names. Dimly, I register that Luca's mom has been joined by quite a large family.

The photographer checks her shot, then goes in for another. Luca pulls me even closer, whispering, "Raff. *Raff.*"

I glance at him, sensing the mischief in that grin immediately. He's going to go in for a kiss, isn't he?

Now, this particular kiss is a work in progress. *Has* been a work in progress. It began a long, long time ago with me sitting among the shredded ruins of our costumes in a hotel room. It gathered within the sudden and shocked silence between us in the weeks after, like threads twisted tighter and tighter until they formed an ugly knot. It sealed itself in a grudge. It warmed, just slightly, in the sunlit hallway overlooking Controverse. And then it stitched itself together, glued itself together, bedazzled itself completely, as

Luca and I found our way back to each other over the re-creation of the costumes that broke us.

The kiss, like all epic kisses, is the final touch of everything that led up to it. Luca's lips brush mine, then mine brush his. We kiss, sharing one breath for what feels like minutes, the crowd cheering us on until finally, Luca lets me go. Just an inch. Just enough to let me know I should maybe keep my wits about me. We are still in public, after all.

"We did it," I say.

"We did it," he says back.

Our time in the spotlight ends, and we shuffle to the side with our gigantic check, trophies, and medals. I spot May at the front of the audience and throw up a V for victory.

Waldorf Waldorf asks for silence. Then he hands the mic off to Irma Worthy herself as she steps onto the stage.

"Every year, we at Craft Club are simply dazzled by the talent, ingenuity, determination, and spirit of you amazing cosplayers. What you do is special. What you do is magical. We're so happy to serve you and so proud to call Boston the home of Craft Club."

Awwww, goes the crowd.

Clubbers usher the two remaining teams forward. Inaya's jaw is set, her nostrils flared. Christina smiles big, not a trace of her former cunning visible. The Satoh twins stay completely in character, their confidence radiant.

"And now, it's my honor to name our Controverse Champions of Cosplay. This year, the grand prize goes to…"

The lights zip over the crowd, up onto the glassy ceiling, and then back down.

"Christina and Inaya with Eternal Sailor Moon!"

Now we all start jumping. The makeshift stage rocks beneath us, setting off a metallic squeal that cuts through the bright air of the arena. Is there bitterness to not winning? Of course. But does it affect the blitz of joy that goes off in me at seeing Inaya's shocked face as she's awarded this title? Not at all. Even if I were mad, I'm still a crafter first. I know that Inaya does incredible work, and I want that work to be recognized no matter what. She earned this. They both did.

Luca and I throw down our check and raise Inaya up. Her wings batter against Luca's, and it's clumsy, and I'm pretty sure Irma nearly faints at what looks like an impending lawsuit, but it doesn't matter. We hoist our friend up like it's nothing, and she grips our shoulders like she trusts us, and for the first time in a long time, I feel like our little group might have a future.

When we put Inaya down, she and Christina are led to the front, where they're crowned as champions. Luca and I slip from the stage and into the back area so Luca can get changed. We have to be quick—already, crews are starting to disassemble the makeshift studio—but this doesn't stop Luca from using the brief privacy to back me into a kiss. This time, I don't see it coming at all. It just happens, like a gift. Like a surprise birthday party. In my mouth.

"Sorry," he says, breaking off. "Is this okay?"

"It's more than okay," I say, and we kiss until a clubber clears their throat.

"Your phones?" he says, offering us back our devices.

I take mine without looking at it while Luca scrolls through the onslaught of notifications that have been flooding in. He laughs and whistles and gasps, then tries to show me something. He notices I'm not looking at my screen and picks up on why right away.

"You're nervous about Evie?"

I nod. He takes my phone.

"Want me to turn it on?"

I nod.

As soon as he does, Evie calls.

THIRTY

The trash barrels roll and scrape as I drag them out to the curb. I arrange the two barrels lovingly, correcting their alignment twice before I'm satisfied. I'm doting. Fussing. Stalling.

The barrels are stuffed with Phobos and Deimos, laid to rest in these two upright coffins. It was the first thing I did after Inaya dropped them off on my stoop a few days ago. It's not that I'm done with cosplay; I'm just done with these birds and everything they remind me of. I'm done with distraction. Done with Luca. All of this just confirms that the only person I can count on is myself.

Right now, I'm trying to focus on what comes next. I don't know what that is. I only know that I'll definitely be doing it alone.

My resolve lasts right up until I need to walk away from the trash cans. Instead, I just sit down. Right on the lawn, next to the driveway. It's not like I'm obsessed with the trash cans. I'm not, like, sobbing adoringly while caressing their plastic bodies. But like magnets, a force greater than me and mysterious to me keeps me in their orbit.

Mysterious is maybe not quite what this is. It's the sense of starting fresh. It's hope, but it comes with the painful truth: I am alone again. Luca and I are done. Luca is gone. He's not in the trash can, but he might as well be rolled up with all of the broken wings we created, now rent apart and collapsed into layers of foam and glue and fabric.

The sense of him being near me is so vivid. Even though I am sitting on the lawn, I let my face crumple into my knees. My sobs are quiet, but they echo in the small cavern I have created with the knot of my body. I stop as quickly as I started—I know Evie is likely in the house, and even though I feel like she'd sort of respect the performance piece of me sobbing beside some trash, I just cannot take any questions from her about my strange, melancholic behavior today.

When I lift my head up, a car has pulled over to see if I'm okay. I'm so shocked by the sudden appearance of the big metal beast that I don't recognize it until the driver's window rolls down and May shouts, "Did someone call for a pick-me-up?"

"That's a horrible joke," I say, getting into the passenger seat of her dad's car. It's just us. "How did you know to come?"

"Just knew."

We drive for a bit. Then she sighs.

"Actually, sorry, you'll find out eventually if you haven't already seen. Here, did you see?"

She passes me her phone from the cup holder. Ion is already up, specifically Inaya's feed. At the top is, of course, a shot of her at the Blitz Cosplay Games. She's holding a huge check—runner-up, and five hundred dollars richer. I sent her a congrats when I heard. Just Congrats, no hearts or emojis or anything. She sent back a blue heart. I expected her to reach out again after that, but she hasn't yet. I figured she was giving me space, which is what I wanted, but now I see there's a bit more to it as May scrolls further down Inaya's feed, into the older posts.

"You didn't see this one, did you?" May asks, opening a post entitled "Blitz Vlog."

"Nope."

"You're not curious about what happened that day?"

"I know what happened that day. It happened to *me*."

"No, no, I mean what else happened. After you left."

I don't answer, and May pauses. Then she says, "I guess he wouldn't have posted any of this himself, but I figured you'd have at least stumbled upon it watching Inaya's stuff. I guess you avoided everything, though."

Everything. May's dire tone distresses me. What could be so bad that she drove all the way here to make sure I didn't see it alone?

"Here." She hands me her phone again.

Inaya's vlog starts with a sleeping shot of me, zoomed in on my curls. Then it jumps to her opening the shower door and

Luca yelping at her to *get out, get out*! He throws a tiny bottle of shampoo at her, and they dissolve into shushed giggles. Then it's back to me, sleeping through it all. Eventually, they're down in the lobby, getting breakfast, and lo and behold, they did go to Dunkin'. Luca is on his phone behind Inaya as she talks to the camera about what they're up to.

"We should probably be getting dressed, but my prejudging isn't until this afternoon, and I kinda don't want to put on that corset until I *have to*. Plus it's warm, and there's no way my makeup is gonna last more than a few hours. So for now we're killing time. We'll probably pop into Blitz for a bit before taking a break to get into gear. Right, Luca?"

Luca almost misses the question, he's so absorbed in his phone. Then he catches on, and the clouds clear from his eyes.

"Yeah, you got it," he says.

The video moves on, but I don't. What Luca was reading—it must have been a continuation of that fight with his family. I know those clouds. And I know that overbright smile shining through.

Inaya's vlog takes her through the morning. Turns out they were inside the Omni, an attached hotel, meeting up with a few of Inaya's friends. Luca is on his phone in the background of every shot until he's not there at all. Then Inaya's inside the con, holding up some prints she scored at the Blitz Art Mart.

"I know," I say to May, handing her the phone. She pushes it back into my hands, saying, "Just keep watching."

We speed through Inaya's shopping, and then there's a jump

in time. At least a few hours, because the next shot is of the hotel room, and the early morning light has been replaced by midday gray. It must be a while after I left. Inaya is getting ready, her camera propped up on the bed. And in the background, picking through the pieces of the costume I ruined, is Luca.

My grip tightens on the phone with each second as I watch. Luca helps Inaya get into gear. She's got some spare red contacts, and he puts them in, otherwise staying in his regular clothes. They head to prejudging, and Luca acts as her handler. She films him trying on wigs at Arda and posing with a DBZ display while flexing. They spend almost all day goofing around, and then Inaya heads into the competition. At that point, Luca vanishes from the video. Inaya wins runner-up, and the last clip is a zooming close-up of pizza.

I know I'm breathing, but I don't feel like I'm getting any air.

"He went back?" I say. "Why did he go back?"

"I asked Inaya that, too," May says quickly, launching into a prepared balancing act. "She found him when he was trying to leave and got him to talk it out with her. I guess she even talked his mom down on the phone, saying she convinced him to go. You know how good Inaya is with parents. They ended up letting Luca stay for the day."

I kind of hear this. A rushing fills my ears, sweeping me into a sickening dizziness. I hold on to my seat, pushing May's phone away. This just confirms what I've always suspected: The dark secret of Luca's life was never cons or cosplay. It was me. The boy who brought him into that world but could never be seen standing beside him. All it took for him to stay was replacing me with Inaya.

May hugs me while I cry. I have no choice but to cry. I just wanted to be enough for this one person, and for a long time, it seemed like I was. I got used to it. I got used to the way he looked at me. I got used to the joy of creating with him. And seeing this, knowing he can be in this world without me and be just fine? It makes the last year feel ruined.

I pick up May's phone again, looking at the slew of videos of Inaya and Luca. The commenters are infatuated with him, of course.

Who is that boy?????

A wild Luca appears!

What did she use to summon this BOY? A baseball bat carved with sigils?

I stop when I get to a comment from Inaya herself, responding to all the questions.

omfg Luca is NOT my bf, gross.........but you guys did convince him to join ion. world, meet @StrikerCosplay. He's new, be nice. xx.

@StrikerCosplay has no posts. But he does have a picture (of him in those stupid contacts), and he's already got 189 followers.

For doing *nothing*.

I find myself opening up a comment, still on May's account.

May snatches the phone away from me as she pulls into a parking spot. She kills the engine and rushes from the car, then pulls me out of the passenger seat. We're in Davis Square, near May's bubble tea place, Boba Yoga (it's Baba Yaga themed, and yes it's part of a yoga studio). She must have called ahead to order, because she doesn't even let me come inside. She just ducks in and grabs two drinks, hands me one, and then we're walking behind the old movie theater, where a small park provides just enough privacy for me to fully lose it.

May lets me go on and on for about twelve minutes—extremely benevolent of her, to be honest—before winding me down.

"I created him. And I can destroy him," I say. I slash the words into the dusk, a violent phrase with a violent meaning. No matter how much I talk, the hurt just keeps coming.

"Maybe you enabled him, but he's always been Luca. Stop talking like an anime villain."

She's right. I didn't create him. At most, I showed him it was okay to be himself. For a long time, I thought he was doing the same for me, but now I don't know. Being with Luca was great, but it was also disruptive. It changed the way I worked and lived, and it gave me a new form of happiness, but it also cost me things. Was that worth it? Right now, it doesn't feel like it.

"I miss him," I say. It's all I know for certain. I am angry, maybe, and probably broken, but those feelings flash in and out of my heart like flitting butterflies. What stays, what sticks, is loss. I miss him. I miss us.

"I'm sorry, Raffy. The whole situation is bad, and I'm sorry it ruined Blitz."

I shrug. I have a lot of shrugs for people these days. It's an easy way to evade the expectations that people try to place on your shoulders.

"I'm sorry, too," I say. "Thank you for showing me. I didn't know about any of that. I haven't touched Ion."

"You've got a lot of people asking about the build you were doing leading up to Blitz."

"I guess they'll never know."

May chews a tapioca pearl. "You could talk about it, you know. You don't owe Luca anything anymore. You get to tell your own story and do whatever you want with it."

I think this is an odd thing to say. Would she actually support me going off, on camera, about Luca?

"What would *you* do with this?" I ask her.

May answers right away. "I'd draw it."

She would. I know that about her. May has always had a gift for processing things with her hands. The worst tangles comb to threads when she picks up her pens. I guess that's true for me, too, but I don't know what to do with this knot. It feels too alive to pull apart. It has a pulse. When I try to unravel it, I feel a powerful grudge radiating from it, and the bad part of me isn't ready to let that go, either.

"I'm not sure I could turn a bad breakup into a cosplay," I tell May.

"I know, I know," she says. "But you can turn it into something better."

"What?"

"Time. You were always saying you felt like you had to pick between spending time with Luca and spending time making stuff. Now you don't need to choose."

It's so dumb, but this helps me a ton. I blink away a few tears that have sprung up on me. It's a pitiful consolation prize for a broken heart—to have all the time I need to sit and mend other things. But May is right. If creating is what I do best, creating is what I must do, and now I have nothing but time to do it.

"So." She puts her hands on my knees. "What are you making next?"

I answer right away.

"Absolutely not another gay bird."

"Oh, thank you, Jesus," she sighs dramatically, falling over me in mock relief. Her breath smells like strawberry matcha as she lets out a celebratory whoop that fills the park. "Oh, thank you, cosplay Jesus. My boy is free."

I'm laughing as May tumbles over me, and I nearly drop my bubble tea. But behind my smile, I'm thinking: *Free?*

Free is what I felt when I was with Luca, when I finally

stopped worrying about the end and just focused on the creation. Freedom is what I glimpsed that day we were in Craft Club, just exploring, before Evie showed up and ruined it all.

Maybe free is what I am, but I don't feel free right now. I just feel alone.

THIRTY-ONE

Luca and I look at my buzzing phone. Evie's name stares back at me.

Not Mom. Not Mother. Evie. Just Evie. And a skull emoji.

"Want me to send her to voicemail?" Luca offers.

"No, I can do this," I say. I take the phone from him and move away from the makeshift Craft Club to where it's quiet. I take too long to pick up, and the call goes to voicemail, but Evie just keeps calling.

I pick up. Before I even say hello, Evie's silky voice bites into my ear.

"So you're not dead. Fantastic."

"Hi, Mom. I'm alive."

Anything could come next. A diatribe, surely. A sermon, certainly. I can even picture my phone erupting into snakes, such is the dark dread coursing through my whole body. I begin to shake. I find a wall and lean on it, doing my best to survive the excruciatingly long pause Evie makes me wait through.

"I'm…I'm sorry," I begin. "I'm sorry for not showing up for the trip. I value the chance at a great opportunity, but something really important happened for me today, and I couldn't say no to it. Another opportunity. I don't expect you to understand, and you don't have to, but—"

Evie's voice is distant when she butts in.

"I said sparkling. This is tap. I can taste the Delaware Watershed."

"What?"

"One moment, Raffy, we're ordering dinner. I'm with Tobias. Here, talk to him."

I burn a new, inventive shade of red. Did she not hear a word I said?

"Raphael! We've been watching the stream. Congratulations!"

Tobias has a profoundly rich voice. It sounds like I am talking to a dragon. A gay dragon who finds new vowels in the middle of every world. *CongratulaaAAaAaations!*

Then I register what he said.

Wait.

WAIT.

"You watched the Controverse Championships?"

"Well, not all of it," Tobias says. "Just the final few hours. You were spectacular! I haven't seen the show you referenced, but what a garment. You're just as talented as your mother says."

"Thank…thank you."

In the background, Evie can be heard haggling with the waiter about watercress.

"Your mother says you may one day make a great designer. I was just telling her I think you've got way more going on than that. I can't remember the last time I was allowed to incorporate PVC pipe into a fashion collection. But you really did get me thinking. And those wings. What wonders! Your model is lucky."

Ha. Luca, my model?

"Thank you," I agree, leaving the blithe compliment intact.

There's a scuffle, and then Evie is back on the phone. I straighten up.

"Raphael. Raphael, are you still there?"

"I'm here."

"Listen, I can't talk long. You called at a bad time, right as we were sitting down."

I choose to ignore the fact that *she* called *me*—six hundred times, probably.

"But I wanted to check in. And…I wanted to congratulate you. Tobias has been telling me all about his own cosplaying pursuits. I'll admit, it's not something I was really interested in learning more about. But I trust Tobias. He's a man of great taste. And talent."

I don't know how to respond to this. It's an endorsement of Tobias, after all, not of me.

"And…" Evie slows, which I enjoy. She's never this careful with her words. "And I should have trusted you. If this is your creative path, then it's your path. I apologize if I made you feel less than…" She pauses again. "You know what I mean, I'm sure."

"Thanks, Mom," I say, smiling.

"I assume you'll need space to keep working on your…projects?"

"You mean my *arts and crafts*?"

"Raphael, do not push me. I'm trying."

"Fine, projects."

Evie sighs. "Well, we have guests in November, so we can't have you in the studio. How about the basement? I've been looking for an excuse to gut it."

I glance up. Luca has come to find me. May is with him. They look positively horrified to find that I'm still on the phone with Evie. *It's fine*, I mouth to them. I turn the phone to speaker.

"That sounds good," I say to Evie. "Listen, I have to go. Luca's family invited me over for dinner."

Evie doesn't immediately hang up. I sense her waiting for something else, so I say, "If that's okay with you?"

"Why wouldn't it be okay? Are they cannibals?"

"We're Italian," Luca blurts before May gets a hand over his mouth. I hang up the phone as quickly as I can. I scream when I get a text a second later:

> Have fun. Good work today. See you next week. Mom.

Luca and May read the text.

"Aw, Raff, she's *tryyyyyyying*," squeals May.

"She's certainly doing something."

Luca flips through the notifications in my phone. Most are from Ion. He stops, pointing at a few.

"Do agents typically reach out to you through DMs?"

I grab the phone. I scan two lines of the message, finding the words *representation* and *opportunities*. Then I black out, probably. I don't know. I'm scrolling, ignoring the voicemails from my mother, and digging into a few other DMs from people with official-sounding titles. People with check marks next to their names. People asking what's next for me, where I'm going, what I'm doing. Businesses asking to work with me and other hobbyists just asking for advice.

I turn off the phone. There's time for the future in the future. I look up, and May and Luca are gone. No, they're right behind me, reading the notifications over my shoulder. Their eyes are wide.

"So. Dinner?" I ask, suddenly shy.

Luca loops an arm around my waist. "You sure you want to come over? It's a big family."

I definitely don't want to go home to an empty house. Not yet. Even with Evie's change of heart, home still feels haunted with the person I was before this day transformed me. Before I let myself change, I guess. I feel older now, but also brand new, like I can handle anything. I can handle this new evolution of Evie. I can handle my own ambitions. And I can handle my heart, knowing now how much stronger it is after I put it back together.

But I don't dwell. I'm not worried about handling anything right now. I'm just happy.

"I'm sure," I say.

"I, too, am sure," says May, with an air of magnanimous invitation (to herself).

"Inaya's busy, but she said she'd catch us later for karaoke, if you're not too bitter."

Luca and I share a smile.

"We're not," I assure May.

"Then it's settled." Luca claps his hands ceremoniously. "Let's go!"

And we do.

ACKNOWLEDGMENTS

I've always loved to make stuff, and I'm incredibly grateful to the many people in my world who have taught me about crafting, making, morphing, transforming, and so on. Thank you for helping me create on my own terms.

First, I want to thank my family, and even before that, you should know my own mother is nothing at all like Evie. She's loving and supportive and, alongside my step father, provided me tons of space of resources to figure out my art. Same with my father, who let me draw sprawling fantasy maps on x-ray boards brought home from the hospital. I've been fortunate with three—and now four! Welcome, Mary!—parents who have raised me to be curious and brave, and I'm thankful for this above all else.

Same toward my siblings, Blase, David, and Julia, all equally supportive across the many realms our family spans. And same to the rest of my loud, always-laughing family. Especially my cousin

Douglas, who gave me a genius artist right in my family tree to follow behind.

Art has always provided a larger family for me, too. This book wouldn't have been impossible without the ingenious, bafflingly creative community of cosplayers that tirelessly turn every con into a crafter's heaven. Creating is one thing, but making creation accessible is another, and I am indebted to the many makers who work tirelessly on tutorials, how-tos, streams, and panels. You make *making* possible, for everyone. Thank you for letting me play in your world.

For this book, I spent a considerable amount of time watching Kamui Cosplay tutorials. Svetlana and Benni, you don't know me, but I adore you (and your dogs). I also got to witness several patterning and corseting lessons by Cowbutt Crunchies Cosplay, all of it used in this book. Finally, my biggest thank-you goes to my friend and idol, Jacqui, of Alchemical Cosplay. Thank you for taking a chance on the random writer who showed up in your life after seeing you on stage at NYCC. And thank you for letting me cosplay as your handler in Boston. You made Raffy's story possible. You are his idol.

I also went to many cons and want to thank my own little con fam. Sal, you get the first thanks for obvious reasons. Christina, May, Brian, Jen: you all taught me that cosplay is a team sport. I can't wait four our next, best cosplay outing.

Elizabeth Graham, you're a vision, and I am so grateful for your friendship and insight into the world of elite art, curation, and galleries. For anyone wondering, Elizabeth is a gem with exquisite taste and shares none of Evie's acidic points of view.

And I need to thank a few other writers who were invaluable in keeping me going when this book was kicking my butt. Claribel and Phil, not even Olivia Satan could have done a better job. Fern Brain Chat, ilu even when you drag me within an inch of my life.

I for sure want to thank the rest of my close friends, too. So many costume parties, such unflinching endorsement of ridiculous craft projects that were still drying by showtime. It's an honor to come from a group of people so committed to such a high level of absolutely pointless theatrics. Jess, you specifically. I love you all!

And of course, when it comes to making, I need to dedicate a TON of gratitude toward my publishing fam. Veronica Park, my agent, who turned this whimsical idea into something real; Annie Berger, my editor, who is as smart as she is creative as she is patient; Cassie Gutman, my production editor, who perhaps has the hardest job of all (debating which bad puns make it in); Lizzie and Beth and Mallory, who handle publicity and marketing, along with Michael, Margaret, and Caitlin, my conference team—you all have arguably an even tougher job keeping track of me, and I thank you for your hard, hard work; and of course Dominique Raccah, my publisher, who inspires me to no end.

I also want to give a special thanks to the artists who turned my book about art into art itself: Danielle McNaughton on internals, Nicole Hower on art direction, and the astounding Maricor/Maricar, the embroidery master behind the cover art that begins this book.

All of you are superstars in the constellations of Controverse.

I'm going to stop before I start thanking the craft suppliers who have been bankrupting me. You get the point. It takes many, many people to make a book and many more to inspire it. I wrote this, but we all made it together. So I'll leave you with Irma Worthy's well-earned advice: Measure twice, cut once, give up never.

Happy crafting!

ABOUT THE AUTHOR

Ryan La Sala grew up in Connecticut, but only physically. Mentally, he spent most of his childhood in the worlds of *Sailor Moon* and *Xena: Warrior Princess*, which perhaps explains all the twirling. He studied anthropology and neuroscience at Northeastern University before becoming a project manager at a web design agency. He technically lives in New York City but has actually transcended material reality and only takes up a human shell for special occasions, like brunch, and to watch anime (which is banned on the astral plane). You can find him on Twitter @Ryality or visit him at ryanlasala.com.

FIREreads
🔥 #getbooklit

Your hub for the hottest young adult books!

Visit us online and sign up for our
newsletter at FIREreads.com

 @sourcebooksfire

 sourcebooksfire

 firereads.tumblr.com